THE SECRET KINGDOM

LEOPARDS' GOLD

JENNY NIMMO

EGMONT

EGMONT

We bring stories to life

Leopards' Gold first published in Great Britain 2013
by Egmont UK Limited
The Yellow Building, 1 Nicholas Road, London W11 4AN

Text copyright © Jenny Nimmo 2013

The moral rights of the author have been asserted

ISBN 978 1 4052 5734 3

1 3 5 7 9 10 8 6 4 2

A CIP catalogue record for this title is available from the British Library
Printed and bound in Great Britain by the CPI Group

47187/2

www.egmont.co.uk

EGMONT

Our story began over a century ago, when seventeen-year-old
Egmont Harald Petersen found a coin in the street. He was on
his way to buy a flyswatter, a small hand-operated printing
machine that he then set up in his tiny apartment.

The coin brought him such good luck that today Egmont has
offices in over 30 countries around the world. And that lucky
coin is still kept at the company's head offices in Denmark.

For Richard Simpson

Contents

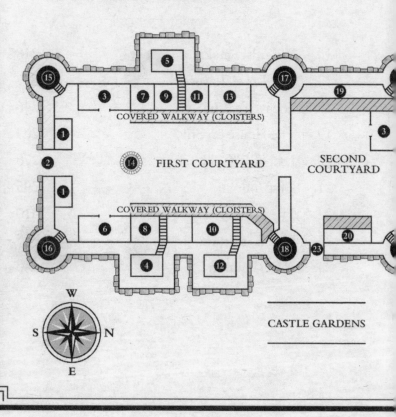

GROUND MAP OF
THE RED CASTLE

5

15   3   7   9   11   13   17   19

COVERED WALKWAY (CLOISTERS)

1   3

2   14   FIRST COURTYARD   SECOND
                                   COURTYARD

1

COVERED WALKWAY (CLOISTERS)

6   8   10

16   18   23   20

4   12

W
S   N
E

CASTLE GARDENS

1	Guardroom	9	Children's Dining Hall
2	South Gate	10	Great Hall
3	Stables	11	Chancellor's Office
4	Library	12	Children's Bedchambers
5	Chancellor's Apartments	13	Meeting Hall
6	Kitchens	14	Pump and Well
7	Schoolroom	15	Grey Men's Chambers
8	Hall of Corrections	16	Bell Tower

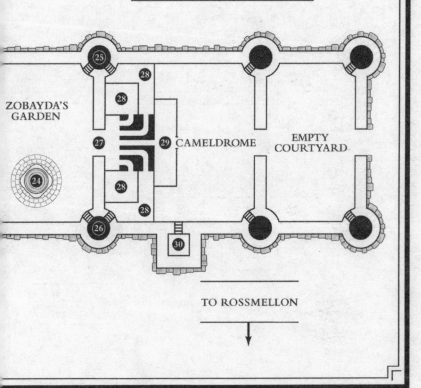

RIVER AT BASE OF DEEP RAVINE

ZOBAYDA'S
GARDEN

CAMELDROME

EMPTY
COURTYARD

TO ROSSMELLON

Characters

In the Red Castle

Timoken

An African king. When he was born his mother wrapped him in the web of the last moon spider. It was a gift from a forest-jinni who said that it would give Timoken immortality and exceptional powers. When he was eleven, Timoken's parents were killed by another tribe, aided by demons from the forest. Timoken escaped from his kingdom with his sister, Zobayda, and together they travelled the world, eventually coming to Britain. Timoken is now nearly three hundred years old. The moon spider's web has become his cloak.

Zobayda

Timoken's sister. She wears a ring made from the web of

the last moon spider. This gives her some protection but does not make her immortal. She is clairvoyant and has aged faster than her brother.

Berenice

Born in the Spanish Kingdom of Castile, her father was the greatest swordsman in the land. She was kidnapped when she was twelve, but rescued by Timoken. They were later married.

Eri

A wizard. He escaped from Castle Melyntha with Timoken when it was taken over by the conquerors. Eri is one of the ancient Welsh/Britons.

Llyr

Eri's grandson, and also a wizard. Llyr's parents were murdered by the conquerors.

Thorkil

Son of the Saxon earl, Sigurd, who was murdered by the conquerors. He is now King Timoken's chancellor.

Edern, Mabon, Peredur and Friar Gereint

Welsh/Britons who were kidnapped when they were children. They were about to be sold as slaves when Timoken rescued them. They are now his most faithful knights, except for Gereint who was brought up in a monastery.

Rigg

Bellman of the Red Castle.

Wyngate

Investigator of the Red Castle. He escaped from the town of Innswood when it was burnt down by the conquerors.

Chimery

Married to Thorkil's sister, Elfrieda. The chancellor's right-hand man.

The King's Children

Borlath

Aged nineteen by the time of this chronicle. He can burn objects with his fingers.

Amadis

Aged eighteen. He can communicate with animals.

Lilith

Aged sixteen. She can bewitch others with clothing.

Cafal

Aged fourteen. A were-beast.

Olga

Aged thirteen. She can move objects with her mind.

At the beginning of this chronicle, the king's younger children have not discovered their talents.

Guanhamara Aged eleven.

Petrello Aged ten.

Tolomeo Aged nine.

Vyborn Aged six.

In the Forest

Tumi
Friend of Timoken and son of a fisherman.

Sila
Tumi's wife.

Karli
Tumi's friend.

Esga
Karli's wife.

All four were children when the conquerors burnt down their homes in the town of Innswood. They escaped and lived in the forest.

Osbern D'Ark
Steward to Prince Griffith of Melyntha Castle. When the prince was killed in battle, Osbern, a conqueror, began to take control of the castle. All Welsh/Britons had to leave or be killed.

The Damzel of Decay

An evil spirit who lives in the forest. An enemy of sunlight, she embodies all the death and decay that occurs in the damp and the dark. She hungers for the Red King's cloak.

The Conquerors

People of Norman/French descent referred to as conquerors because their ancestors invaded England in 1066. Since then conquerors have occupied the English throne.

Animals

Gabar

A camel. He came from Africa and has travelled the world with Timoken. He is also nearly three hundred years old, having drunk some of the Alixir the forest-jinni gave to Timoken's mother.

Enid

A dragon. She feels that she belongs to Eri, the wizard. She loves Gabar.

Greyfleet

A wolf. Leader of the pack and friend to Amadis.

Sun Cat, Flame Chin and Star

Leopards. Timoken wrapped them in the moon spider's web when they were cubs. Now they are immortal and magical.

Isgofan

Amadis's black horse.

Elizen

The queen's white horse.

Chapter One

The Vanishing

The spell began at their feet. Eri, sitting on a tree-stump, hummed; his voice broke often and he paused in his chant. He was now very old and couldn't hold the notes for long. It was his grandson, Llyr, who murmured and sang as he walked beside the wall of leaves.

Every autumn, children from the castle would gather freshly fallen leaves and build up the wall until it reached their knees. It would remain throughout the winter, but in the summer months the leaves would sink a little and the wall had to be built up again, and then, when the wizards chanted, everything inside the wall would become invisible.

The spell-wall extended deep into the forest. It encircled the castle, whose sixteen towers rose above the trees. As Llyr sang, the spell crept through the grass until it reached the great yews that stood on either side of the high castle gate. The yews and the gate were slowly swallowed. The spell drifted over the castle gardens, it covered the banks of roses and the marble statues. Hedges of rosemary, hawthorn and sage were gently shrouded in a white mist.

The pond melted into gossamer, the stone steps dissolved, the great castle doors disappeared along with the high red walls and, finally, the sixteen towers.

The castle and its inhabitants were now invisible to the outside world. Humans and animals were also floating. This was the only drawback to invisibility, and a bell was always rung to warn the people that soon they would be swept off their feet, or out of their beds.

Llyr returned to Eri. 'It is done. You can rest now, grandfather.'

'Did you hear the bell?' asked Eri.

'I was listening to our chant. I heard no warning. But I told the bellman the spell would soon begin.'

'It never came. Timoken will be annoyed. His sister is frail and shouldn't be tossed out of bed without warning.'

'It could be worse,' said Llyr. 'At least the beds don't move now, and the chairs all stay in place.'

A hint of a smile touched Eri's lips. 'No. You've done well, Llyr.'

'A little more work,' said his grandson, 'and I'll be able to keep them all grounded when the disappearing starts.'

Eri looked towards the vanished castle. 'I wonder how they're doing in there. Without the warning bell there'll be a few bruised heads.'

'And what has become of the bellman?' said Llyr with a frown.

Petrello woke up to find himself in the air. His brothers were floating just beneath him. Tolly, his brown curls bobbing, twisted and turned, his arms flailing, his hands reaching for something to grab. Vyborn lay on his back, spread-eagled inches above his bed. He glared up at Petrello accusingly.

'It's not my fault,' said Petrello.

'The bell didn't ring.' Tolly kicked in the air. 'I'd have held the bedpost if I'd had a warning.'

'Perhaps we didn't hear it. Or perhaps the wizards had no time to call the bellman.'

Petrello's feet skimmed the floor and his head jerked back, hitting a bedpost. 'Ouch! That doesn't usually happen. What's going on?'

Vyborn's small body had drifted higher. He had rolled over and was now staring down at Petrello. Petrello hoped his brother wasn't going to be sick. Vyborn was often sick. He was only six years old and sometimes ate more than he should, though he was still a scrawny boy. He had a face like a bad-tempered owl.

Petrello swam over to the window and, reaching for the sill, clung on. In the pale dawn light he could make out the lines of rose trees in the castle gardens, and the low hedges of medicinal herbs. Two stately yews marked the end of the garden and the track that led east to the small town of Rossmellon. To the south the great forest of Hencoed spread as far as the eye could see, to the north the mountains rose like ghostly towers, their snow-capped peaks lost in the night clouds.

Two men appeared between the yews. Both wore blue cloaks edged in gold. The men carried long staffs that glimmered softly as they moved through the garden.

'The wizards are returning,' Petrello observed. 'They have a lot of ground to cover now that the castle has grown so vast.'

'And it's still growing.' Tolly gulped the air as the wizards' spells tossed him to the ceiling.

4

It was true. Even the king had begun to wonder if his castle would continue to expand. It had been built by his African spirit ancestors twenty-seven years before. For some reason, they considered the building incomplete and would arrive now and again, in the dead of night, called perhaps by an old song the king had thoughtlessly hummed on his way to bed, a rhythm that had remained in his head ever since he had fled his secret African kingdom.

Try as he might, the king could never discover the precise sounds that called his spirit ancestors. The great Red Castle now sprawled for almost a mile, along a cliff that rose sheer from the river Dolenni.

Petrello couldn't see the river, but he never tired of the view from his window and he marvelled that while he could see so much, the castle and all its inhabitants were invisible to anyone outside.

The wizards were responsible. Their spells kept the castle safe. If the king of England were ever to know that in the northern forests there was a castle larger than his own, he would consider its owner – especially since he was a foreign king – a threat to his throne. An army of conquerors would be despatched and the castle burnt to the ground. If they survived the fire who knew what would happen to an African king and his family, once they were prisoners of the conquerors' king.

'I wish the spell wouldn't do this,' said Tolly as Vyborn floated above him and dribbled on to his bare foot.

'Llyr will refine it,' said Petrello. 'It's already better than it was. Remember, we used to see through all the walls, as if we were in a giant bubble. And the furniture floated. Now it's just us.'

'I don't remember,' grumbled Vyborn.

'You were only two,' said Tolly. 'But I remember because I was five and Trello was six.'

An angry roar echoed down the passage outside the boys' bedchamber. 'Senseless! Ludicrous! Pointless!'

'Borlath!' Tolly made a face.

Borlath, the king's eldest son, was always angry. If he'd had his way, the wizards would have been banished long ago and the castle left to be defended by the king and his knights.

Borlath's fingers could burn like fiery pokers. It was an endowment inherited from his father, though the king never used his fingers in anger. In Borlath's bad moods it was best to avoid him.

'Sometimes I wish he'd burn himself on his own fingers,' Petrello murmured.

The wizards were drawing closer. Llyr supported his grandfather on his arm. Old Eri limped badly, his back was bent and the hem of his cloak heavy with dew, but he still wore a mischievous smile.

Llyr was tall, his face paler than his grandfather's. Llyr wasn't smiling. Spells were a serious matter. If they were not right, their power could be reversed. He was forever lecturing the children about the misuse of magic. The wizards themselves never floated. Even they were not sure how they managed to avoid it.

'What's the danger, Trello?' asked Tolly. 'Can you see any soldiers?'

'I see the wizards,' said Petrello. 'No one else.'

'Then why are we floating?' grumbled Vyborn.

'Danger can't always be seen.' Petrello watched the two wizards approach the entrance to the castle. They passed out of sight and he heard the great doors grinding open as they obeyed the touch of Llyr's staff. Petrello never failed to wonder how the doors would glide apart at a tap from a slim wooden staff when usually it took two men to unbolt and open them.

The light in the eastern sky began to brighten, sunbeams slid over the distant hills and the dark forest became emerald green. And still those in the vanished castle swam in the air of their bedchambers, in the rafters of the kitchens, the stables, the guard rooms and the Great Hall.

The dogs and horses had become accustomed to the weightlessness that would suddenly overcome them. They knew it did them no harm, and yet they became unusually silent at such times, as though the spell that held them aloft had stolen their voices for a while.

The sun rose above the hills, but the floating persisted.

Petrello's arms began to ache. He let go of the sill and as he swam free he felt his leg dropping. The air beneath him was getting thinner, his feet touched the floor and he heard his brothers land behind him. Llyr always made sure the bonds of a spell were gently loosened.

Vyborn sat scowling on his bed. Tolly lay on the floor laughing. Sunlight touched his forehead and he suddenly stood up, looking anxious. 'I shall be late.'

'Late for what?' asked Petrello.

'Can't tell.' Tolly pulled on his woollen hose, stepped into his breeches and slid into his shoes. The next moment he was running through the door.

'You forgot your jerkin, brother!' called Petrello.

'Too late!' sang Tolly.

They had never had secrets from each other. But for twelve days now, Tolly had run off before the morning meal, never telling his brother where he was going, or why. Petrello was puzzled. Next morning he would follow his brother, he decided.

'Where does he go?' asked Vyborn.

'How should I know, brother?'

'You must know because you and he are best friends. You know everything Tolly does. I know nothing, nothing about anybody.' Vyborn's black eyes were expressionless.

'I'm sure you know things about your friends,' Petrello said lightly.

'I don't have any friends,' Vyborn muttered. 'I don't know anything.'

Petrello felt a twinge of pity for his small, melancholy brother. 'You will one day,' he told him.

'Yes,' Vyborn agreed. 'One day I'll know a lot.'

Petrello dressed quickly and made for the door.

'So where are you going?' Vyborn asked. 'I suppose that's a secret too.'

'Not at all. I'm going to see the wizards.'

'Why?'

'To ask about the bellman.' Petrello glanced at this brother's frowning face, stepped into the passage and closed the door.

The wizards' room was at the top of the seventh tower. Once there had been four towers; now there were sixteen. Who knew how many more there would be before the spirit ancestors considered the castle to be complete. When the seventh tower had appeared, fifteen years ago, Eri decided to claim it for his own; a place where he could instruct his grandson in the rules of magic and the practice of healing.

Petrello climbed a winding stone stairway. He no longer averted his gaze from the bones that rattled as he passed. The bones came from creatures that were long dead when Eri found them. Creatures whose like might never be seen again. They hung on iron nails protruding from the walls on either side of the narrow stairway; Petrello could sense their potency, though he could never guess why the wizards kept them there. When he had asked, Eri merely replied, 'The past has strength, young man, if you believe in it.'

At the top of the steps stood a blackened door, its rough surface carved with stars and circles, pentagrams, crescents and other mysterious symbols that held meaning for the wizards but no one else.

Petrello put his hand on the great ringed handle but didn't turn it. There was safety here, but also danger. A scent of deep earth lingered round the door, and a waft of scorched herbs.

Petrello knocked three times on the thick oak, and a voice called, 'Who is there?'

'Petrello!'

'Enter.'

Now came the moment Petrello treasured. He turned the handle and the door opened with a low groan. Petrello stepped into a room the wizards called their Eyrie, their eagle's nest. It was easy to see why. All that could be seen from the wizards' long windows was sky.

On the back of the door two blue cloaks hung from a peg; their hems, stained with mud, dripped on to Petrello's boots as he closed the door.

'Good morning, Petrello, I can guess why you're here.' Llyr was seated behind a long table covered with neat lines of dried plants, books, bottles, smooth pebbles, winking crystals and gleaming polished bones. 'You won't be our only visitor. Everyone will want to know why the bell was silent.'

Petrello approached the table, the better to see those enchanting crystals. 'Why *was* the bell silent, Llyr?'

'We may never know.' Llyr stood up. Sunlight from the window behind him sent his long shadow across the table and over Petrello's head. The wizard's thick hazel-brown hair was unusually tangled, his slim fingers scratched and stained.

Llyr glanced at a sleeping figure on the couch by the window. A red blanket had been pulled right up to the sleeper's chin, but the great nose pointing at the ceiling could only belong to the wizard, Eri. At the foot of the couch, curled into the folds of the blanket, lay the dragon, Enid. She too was asleep. Thin spirals of steam issued from her quivering snout and she growled in her dreams.

'Why, Llyr?' Petrello walked to the end of the table and daringly touched one of the crystals. 'Why might we never know?'

Before Llyr could answer, the door swung open again. Only the king would enter the Eyrie without knocking. Petrello's father stood on the threshold: taller even than

Llyr, his red cloak was pinned at his shoulder with a golden circle, studded with rubies; his sword in its silver and gold scabbard was buckled to his jewelled belt; and in his thick black hair a gold crown glistened like an almost hidden circle of stars.

'Why was the bell silent?' the king demanded. 'The bellman should have been warned before you set us all topsy-turvy. My sister is old now, she was quite shaken.'

'We did warn the bellman.' Eri had woken up, but remained lying where he was.

The king looked puzzled. 'Did he ring the bell then? Are we all going deaf?'

'No, Your Majesty. You are not going deaf,' said Llyr.

Petrello saw deep concern enter his father's face. The king didn't like the comforting rhythm of his castle to be disturbed. 'Then what . . .?' He spread his hands.

'It was Rigg's turn today. He is an efficient bellman, never late,' Eri said from his couch. 'I warned him there were soldiers in the forest. I saw them in the crystal and knew they were there. "Ring the bell, Rigg," I said, "quickly before the Vanishing begins." We saw him mount the steps to the tower. We hastened away to cast the spell, but we heard no bell.'

'He disobeyed?' The king shook his head in disbelief.

'We went to the Bell Tower on our return,' said Llyr.

'And found it empty.' Eri sat up and rubbed his eyes. 'There was blood on the steps, but no sign of Rigg.'

The king's jaw dropped. He gazed about him in dismay, until his eyes found Petrello, backing away from the crystals as discreetly as he could.

'Someone attacked the bellman?' said the king. 'Why was I not told as soon as you saw the blood?'

'I was coming, sire,' said Llyr, 'but we thought Rigg might merely have fallen and cut himself. Grandfather wanted to sleep and dream before we caused a stir.'

'I did not dream,' sighed Eri. 'Rigg was most likely attacked, for he's certainly disappeared.'

Chapter Two

The Investigator's Message

No one had ever disappeared from the Red Castle. The inhabitants died of illness and old age. Beyond the castle gardens, beyond the wizards' protective wall of spells, men fought each other and died. The English king's soldiers swept through the countryside unchecked, murdering and stealing, capturing and burning, but in the Red Castle, everyone had always been safe.

'Petrello,' said the king. 'Come with me.'

'Yes, Father.' Petrello moved quickly to his father's side.

'Return soon, young man,' said Eri. 'We like your company, don't we, Llyr?'

'Indeed we do.'

Petrello made a small bow. 'Thank you, wizards.'

The king was already descending the steps, two and three at a time. Petrello hurried after him. The king muttered to himself. He had taught his children to understand the language of his secret kingdom, but today his voice was quiet and quick, and Petrello could only catch a few words.

They reached the passage that connected the Eyrie to the Book Tower. The king increased his pace and Petrello had to run to keep up with him.

A bell rang out, the call to breakfast; faint and light, it bore no resemblance to the great warning bell. The king paid no attention to it. 'How old are you, Petrello?' he asked.

'Ten years, Father.'

'Of course. Forgive me. I knew it, but sometimes I forget. There are so many children here.' The king smiled and rubbed his head. His slim crown glinted as they passed the embers of a torch in an iron bracket on the wall. 'Soon I shall forget which room is where,' went on the king. 'What tower contains our stocks of corn, where I can find the schoolroom or where the ice is kept.'

'Will the ancestors never stop building, Father?' asked Petrello.

The king laughed out loud. 'Who knows, my son.' He stopped at an archway leading to another flight of deep stone steps. 'Here we are. The investigator is working in the library. Tell him to hurry to the Meeting Hall. I shall be with the knights.'

The king strode on while Petrello leapt up the steps. It was a short flight this time. The library was on the first floor of the Book Tower. There was no door, merely an arch, so low that most grown men had to duck beneath it.

Children seldom came to the library. They were not allowed to touch the precious books, though occasionally they were permitted to creep in and listen to a story told by the bard, Adam.

Petrello had the impression that the very walls were made of books, for they stretched from floor to ceiling, covering every inch of space. A narrow window between two shelves allowed very little light into the room, and Moreau, the Book Guardian, always had a candle burning on his desk. Today he was scuttling about the library, tucking books into the shelves and picking up others that had been dislodged by the Vanishing.

'Yes?' said Moreau, glaring at Petrello. He was a very small man with crinkled white hair and eyelids wrinkled and red from all his reading.

'The king sent me to find the investigator, sir,' said Petrello.

Moreau nodded in the direction of one of the low, velvet-covered tables. Wyngate, the investigator, had his back to Petrello, but there was no mistaking the feathered cap that he always wore. His head was bent over a very large book, his long fingers tracing the letters that ran across its yellow pages. The candle at his elbow had burnt to a flickering stub.

Petrello went across and tapped the investigator's shoulder.

Wyngate jumped. 'What . . .?' And then he saw the boy. 'Petrello, what brings you here?'

'The king wants you in the Meeting Hall, sir.'

Wyngate frowned. 'Now? But only this morning he sent me to the library, and I am not nearly finished with the land investigation he set me.'

'The bellman has disappeared, sir. Captured, the wizards said, because there was blood. That's why he . . .'

'Blood? Captured?' Wyngate stood up, sending his stool crashing to the floor. The Book Guardian looked at him accusingly and shook his head.

'So that's why we weren't warned of the Vanishing.'

Wyngate strode to the arch with Petrello at his heels.

'Books should be returned to the shelves,' grumbled Moreau.

'I'll do it later,' said Wyngate, ducking under the arch. 'Where was the blood?' he asked as he sped down the steps.

'On the Bell Tower stairway they said,' Petrello replied.

'Tell the king I'll be with him as soon as I can. But I have to visit the Bell Tower first. There might be clues.'

'What else, Wyngate?'

'What else?'

'What else can I do to help?'

'Search, Petrello. Look for signs, for anything that might indicate where our bellman has gone.' The investigator ran back towards the Eyrie, leaving Petrello at the foot of the library steps.

The Meeting Hall lay on the other side of the castle, and as Petrello ran across the courtyard he passed groups of people talking urgently to one another. Two words were on everybody's lips. 'No warning!'

He was approaching the door to the Meeting Hall when his arm was suddenly grabbed and a gruff voice said, 'Where are you off to in such a hurry?'

Borlath, oldest of the royal children, tightened his grip

on Petrello's arm. Behind him, his younger brother Cafal hopped from foot to foot, smirking. His sandy hair stood up from his head like the bristles of a wild boar.

'Tell me where you're going.' Borlath's smile was never friendly. His black brows hung thick and heavy over his small black eyes, giving him a perpetual scowl.

Petrello tried to twist away from Borlath's grip. 'I'm on an errand for our father.'

'Something to do with the bellman?' Borlath's fingers were getting hotter; soon they would burn through Petrello's jerkin and into his skin. Cafal watched his older brother with admiration. He gave Petrello a pitying grin that stretched his freckled skin into a dog-like mask.

'Why must you know everything, Borlath?' Petrello protested.

'Stupid question.'

Petrello felt a stinging burn. The pain was so intense he thought he would faint. Cafal began to laugh, his voice inhuman, like the shriek of a wild creature.

There was a sudden low growl behind them.

Borlath loosened his grip on Petrello, and with a petrified howl Cafal turned and ran. A wolf, grey as a storm cloud, bounded up to them. Borlath stiffened at a second low growl, not from the wolf, but from another of the king's sons: Amadis emerged from a group of young men and walked up to his brothers. Resting a hand on the wolf's head, he grunted softly and murmured, 'Greyfleet.'

The wolf backed a little and sat close to his master's feet.

The air between the brothers bristled with hostility. Amadis and Borlath could not have been more different. Amadis had hair as pale as straw and his eyes were the colour of dark wine. Like his father, his quiet voice could speak the language of any creature.

'What do you want?' Borlath snarled.

'Let our brother go,' said Amadis.

Borlath had dangerous fingers, he was broad and heavy, but he was afraid of the grey wolf whose eyes never left Borlath's face.

'The Knight Protectors are wanted in the Meeting Hall,' said Amadis. 'Didn't the message reach you?'

'What if it did?' growled Borlath. He let go of Petrello's arm and Petrello, taking his chance, twisted away and dashed through the crowds. From the other side of the courtyard he watched Borlath follow his brother to the Meeting Hall. Only then did Petrello remember the investigator's message to the king. He should have passed it on to Amadis, but Borlath's burning assault had swept everything from his mind.

Within seconds Petrello was speeding down the open passageway towards the Meeting Hall. The doors were open and the Knight Protectors were still arriving from their quarters in other parts of the castle. They had been summoned hastily, but many were expecting the call. A Vanishing without warning was a grave matter and many Protectors had hurried to the Meeting Hall without finishing their breakfasts.

When Petrello reached the door he found the hall so crammed with jostling knights, their weapons rattling and clanking from hurriedly buckled belts, he knew it would be impossible for him to speak to the king.

'Be off now, young 'un,' said the guard. 'This isn't the place for you.'

'But . . .' Petrello began, and then he saw his father's friend, Sir Edern. He was one of the last to arrive, and came marching across the courtyard, his belt unbuckled and his red beard dotted with crumbs.

'Sir Edern!' Petrello ran up to the untidy knight. 'The investigator will be coming later, please tell my father he has gone to the Bell Tower to . . . to . . .'

'Investigate?' laughed Sir Edern. 'I'll tell him, Petrello. Is my beard clean?'

'No, sir,' said Petrello.

Sir Edern laughed again and pulled at his beard. 'Bless you for your honesty,' he said. Patting the boy's head, he hurried on.

Petrello watched the doors close behind the last knight. He wished he could have slipped inside before the guard saw him again. What would the king say? If the bellman could not be found in the castle, then the knights would ride out with the king at their head. They would search the forest, and then perhaps the hamlets and the towns, and then the mountains.

The king often led his Knight Protectors out into the fields and forests, looking for people who needed their help. The poor country folk had no one to defend them. Troops of soldiers would suddenly descend, taking everything their lord demanded; land that the poor had always considered free was now owned by the conquerors. Anyone who resisted them would be cut down in an instant. Women were not spared, and nor were children.

The first time King Timoken and his knights appeared,

as if from nowhere, the people were terrified. Who were these men on their fine horses? Their helmets gleamed and their belts were encrusted with gold and jewels. Their leader's shield and tunic were emblazoned with a burning sun; his face was dark, his cloak a vibrant red. The people could hardly believe it when they learned he came not to loot and kill but to protect them. They began to call him the Red King. His knights were so skilful, their weapons so deadly, that the conquerors' men often turned tail rather than meet them.

But if the soldiers stood their ground, there would be a bloody battle.

Petrello had seen the king and his knights return from one of these more violent skirmishes, their tunics ripped and muddied, their weapons bloodied and their shields bent out of shape.

But a search is different, thought Petrello. There could be no danger in a hunt, unless a wild boar was caught up in it.

'Brother, why are you dreaming?' called a voice.

The anxious crowds that only a moment ago had filled the courtyard were now breaking up and hastening to breakfast.

A girl came running up to Petrello. She took his hand and shook it gently. 'You and your thoughts, little brother.'

'Not so little.' Petrello might have been younger than his sister Guanhamara, but she was small for her eleven years. With her wide hazel eyes and shiny chestnut hair, she reminded Petrello of a startled fawn.

'Did the Vanishing shake you? I didn't hear the warning and flew right up to the ceiling and banged my head.' Guanhamara rubbed her forehead and giggled.

'There was no warning,' Petrello said gravely. 'Rigg the bellman has disappeared. The investigator asked me to look for signs. Will you help?'

'Of course! But have you eaten?' asked his sister. 'The bell went ages ago.'

'I didn't notice. I've been busy.'

'Let's go together. I'm hungry, and you can defend me from the ogress.'

'Nurse Ogle? I'm not a good choice, Guan.'

Petrello and his sister hurried to the Children's Hall. They found the table almost bare. The excitement of a surprise Vanishing had given the other children a huge appetite. Even Nurse Ogle had failed to stop the grabbing and gobbling of twenty-five hungry children, all of them under twelve.

The hot pottage had all gone but Tolomeo had saved some bread and cheese for his brother. 'Sorry, Guan. I thought you had eaten,' he told his sister.

'I bumped my head,' Guanhamara said ruefully as she slid next to Tolomeo on the bench.

'You can have some of mine.' Petrello squeezed in beside her and tore his bread in half. He was just about to cut the cheese with his black-handled knife when a high voice drowned out the surrounding chatter.

'Where have you two been?' From the head of the table, Nurse Ogle glared at the latecomers.

Silence fell. Everyone stared at Petrello and Guanhamara.

'As a matter of fact, I've been very busy,' Petrello said, a little too self-importantly.

'Busy? You?' sneered Nurse Ogle. 'You, Petrello, the foolish. You who cannot write your letters correctly, who cannot remember your numbers, who forgets what day it is.'

A quiet sniggering ran down the table.

Petrello clenched his fists, his fingers tingled, the

muscles in his arms contracted and he felt himself begin to shake. The sensation was familiar. Nurse Ogle's ridicule was hard to bear, and how she enjoyed his discomfort.

The sniggering grew louder.

Guanhamara took his arm and squeezed it tight. 'Don't let her hurt you,' she whispered. 'Tell her straight.'

Petrello stood up. 'I was on an errand for my father, to find the investigator. And when I found him, he set me a task.'

'The investigator?' Nurse Ogle's eyebrows lifted to the edge of the white wimple that she wore tight over her grey head. 'A task? What task?'

'To find signs,' Petrello stated. 'For the bellman has disappeared.'

The sniggering stopped and an animated buzz broke out.

Nurse Ogle appeared at a loss for once. 'I see,' she said at last. 'And that is why there was no warning before the Vanishing.'

'Exactly,' said Guanhamara.

'You would have to poke your nose in, wouldn't you, Guanhamara?' Nurse Ogle rose from her seat and swept to the door. 'Wash your platters and stack them,' she called as she left the hall.

The children filed out, taking their platters to the pump in the courtyard. As they were replacing them on the long table, a boy came up to Petrello and asked if he could help in the search. It was Sir Edern's son, Selgi. He was red-haired like his father, and always wore an eager smile.

'You have to do your lessons, Selgi,' said Petrello.

'So do you,' Selgi retorted.

'I have permission from the king,' lied Petrello.

'So do I,' said Guanhamara, adding another lie. 'We wouldn't want to get you into trouble, Selgi.'

For a moment Selgi lost his smile. 'Then I shall help when lessons are over,' he said.

'Agreed,' said Petrello.

'Tell Friar Gereint why we are absent,' Guanhamara called after the departing Selgi.

'I will.' Selgi waved a hand.

'Where shall we start?' Guanhamara grabbed her brother's hand and pulled him towards the kitchens.

'Why the kitchens?' Petrello protested.

'It's a good place to hide. There are cellars.'

'But, Guan, I don't think Rigg is hiding. Didn't I tell

you? There was blood on the steps and the wizards believe he was taken. To tell the truth, I don't know what sort of signs I'm looking for.'

'Oh! Then how –' Guanhamara stopped when she saw the investigator hurrying from the Bell Tower. Putting a hand on his feathered cap, he began to run. 'Look! It's Wyngate. I think he has made a discovery.'

'It's grim, by the look on his face,' said Petrello.

Chapter Three

The Hall of Corrections

Brother and sister stood half-hidden behind a pillar. The door to the Meeting Hall was only two paces away, yet they dared not go closer. They could hear the investigator's raised voice, but his words were muffled behind the thick door.

The guard stared at the pillar. He could see Petrello's shoulder and the hem of Guanhamara's blue robe. The bell for lessons rang out, but the children didn't move. All at once the doors opened and the king strode out; his lips were compressed, his eyes troubled.

A crowd of Knight Protectors followed. Some made for the armoury, others went to the stables. The guard began to close the doors, but a solitary figure suddenly walked out. The investigator nodded at the guard, then turned away. He rubbed his chin, his expression puzzled rather than concerned.

'What has happened, Investigator?' asked Petrello as Wyngate passed.

'Ah, Petrello.' The man stopped beside the children.

'Has the bellman been found?' asked Guanhamara.

Wyngate shook his head. 'He won't be found within the castle. There's no need for a search now.'

Petrello was disappointed. He had wanted to find Rigg, to spite Nurse Ogle and prove that he could do something right. 'Have you found something, Wyngate?'

The investigator looked at Petrello and his sister. They could see that he wanted to speak, but hesitated, perhaps because they were children.

'We swear on our father's name that we will never speak of what you tell us,' said Petrello.

'Except to each other,' Guanhamara added quietly.

The investigator smiled. 'You are growing up. Both of you. There are those in this castle whom I could not trust. But I know you would keep your word.'

They waited, silent and eager.

'There is a traitor in the castle.'

Shocked, the children stared at the investigator. They had heard of traitors, but none had ever been found in the Red Castle – as far as they knew.

'How can you tell?' asked Guanhamara.

Wyngate touched the jackdaw's feather in his cap, as if for luck. 'There is a window on the second level of the Bell Tower,' he said. 'It was not latched. Attached to the central beam of the casement I found threads of a rope that had been tied around it. The window can only be unlatched from the inside. And only someone inside the castle could have tied a rope around that beam.'

'So Rigg was wounded, and maybe knocked unconscious by a person we know?' Petrello was now more intrigued than horrified.

'Either that, or the traitor assisted a stranger from outside.'

'But the guard on watch would have seen,' Guanhamara pointed out.

'Exactly,' Wyngate agreed. 'And so I have had the guard arrested. He is to be questioned by the king and Chancellor Thorkil in the Hall of Corrections. I am on my way there.'

'Can we come?' Petrello asked, knowing the answer, but unable to contain his curiosity.

Wyngate smiled. 'Of course you may not, cheeky boy. Off to your lessons. You are late.'

'We were searching for signs,' said Guanhamara.

'Too late.' The investigator hurried off, calling over his shoulder, 'Rigg is long gone from this castle.'

Petrello and his sister watched the investigator's bird-like steps across the cobblestones. The feathers in his cap caught a ray of early sunlight and glinted blue, then green and then the same shade of purple as his flying cloak.

'I am afraid of Chancellor Thorkil,' Guanhamara said in a low voice.

Petrello looked at his sister, surprised by her tone. It was unlike her to be afraid. 'Why?'

'There is a coldness about him,' she said. 'I wouldn't want to be that poor guard.'

'Perhaps he's not so poor,' said Petrello. 'Perhaps he is in on the plot.'

'You and your plots,' Guanhamara laughed. 'How you love intrigue, brother. But I want to hear what the guard says. Come on!' Lifting her hem, she began to skip across the courtyard.

Petrello looked around nervously. Children were commanded to go to their schoolroom as soon as they heard the second bell. But today knights and courtiers hurried past, hardly glancing at the truants.

'Come on!' hissed Guanhamara. She ran into the shadowed cloisters and Petrello followed her.

'Where are you going, brother?' The shout came from behind them.

Petrello looked back. Tolomeo came racing up to him.

'I'm not telling you where I'm going,' said Petrello, 'unless you tell me where you go every morning.'

'I can't!' Tolomeo said emphatically. 'I'm sorry but I promised . . .' he clamped his lips together.

'Who did you promise?' Petrello persisted.

'Stop arguing and hurry up,' called Guanhamara.

Petrello didn't want to attract attention. He barely raised his voice to say, 'Tolly's here.'

Guanhamara turned and hurried back to them. 'Good,' she said. 'Tolly, you can tell Friar Gereint that Petrello and I are on an errand for the king.'

'Are you?' Tolly was impressed.

'We were,' said Petrello.

Tolly frowned. 'Why won't you tell?'

'We're wasting time,' Guanhamara tapped her foot. 'Tolly, we're trying to find out why the guard didn't see

Rigg the bellman being abducted.'

'Was he abducted?' Tolly's eyes grew round. 'Can I come with you?'

'If you tell us where you go every morning,' said Petrello.

Tolly buttoned his lip. Guanhamara sighed and said, 'We'll miss everything if you don't hurry. And who's going to make our excuses to Friar Gereint?'

'We'll think of something,' Petrello said quickly. 'Well, Tolly?'

It was Tolly's turn to sigh. 'I might tell you after we've done whatever it is you were going to do.'

'We're going to the Hall of Corrections.' Petrello turned to see Guanhamara pacing ahead of them. She stopped and looked back at the boys, putting a finger to her lips.

'I knew this would happen,' whispered Petrello. 'There's a guard outside the hall and he's looking straight at us. We'll never get past him.'

Guanhamara took a few steps towards them. 'We just need to slip inside. The steps to the next floor are right behind the door, and see, it's still open. They must be waiting for someone.'

'How do we get past the guard?' Petrello nodded at the man.

'I know him,' said Guanhamara.

'And so . . .?' Petrello noticed that the man was now frowning at them.

'And so I know that he's the best and proudest rat-killer. He can't resist them. I've heard him boast that his tally is seven hundred and fifty-three.'

'Must we find a rat?' Tolly wrinkled his nose.

Guanhamara stared hard at her brothers. Petrello had never seen such an expression on her face. She looked both expectant and somehow defiant. 'I did something yesterday. Something I've never done before. In two minutes I shall repeat it.'

Tolly and Petrello didn't know what to say, or what to expect. They watched their sister stare at the guard's feet. They heard her murmur. The sound was tuneful but came from deep inside her throat; her lips were barely parted. They followed their sister's gaze. Tolly gave a light gasp and Petrello grabbed his arm. There, sniffing at the man's boots, was the biggest rat they had ever seen.

'A-a-a-a-agh!' The guard lifted his foot. The rat leapt.

The guard brought down his pike. 'A-a-a-a-agh!' he roared again. The rat ran and the guard gave chase.

'Now!' Guanhamara plucked at her brothers' sleeves and ran towards the door.

Petrello found himself racing after his sister, his head full of questions. How did she do it? Was the rat flesh and blood? Could it be killed? He slipped past the open door and up the narrow steps, his eye on the hem of his sister's gown, fast disappearing up the winding steps. Tolly came panting behind him.

They reached the empty room above the Hall of Corrections. Guanhamara tiptoed carefully across the floor to the other end of the room. She knelt down and beckoned her brothers. They were not so light-footed. Even though they walked on their toes, the boards creaked under their boots. But the king's deep voice in the room below drowned out almost every other sound.

Tolly and Petrello reached their sister and knelt down beside her. She nodded approval and pointed to a gap between the floorboards directly in front of her. The inch-wide space ran for several paces before the boards closed up again.

Guanhamara lay full-length on the floor, one eye pressed to the gap. Petrello found it hard not to laugh. His sister was obviously something of a spy; she had done this before. He lay beside the gap, his head touching hers, his feet in the opposite direction. There was a soft bump as Tolly dropped down behind him. Now all three had a narrow view of the room below.

The king was out of sight, sitting at the far end of the room. Lord Thorkil couldn't be seen, but they could hear his voice. However, when the guard was led in by two soldiers, they stood directly beneath Petrello. He couldn't see the prisoner's face but his helmet had been removed and his bald head looked familiar. The soldiers pushed him forward and then stood behind him.

'John, you know why you are here?' said the king.

John bowed his head. 'I'm told that Rigg the bellman has been taken, Your Majesty.'

'Were you asleep, John?'

There was no reply. The prisoner remained with his head bowed, his hands clasped before him.

The silence lasted so long, Petrello raised his head. He found himself looking into his sister's eyes. Guanhamara shrugged. Was the man in a trance?

'I asked you a question, John.' The king's voice was stern, yet patient.

'I was not asleep, Your Majesty.'

'We're glad to hear it.' This voice had a high, brittle quality. There were several slow, precise footsteps on the flagstones below, as though someone wanted to give John time to think. Petrello put his head to the gap. He made no sound but the man who had just walked into view looked up. Lord Thorkil's eyes were a bitter blue. Petrello tried hard not to blink. Could the chancellor see the three pairs of eyes peering down at him?

Lord Thorkil turned his gaze on John, the guard. 'Your post on the South Wall commands a view of the Bell Tower, does it not?'

'It does, my lord.' John's voice was dry and fearful.

'So how is it that you failed to see anything unusual outside the tower earlier this morning?'

'I . . . I . . .' John hung his head. He wriggled his shoulders as though trying to escape invisible bonds.

'Perhaps you did see something, John,' said the king. 'Are you too afraid to tell us?'

John's head came up. He was the same height as Chancellor Thorkil and looked directly into his eyes.

Petrello couldn't see either of the men's faces, but he sensed that a look passed between them; a look unseen by the king.

'It is true . . .' the guard quavered. 'I witnessed a dreadful act, but I was threatened with my life not to divulge what I had seen.'

'Tell us, John.' Lord Thorkil's voice was now smooth and persuasive. 'Don't be afraid. You know that the king is just.'

Words now tumbled out of John. How he had seen two men approach the tower, how a high window had opened, and a rope, thrown by one of the strangers, had been caught by someone behind the window, and tied to a beam.

'And did you not think to alert us at this stage?' The king paced across the floor and now stood beside the chancellor.

John squirmed and hung his head again. One of the soldiers prodded him in the back, and he murmured, 'I could not.' Then, clearing his throat, he added, 'I had been warned to look the other way, but I was curious to see . . . how it would be achieved.'

'So, you knew what was going to happen?' said the

chancellor. 'And did you see Rigg being taken?'

John nodded miserably. 'He was tied to the rope and lowered. He was unconscious, his head bloody. As they carried him away the Vanishing began, and I was in the air – I saw nothing more.'

The king stood very still. He rubbed his head, touching the crown. He seemed reluctant to ask another question, yet all three children lying above knew what it would be.

'Who warned you? Who threatened you?'

John wrung his hands. He stared at the motionless chancellor, and then looked away.

'Tell us, John,' the chancellor said evenly.

After a long pause the desperate prisoner blurted, 'Your son, Your Majesty.'

The king's hand fell to his side. 'You lie!'

John shook his head, almost like a dog shaking water from its coat. 'Forgive me, Your Majesty, but I do not lie.'

Petrello looked up and once again found himself looking into his sister's frightened face.

'I have six sons, John,' said the king. 'Three of them are children. Which of my three elder sons do you accuse?'

John squirmed. He looked at the chancellor and then

at the floor. 'Prince Amadis,' he mumbled. 'He threatened to set his wolves on me.'

Petrello was so shocked he sat bolt upright, bumping into Tolly kneeling behind him. Guanhamara was sitting now and frowning in disbelief. Of all their brothers, Amadis was their favourite, and the one least likely to threaten anyone.

The children's sudden movements made a rustling and a scraping, but the atmosphere in the room below was now so tense no one seemed to notice the sounds above their heads.

Guanhamara mouthed the words, 'Not Amadis. It can't be.'

Petrello pointed to the other side of the room, where the steps began. He wanted to run and warn Amadis, but his sister shook her head. There were footsteps below them. The king was leaving the Hall of Corrections, followed by the chancellor, the prisoner and his guards.

'What will our father do now?' asked Tolly.

The others couldn't answer him.

Chapter Four

Caught in the Forest

'We must warn our brother.' Tolly jumped up and ran to the steps.

Petrello followed. 'He'll be with the Knight Protectors.'

'You two run.' Guanhamara shooed them with her hands. 'I'll investigate. Why did that guard lie?'

Petrello looked back. 'He was afraid of the chancellor. A look passed between them, and the guard went kind of tense. Didn't you see?'

'I'm not sure.' Guanhamara scratched her forehead. 'I'll tell Wyngate. He'll know what to do.'

'Why not go to our father, Guan?' said Tolly. 'He surely can't believe that Amadis is a traitor.'

'Maybe. Run now, and get to Amadis before the chancellor's men.'

Tolly and Petrello raced down the steps and across

the courtyard. The stables covered a large area close to the East Gate. The grooms were busy saddling horses for the chancellor's men, who stood in groups talking in low voices. They turned to stare at the boys when they entered the stables.

'Why are you not in the schoolroom?' said Chimery, a lean fellow with lank grey hair and a deeply lined face.

'We have permission from the king,' said Tolly, 'to . . .' he floundered.

Chimery clicked his tongue and turned back to his comrades. The boys made out the words 'brats' and 'spoiled', but the men's voices were too low and hurried for them to hear any more.

Although the chancellor's men were not Knight Protectors, Lord Thorkil was a distinguished knight himself, and had personally trained an elite force of ten fighting men. They didn't share the Knight Protectors' easy-going, boisterous lifestyle, nor did they wear the bright colours favoured by the other knights. The chancellor's men were clad from head to toe in grey; from darkest charcoal to palest ash. Others in the castle called them the grey men, though never to their faces.

While the grey men were badgering the grooms, the

boys quickly saddled their ponies and trotted out of the stable. As they cantered through the South Gate, Tolly asked, 'What did you think of the rat, Trello?'

'What did I think?' Petrello grinned. 'I thought, so that's our sister's endowment; making creatures out of air. And then I thought, at last she's going to get her own back on Olga and Lilith.'

Olga and Lilith were their older sisters. Lilith was sixteen, Olga three years younger. People joked that Lilith's sister stuck closer to her than her own shadow. They both had truly unpleasant talents.

It was early spring and green buds were appearing on the ancient trees. But the air was still cold. Not far from the edge of the forest, the boys found Urien, a small, stout knight who always seemed to find himself left far behind the others. His mare was old, but Urien wouldn't part with her. He said that she had always carried him home safely.

'Which path did our brother Amadis take?' Petrello asked Urien.

Urien turned about in his saddle. 'Edern went that way.' He pointed east. 'Peredur, that way.' He pointed south. 'Borlath followed him. Mabon the archer, he went west and so did Ilgar and Edwin. But, um, I saw Amadis

45

riding, um . . .' He pointed north. 'That way.'

'To the mountains,' said Petrello.

'Yes, it would be,' Urien agreed.

'To speak with the eagles,' said Tolly. 'Eagles can see more than earthbound creatures like us.'

'True.' Urien nodded. He took an apple from a bag hanging on his belt. 'What chance do I have of finding the bellman,' he mumbled as he chewed. 'Your brother, Amadis, will come closest.'

'We know.' Tolly gave his pony a light kick and then raced away.

'Good hunting, Urien,' called Petrello as he galloped after Tolly.

The boys had explored the forest many times, but it was so vast they knew it was unlikely that they would ever know every part of it. Paths spread through the trees like the threads of a giant cobweb; deer tracks, goat tracks, paths made by the knights' horses, the almost invisible trails of creatures that were rarely seen, and the paths of the villagers who came to collect wood for their fires, to catch hares and pigeons for their tables.

The Knight Protectors rarely hunted. They didn't have the same urgency as the villagers to fill their larders, for King Timoken could multiply, and the food that was stored in the castle stock house could be doubled in less than a day.

At the base of the mountain the trees began to thin; soon only gorse and wind-blown thorn trees clung to the mountainside. A track made by wild goats led to the summit, where a covering of snow glistened in the sunlight.

Petrello was ahead when they began to ascend the mountain. He was looking up at the eagle hovering above him when he heard a shout. He looked back and saw his brother's pony tossing its head. It stamped and gave a whinny of distress. Tolly had vanished.

Unable to turn his pony quickly on the narrow path, Petrello leapt off its back and ran down into the trees.

'Tolly! Tolomeo! Is this a joke? Answer me!'

A rock smacked into the back of Petrello's head. He tried to keep his balance but, dizzy with pain, he fell forward, his face buried in a thicket. Hands grabbed his ankles, small rough hands. He tried to turn his head but the pain was too great and covering his face with an arm, he had to let his assailants drag him backwards over the stony ground.

'Let me go!' Petrello shouted. 'I have nothing.'

'You ain't got your dignity, that's for sure.' It was a boy's voice, a boy no older than Petrello himself by the sound of it.

It's a game, thought Petrello. He almost relaxed, but then he became angry and yelled, 'Stop this! I'm the king's son.'

'We guessed that!' This was a different voice, pitched higher. Perhaps it belonged to a girl. She sounded hard and spiteful.

They began to tie Petrello's ankles together, their small hands twisting the rope so tightly his bones grated. As they pulled back his arms, he managed a quick look over his shoulder. He saw curtains of thick brown hair, almost covering a pale face streaked with mud. The girl grinned, showing a toothless gap in her lower jaw. She couldn't have been more than eight or nine.

Once his feet and hands were bound, Petrello was allowed to roll over. He found himself in a dark cave, the ceiling a damp rock veined in green moss. His brother lay in a corner. Tolly's hands and feet were bound and his eyes were closed, but he appeared to be breathing.

'What have you done to my brother?' Petrello glared

at the two ragged children grinning down at him.

'Knocked him on the head,' said the boy. He looked very like the girl, though his hair was shorter and his chin wider. 'He'll be all right,' went on the boy. 'I've been hit on the head worse than he has, haven't I, sis?'

'That you have. And you ain't dead,' the girl cackled.

Tolly began to moan. His eyes opened and he mumbled, 'What happened?'

'See?' said the girl. 'I told you. He ain't dead.'

Tolly began to wriggle into a sitting position. 'Aw, my head. Trello, where are we?'

'You'd better ask them.' Petrello nodded at the two children.

Tolly looked up at the mud-streaked, smiling faces. 'We can't give you anything. We haven't got money, or jewels.'

'You got ponies,' said the girl.

'I suppose you could take one,' Petrello said reluctantly. 'But leave us the other, so we can get home.'

The boy pouted. 'Don't want your ponies.'

'What do you want then?' Petrello wondered if he and Tolly were to be dragged away by the children's family; bandits, no doubt. Would they be killed, just for being the sons of a king?

'We want to come and live in your castle.' The girl had lost her smug little grin. She squatted in front of the brothers and her voice became soft and confiding. 'We've heard about the Red King who can multiply anything, so his people never go hungry. They say he can make rain come and go and he talks to wolves and eagles, and all sorts of animals, just like they were friends.'

'And thunder,' added the boy, kneeling beside his sister. 'He can make clouds, can't he, and rainbows? And we know about the castle that disappears . . .'

'And the loveliness inside.' The girl was almost crooning now. 'And the fine clothes you wear. Look at your jackets: they're like magic, not what normal people wear, even lords and ladies.'

'And your boots,' said the boy. 'I wish I had those.'

'But we're not going to take them,' the girl said quickly. ''Cos we're proud. We just want to live in the Red Castle.'

'So we're going to ransom you,' they both said with satisfaction.

'Ransom?' Tolly and Petrello said together.

'Yeah. That's right.' The girl's eyes were shining now. 'We send a note to the castle. We tell them we've got princes. But we'll give them back if we can come and live in the castle.'

The brothers stared at the ragged children. Their sudden cheerfulness made Petrello feel uncomfortable. He had never given his clothes a thought, nor the food he ate. Were they so fine?

'You'll have to write the letter,' said the boy, 'because we can't.'

'Have you been planning this for a long time?' Petrello asked thoughtfully.

'We saw you on your ponies with their fine harnessing and pretty saddlings,' said the girl. 'And Gunfrid just thought of it. "Let's catch them and ransom them," he said.'

'Because Zeba and me'd been wondering how we could get into your castle,' Gunfrid smiled. 'And there you were.'

The boy looked so confident, Petrello felt sad. Their plan was hopeless. The two half-starved children would be caught by the guards as soon as they showed their faces. He shook his head. 'It won't work.'

'Will!' Gunfrid and Zeba shouted.

'You don't know . . .' Gunfrid stopped and looked

51

up at the roof of the cave. Dust fell on to his face and he sneezed.

A series of dull thuds echoed around the rocks. Hoof beats. There was a horse above them.

Petrello opened his mouth and then closed it. There could be worse than these children out in the forest. Zeba and Gunfrid were of the same mind, it seemed. They froze, their eyes wide with apprehension.

Tolly didn't share their fears. 'Here!' he shouted. 'Help!'

Gunfrid brought up his fist, his face an angry red, but he didn't hit Tolly. It was an empty threat.

Petrello peered through the low cave entrance. He could see the black legs of a horse, but the rider was out of sight. Gunfrid and Zeba had their backs to the entrance. Now that Tolly had given them away, Petrello felt he had nothing to lose. 'Here!' he shouted.

The man outside dropped to his knees and looked into the cave.

'Amadis!' cried the brothers.

In one glance Amadis took in his brothers' bound hands and feet and the two ragged children. 'What mess have you got yourselves into, little brothers?' he said.

Gunfrid and Zeba scuttled over to the brothers. Gunfrid

produced a small knife and held it to Tolly's throat.

Amadis shook his head. 'Boy, put down your knife!'

'I will not,' Gunfrid said defiantly. 'I will cut your brother's throat, if you . . . if you . . .' He looked imploringly at his sister, who shrugged her thin shoulders and grimaced.

Amadis made a strange noise in his throat. Petrello recognised the sound. He knew what would happen next.

The wolf, Greyfleet, slipped past Amadis and walked into the cave. Gunfrid and Zeba began to scream, even before the wolf revealed his long fangs.

'Hush,' said Amadis. 'The wolf will not hurt you, but I suggest you use your knife to cut my brothers' bonds. If you do not, Greyfleet here will be on you in a moment, and then nothing can save either of you.'

Zeba had wriggled into the darkest corner of the cave, and there she stayed, her eyes never leaving the wolf.

Greyfleet moved not a muscle. Petrello and Tolly knew him well. He would do anything that Amadis asked of him, but he was a wild creature for all that, and would revert to his savage nature in a second.

Gunfrid rapidly cut through Tolly's bonds, but when he began to sever the rope around Petrello's ankles, his small hands began to shake.

'Don't cut my flesh, I beg you,' said Petrello with a laugh.

He had hoped to calm the boy with a joke, but there was a sob in Gunfrid's voice when he replied. 'I don't mean to cut. I'm doing my best.' He crawled around Petrello and quickly released the hands tied behind his back.

Bending his head to avoid hitting the low cave roof, Petrello moved swiftly past the wolf and joined his brothers outside.

The two children sat very close to each other, staring at the wolf. Greyfleet still hadn't moved. When Amadis made a sound low in his throat, Greyfleet's ears flicked. He turned and loped out of the cave. Amadis touched the wolf's head as he passed and then Greyfleet was gone, gliding into the trees until he became one of the many shadows that moved incessantly across the forest floor.

'I found your ponies.' Amadis told his brothers. 'We'd best be getting home.'

'You can't go home, Amadis,' Petrello said gravely. 'That's why we're here. We came to warn you.'

Amadis gave Petrello a quizzical look. 'You speak in riddles, brother. What do you mean?'

Tolly said breathlessly, 'The guard on the South Gate

has accused you of being in league with the bellman's abductors.'

Amadis did something unexpected. He chuckled.

'Believe us,' begged Petrello. 'He says you threatened to set your wolf on him, if he prevented the bellman's capture. The chancellor's men are searching for you. You must ride away; now, Amadis, before they find you.'

Amadis gave a small frown, but the next moment he was smiling and then he was laughing.

Petrello, worried for his brother's sanity cried, 'Don't you understand, Amadis?'

'I hear what you're saying,' said Amadis. 'But it makes no sense. I was on my way back to tell the king that the bellman is being taken to Castle Melyntha. The eagles told me. They saw it all. Why would I reveal the bellman's whereabouts, if I had assisted in his capture?'

Petrello couldn't answer.

Tolly said, 'John, the guard, was lying.'

Why? The unspoken question hung between them. Petrello remembered the way the guard had stared at Lord Thorkil, and then looked away, as though he were afraid. 'I think it might have something to do with the chancellor,' he said.

Amadis looked serious for once. 'Come on, boys. I've tethered your ponies. We must unravel this mystery.'

Petrello turned to the cave. Gunfrid and Zeba had scrambled out. They stood together, their eyes darting from one brother to another.

'Please . . .' Gunfrid spoke in a thin, choked voice.

'We must take them with us.' Petrello looked at the homeless children.

'That boy would have killed you,' said Amadis.

'No. He was frightened. Gunfrid and Zeba have nowhere to go, and we have so much.'

Amadis smiled. 'You have a soft heart, Petrello.' He patted his horse Isgofan's neck. 'Come on then, Gunfrid and Zeba. You had better ride with me.'

Chapter Five
Wolves and Eagles

Amadis lifted the two ragged children on to his horse and jumped up behind them.

The children were so thin the three of them fitted comfortably on the fine saddle with its golden pommel. It had been a gift from the king on Amadis's seventeenth birthday.

As soon as Petrello and Tolly were mounted, they set off along the forest track. They could hear movements in the trees, the occasional shout and, once or twice, a horse whinnied.

'They're still searching for the bellman,' said Amadis. He cupped his hands around his mouth and called, 'Hey, Sir Edern, Sir Peredur! I have news!'

The other Knight Protectors were obviously some distance away. Perhaps they couldn't make out the words that Amadis was shouting. Petrello was anxious. The chancellor's men might have heard his brother's voice. Amadis would be arrested before he had time to explain.

'Maybe it would be better not to shout, Amadis,' Petrello suggested. 'The wrong people might hear.'

'And you'll be caught,' said Tolly.

'Don't worry, little brothers. I have my guardians.' Amadis gave a soft yelp. 'See!'

He pointed at the thickets bordering the track on both sides.

The boys glimpsed the bobbing head of a wolf, then another, and another. There were four wolves, two on each side of the track. The wolves showed themselves, briefly, then disappeared.

'Greyfleet and his brothers.' Amadis looked over his shoulder and smiled.

Gunfrid and Zeba stared nervously at the undergrowth. They hunched their shoulders and lowered their heads.

Amadis patted the boy's shoulder. 'You're safe with me.'

All at once, Gunfrid muttered, 'In Castle Melyntha they hate the Red King.'

'And how do you know this?' asked Amadis, frowning.

'We come from there,' said the boy. 'Our lord, Sir

Osbern D'Ark, hates the king because he is a magician and his castle is hidden, and because he stole Sir Osbern's bride.'

'That would be our mother,' said Amadis. 'Sir Osbern is descended from a conqueror, is he not?'

'His grandfather was a conqueror,' cried Zeba, suddenly animated. 'One of those men who invaded our country and killed our true King Harold.'

'That was a hundred years ago,' said Petrello, airing his knowledge.

'Yes, when the false King William came,' said Gunfrid. 'But conquerors still come, many, many, many of them, and the new false king gives them our land and our houses and our cattle and our forests.'

'We know our history.' Zeba raised her rough little voice defiantly. 'Our parents told us, over and over, so that we should never forget it.'

'And they hate the Red King as much as the conquerors,' added Gunfrid.

'Why?' Amadis was genuinely astonished.

'Because he never came to rescue them,' said Gunfrid. 'Our parents were children of wealthy merchants who rebelled against the conquerors and were killed for it.

But their children, our parents, ran into the forest and lived there, until they were caught by Sir Osbern's men. Some of their friends escaped and went to live with the Red King. And our parents thought that because the Red King was a magician, and very powerful, he would come to rescue them. But he never did. They waited and waited and waited, and now they are dead.'

'They worked hard even when they were sick,' said Zeba. 'Because they were slaves, and so were we, until we escaped.'

Even Amadis was lost for words. Petrello didn't want to believe the scruffy children, and yet he found it hard to doubt them. Their voices rang with passionate resentment.

'If our father was so disliked by your parents,' Amadis said at last, 'why do you want to live in the Red Castle?'

After a moment's hesitation, Gunfrid said, 'We want to live a magical life and be safe.' He sounded a little ashamed.

Zeba mumbled something and Amadis asked her to speak up, for no one would be angry with her.

Hardly raising her voice, Zeba murmured, 'I want to know why the Red King didn't save our parents.'

'I see,' Amadis said thoughtfully. He whinnied softly and his horse began to canter.

Petrello's pony followed; Tolly, humming to himself, came last.

Amadis seemed eager to get back; his horse gathered speed and Petrello found it hard to keep up. Tolly was left far behind.

There was a sudden, distant shout. Petrello reined in his pony and looked back. There was no sign of Tolly, but the track twisted and turned so often, he could have just been beyond the nearest bend. The shouting grew louder. 'Hey there, Amadis!'

'Hey there, Sir Edern!' Amadis turned his horse just as Sir Edern came galloping up, with Tolly in his wake.

'Young Tolomeo tells me you've news of the bellman,' said Edern, his horse slowing to a trot.

'Indeed,' said Amadis. 'I heard it from the eagles. The bellman is being taken to Castle Melyntha.'

'Aha!' boomed Sir Edern. 'Castle Melyntha.' He took a small hunting horn from his belt and blew several long blasts. 'Well done, lad!' He raised a gloved hand to Amadis, wheeled his horse around and galloped away, calling, 'I'll have to find Peredur. He's gone far south, but the others will have heard my call. Tell the king . . .'

The rest of his words were lost in a thunder of hooves and a crackling of undergrowth, all accompanied by the shouting of Knight Protectors in different parts of the forest.

Amadis smiled to himself. 'One mystery solved,' he said, but another to be fathomed. Come on, boys!'

Petrello thought about the chancellor's men. Had they heard the horn? Perhaps they had gone east, to search the town of Rossmellon. It wasn't far. They might have returned to the castle already.

The trees thinned towards the edge of the forest, and the castle came into view, the South Gate directly facing them. The chancellor's men were stationed in a line before the entrance, the great doors were open on to the courtyard, and a bustling of soldiers could be seen behind the grey men.

Amadis whispered to his horse and it began a gentle walk. His brothers fell in behind him.

'Who are those men at the gate?' asked Gunfrid. 'Their look is fierce.'

'Not for long, I hope,' said Amadis. 'They are Chancellor Thorkil's men, and they take their duties very seriously.'

'Take care, brother,' Petrello said earnestly. 'They mean to make you their prisoner.'

Amadis laughed. 'They don't stand a chance.' As his black horse began to walk up the slight incline to the South Gate, four wolves emerged from the trees. They slipped elegantly alongside the horse then formed a line in front of the group.

One of the chancellor's men drew his sword. Petrello recognised Chimery's lined face. Were four wolves enough to protect Amadis? Even as the thought entered Petrello's head, a stirring in the air made him look up. The sky was dark with silent eagles. They floated on slow currents, their great wings spread wide; there were so many their wingtips almost touched. Amadis had made them forget they were solitary hunters.

One of the eagles swooped down and alighted on the bronze pad that protected Amadis's shoulder. 'If they try to cut down my wolves, the eagles will pluck out their eyes,' said Amadis.

Gunfrid and Zeba shuddered. They had thought that in the company of princes entering the castle would be easy.

The wolves increased their pace; they lowered their

heads, hunched their shoulders and began a swift creeping movement towards the chancellor's men.

'Call off your wolves!' shouted Lord Thorkil.

'Tell your men to stand aside,' called Amadis.

'Not until your beasts are behind you!' Lord Thorkil snarled, drawing his sword.

'Let us through!' Amadis demanded. 'We have news of the bellman.'

'Why do you bring ragged strangers to our castle?' called Chimery.

'They need our protection,' Amadis replied.

'Psha! Wild children are trouble,' said Lord Thorkil. 'Tell them to dismount.'

'I will not. The children can help us. They are from Castle Melyntha, where the bellman is being taken.' Amadis urged his horse forward. The eagle on his shoulder gave a threatening cry and the birds above dropped lower and lower.

The eagles were now so near their heads, Petrello could hear the ripple of their feathers. They seemed to suck the air from his lungs, but he forced his pony to follow Amadis, and Tolly did the same. They were so close, Petrello could touch his brother's outstretched fingers.

'They won't harm us, Tolly,' Petrello whispered. 'A sound from Amadis and they'll go.'

'Are you sure?' croaked Tolly.

Amadis was only a few paces from the chancellor's men, but their line didn't break. Lord Thorkil's hard gaze never wavered from the prince's face. The chancellor seemed poised to move, yet unable to give way. He gave a brief command, and all his men drew their swords.

'You are a traitor, Amadis!' roared the chancellor. 'Give yourself up!'

The prince's answer was a thin eerie cry. The eagle on his shoulder flew straight at the chancellor's men; the other birds swooped and the line of grey men broke. Wolves snapped at their heels, talons stabbed their helmets, great wings beat on their shoulders and the men scattered, their swords waving at empty air. It was a cheering sight, but Petrello feared for Amadis. He would have to pay for this humiliation. Lord Thorkil never forgave an insult.

The soldiers mustering in the courtyard turned to stare at Amadis, their commander throwing a hostile glance in his direction.

'You were no doubt coming to look for me,' said Amadis.

The commander was about to answer, when he was interrupted.

'There you are!' said a woman's voice.

The soldiers parted and Queen Berenice strode up to the three princes. She might have had nine children but she was still beautiful. Her blue dress clung tight about her small waist, where she wore a wide belt studded with jewels. Her golden hair, braided round her head, was only one shade darker than her second son's. She seldom wore a crown. 'What have we here?' she asked, patting Gunfrid's small foot.

'Two more children for you, Mother.' Amadis dismounted and lifted Gunfrid and Zeba from his horse.

The queen laughed. 'You're in trouble, my son, but I told the king he should be ashamed to think you had betrayed us.'

'I have news of the bellman. Got it from the eagles. He's being taken to Melyntha.'

'Melyntha?' The queen grimaced. Turning to Petrello and Tolly, she said, 'And you two, did you catch your brother and bring him home?'

Smiling, the boys slid off their ponies. 'We went to warn him,' Petrello admitted. He could never lie to his mother.

'Come with me, all of you!' She turned away, beckoning them to follow. 'The king is in conference with Wyngate and the wizard. He needs advice.'

'I fear I have upset the chancellor,' said Amadis, pacing beside his mother.

'Outraged him, more like,' said the queen. 'I saw the eagles.' She glanced at the wolves. 'I suppose they must accompany us?'

'Better that way.' Amadis leaned down to touch Greyfleet's head.

The queen laughed again, and Petrello felt the warmth of her voice making everything right, as it always did. He noticed that Gunfrid and Zeba were not with them and, looking over his shoulder, saw the two children standing perfectly still, staring at the stable boys. Three sturdy lads had run out to take care of the princes' mounts and Petrello realised how thin and ragged the lost children were compared to the stable boys, who wore warm, well-fitting jerkins, woollen hose and stout leather boots.

'Come!' Petrello called. 'We'll get you some new clothes.'

Gunfrid and Zeba turned to him. They looked bewildered.

'Yes, you,' said Petrello. 'Come on.'

As they began to follow, Tolly ran to the queen and asked, 'What shall we do with the lost children, Mother, while we are with the king?'

'They come from Melyntha,' said Amadis. 'They'll have knowledge that could help us.'

'Bring them along then.' The queen beckoned the two children. 'The more heads the better.'

'Our mother's approach to a problem is different from others,' Amadis told the waifs. 'She is not cautious.'

'Luckily for you,' said the queen. She looked for the best in everyone. That way, she told her children, people would not want to let her down. Her husband had a more suspicious nature. He claimed it was safer not to trust on sight.

The king was in the Meeting Hall, with Wyngate and the wizard Llyr. The three men sat at one end of the long table; the king at the head, the wizard and the investigator at either side of him. A fire blazed in the great stone fireplace behind him and the room felt warm after the spring chill outside. The three men looked up when the queen and the princes came in. The king saw Gunfrid and Zeba, hovering behind Amadis.

'Beri, what are you up to now?' sighed the king. 'We are in conference here.'

'I can vouch for these two waifs,' said the queen. 'Amadis maintains they can help us. And it's time Petrello and Tolly were brought into our confidence.'

'And you, Amadis,' said the king. 'The chancellor would have you in chains.'

'What nonsense!' The queen lifted the hem of her dress and, swinging her leg over the bench, sat beside Wyngate. 'Thorkil is playing some game of his own. Amadis had nothing to do with the bellman's disappearance. He has brought you news. The bellman is en route to Castle Melyntha.'

Amadis slipped behind the king and sat beside Llyr. 'There is only one track, the eagles are never wrong.'

'Melyntha?' The king's frown deepened. 'Why there?' He looked at Amadis and raised an eyebrow. 'The eagles are certain of this?'

Amadis nodded. 'They're the best spies in the world. They see where all paths lead.'

'Hmm.' The king looked at his hands, resting on the table. He stared at them, twirling his thumbs. 'Why?' he murmured.

A low rumble came from Greyfleet's throat. It was as if the wolf understood the king's thoughts. The king looked at the four wolves and the children, still waiting by the door. 'Come,' he said. 'Sit with us and tell us what you know.'

Petrello, his brother and the two ragged children moved to the table. As they sat all in a row at the far end, the king gave a light bark and, with appreciative grunts, the wolves ran to the fire and sat before the flames.

Gunfrid and Zeba looked anxiously at Petrello. He was about to reassure them when, all at once, the doors crashed open and Borlath strode into the hall. Before anyone could speak, the furious prince uttered a long and strangled, 'A-a-a-a-gh!'

The king stood up. 'Borlath!' His deep voice echoed round the hall. 'You –'

'Why was I not informed?' yelled Borlath, his thick brows drawn together in an angry line. 'Who's the oldest prince? Who's the heir?' He thumped his chest. 'I AM! Yet no one thought to tell me of this meeting. And here sits the one responsible for our catastrophe.' He pointed a flame-tipped finger at Amadis.

'Silence!' roared the king.

The table was some distance from the door but Petrello could feel the heat of Borlath's wrathful fingers on his cheeks.

The king lifted a warning hand. Once he would have used his power to subdue his oldest son, but long ago he had promised the queen never to use magic on their children.

Borlath's angry gaze swept across the room, and found the children sitting at the far end of the table. Now he was truly incensed. 'You let CHILDREN come to your meetings and not ME!' he screeched.

'Enough!' boomed the king.

At the very same moment a lofty bookcase at the end of the room crashed to the floor, sending heavy precious books sliding over the flagstones. Cream vellum pages were horribly creased, and a gold-embossed cover was bent at one corner.

Petrello knew who had done it, even before he saw her. His sister Lilith poked her long face around the door, and there was Olga, in her shadow. Olga who, with her warped mind, could move almost anything she chose.

The time had come for King Timoken to control his children with something more than angry words, but could he break a promise made to the queen?

Chapter Six

The Missing Crystal

The king had no need to break his promise. While he struggled with his conscience, wondering whether to strike his disobedient children with hail or fire, the queen had whirled up from her seat.

'Olga!' cried the queen. 'Come here, this minute.'

Olga was about to slink away after her sister. Lilith had already gone. But Olga found it difficult to ignore her mother's imperious tone. She moved forwards, sulkily, her head down.

'Now put right what you have done!' her mother commanded.

'Can't,' mumbled Olga.

'Don't be ridiculous. If you can push a heavy bookcase over with that clever head of yours then you can pull it back again – and replace the books while you're about it.'

Olga plodded over to the bookcase and stood looking down at it.

'Get on with it, Olga,' said the king. 'We are busy here.'

Borlath stood in the doorway, watching his sister with interest.

'As for you,' said the queen, looking into her oldest son's surly face, 'must the king postpone his urgent meeting while you dally in the forest?'

Anger flashed in Borlath's small black eyes, but he looked away from his mother's withering glance. 'I wasn't dallying.'

'You are a man of nineteen years,' said the queen, 'yet you behave like a truculent child.'

Borlath ground his teeth, half-closed his eyes and clenched his fists. The queen walked away from him and took her seat.

'Sit down, Borlath,' said the king. 'And take part in our discussion, or listen, if you have nothing to say. Amadis was wrongfully accused. He has brought news of the bellman.'

'News?' Borlath moved towards the table, but instead of sitting with the older members of the company, he strode to the far end where the children had gathered. Gunfrid and Zeba watched, their eyes wide with apprehension, as the large knight approached. Red garnets winked on his golden sword hilt, blue lapis lazuli on the handles of the two daggers pushed into his heavy, gold-studded belt. He had been humiliated before them and didn't like their stares. As he passed behind the two waifs he lunged between them and whispered, 'You'd better not get in my way, maggots!'

Petrello and Tolly glared at their brother but didn't dare to speak. The king and queen were listening to Llyr and failed to notice Borlath's menacing lunge, but Amadis saw it, and so did Wyngate.

The waifs shrank down a little, but their faces looked grimly defiant. They were where they wanted to be and a churlish prince wasn't going to drive them away.

All this time Olga had been trying to get the bookcase upright. She would raise it a little way, but then it would come crashing down to the floor again. Petrello reckoned she was doing it on purpose. Either that or she had exhausted her powers when she brought the great thing down. The continual bangs were so distracting it was difficult for anyone to finish a sentence. At last the king became so angry he shouted, 'Do it, Olga. Now. Or your punishment will be worse than you can imagine.'

Olga looked over her shoulder at the king. She remained like this as the top of the bookcase lifted slightly from the floor. And then, with several groans, creaks and thumps it eased itself upright and moved into its former position. The tumbled books flew back on to the shelves and, with a triumphant smirk, Olga flounced from the room.

The king and queen hardly noticed. They were listening intently to Llyr.

'How could this have happened?' the king was heard to say.

'I wish I knew.' Llyr wore a grimace of distress.

'I must see for myself.' The king stood up and marched to the door. 'You still have the bag, you say?'

'Empty, sire!' Llyr ran after the king as he pulled open the door and whirled through it. Wyngate was close on their heels. Amadis and Borlath strode after them, and the children were left with only the queen, who looked as though a thunderbolt had landed right in front of her.

'Mother, what's happened?' cried Petrello.

Tolly ran and looked into her shocked face. 'Tell us.'

'The crystal,' she murmured. 'It's gone.'

'But I saw the crystals, all of them, on Llyr's table only this morning,' said Petrello.

'The others are there.' The queen shook her head. 'But the Seeing Crystal is gone.'

Petrello realised what she was saying. The wizards had a small flat crystal, the size of a man's hand. They kept it hidden, but he had seen it once among Llyr's magical effects. When the wizard held it up to the window, sunlight had blazed through it, bathing the walls of the Eyrie with a thousand dancing colours. And then, at a word from Llyr, the light and the colours had formed an image on the wall. Petrello saw animals drinking from a forest pond, and then a market had appeared where people hurried back and forth with bags and baskets. This picture was replaced by another: soldiers drilling in a castle courtyard.

'That crystal,' said Petrello.

'The Seeing Crystal.' The queen rubbed her forehead with long pale fingers.

Gunfrid and Zeba had crept closer. Aware that something had gone badly wrong, Gunfrid asked, 'What's happened? Ain't we safe no more?'

The queen smiled at him as she stood up. 'Of course

you're safe. Petrello will tell you – I must go to the Eyrie. The wizards might be mistaken, they could have overlooked . . .' She moved swiftly and carried the rest of her words through the door, where they were lost in the sounds of a growing commotion.

Gunfrid looked at Petrello. 'What's a Seeing Crystal? Tell us.'

Petrello hesitated. He had always considered the crystal to be a precious secret, and yet everyone in the castle knew of it, and was comforted by the safety it provided. What harm could it do, to let the orphans know about it?

'It's a crystal that shows the wizards what is happening outside the castle. They can see an enemy approach, soldiers on the move, things that might harm us.'

'They can see into the deep forest,' Tolly added. 'And inside castles with walls thicker than this.' He spread his arms as wide as they would go. 'And into the thunderclouds, and under the ground.'

Gunfrid's mouth dropped open and Zeba's grey eyes looked ready to pop out of her head.

'It's mostly soldiers and spies that the wizards are watching for,' said Petrello. 'So they can go out and cast their spells around the castle to make it disappear.

But before they do that, they have to tell the bellman to warn us all.'

'Because the spell throws us into the air,' Tolly explained.

'We float,' Petrello clarified.

'I'd like that,' said Zeba.

'Me too,' said Gunfrid. 'Unless I banged me head on the ceiling.'

'Hence the warning bell,' Petrello stated.

'But not today,' said a voice, and Guanhamara swung through the door. Behind her came her friend Elin, a tall girl with russet curls and large blue eyes.

'Friar Gereint's been asking for you,' Guanhamara told her brothers. 'And who are these strangers?'

Zeba went up to Guanhamara and touched her dress, pinching the soft blue material between mud-stained fingers. 'What mighty fine clothes,' marvelled the girl.

Guanhamara beamed at her. 'I'll find you some clothes just like mine,' she said, taking the girl's hands.

'Where have you come from, you poor thing?' asked Elin.

'Castle Melyntha, ma'am,' murmured Zeba.

'Not ma'am,' said Elin. 'Just Elin.'

Petrello was eager to follow the queen. Leaving the children with his brother and sister, he ran to the Eyrie. But the king had already gone.

The queen was sitting with her arm around Eri. The old man held his head in his hands, while he ground his teeth and uttered obscure and ancient oaths.

Petrello's presence was ignored.

Enid the dragon waddled around the room, emitting hot snorts of distress and constantly getting in Llyr's way as he ran about, turning over caskets, lifting rugs and feeling in the pockets of the different robes that hung on the Eyrie walls.

Wyngate was methodically sifting through the crystals on the table. 'It might be here,' he said, 'you could have –'

'No,' cried Llyr, motionless at last. 'The Seeing Crystal is always kept in this.' He held up a red velvet bag embroidered with a golden eye. 'I replaced it before we left to begin the Vanishing. Someone has taken it. Let's not deceive ourselves any longer.'

Petrello couldn't help himself. He had to ask, albeit apologetically, 'How do you know when to use the crystal, Llyr? I mean, it's a silent thing, and you can't always be looking at it.'

Eri raised his head. 'It is not a silent thing, boy. It calls us when danger is close.'

'Oh!' Petrello's mouth fell open. 'I see.' He felt foolish.

'Your father will be in the cameldrome,' said the queen gently, 'if you're looking for him.'

'I am,' said Petrello.

As he hastened down the steps, he murmured to himself, 'The Seeing Crystal is not silent.' He should have guessed. How else would the wizards have known when to use it?

Petrello quickly made his way through the crowded courtyard. There were now five courtyards within the castle walls. The first was always bustling with activity, for it was where the most necessary functions of the court had been established. Here were the stables, the dining halls, meeting places and the Hall of Corrections.

In the second courtyard, cooks, carpenters and smiths worked in the cloisters. In the third, the king's sister, Zobayda, had recreated a Spanish garden with fountains, palms and climbing roses. A gentle warmth constantly permeated this quiet place, a climate created by the king especially for his sister. Zobayda was almost always there, reclining on velvet cushions and reading, or sewing clothes for her nephews and nieces.

The fifth courtyard lay empty; it had only been in existence for a year. The fourth had been filled with sand. It was here that the king kept Gabar, the camel that had accompanied him all the way from the secret kingdom. King Timoken still liked to share his problems with Gabar. The camel was his oldest friend.

Today, the third courtyard appeared to be deserted. Zobayda was still in her room, recovering from the shaking she had endured during the unexpected Vanishing.

Petrello could see his aunt sitting in her window, watching the fountain below her. Or was she? Petrello waved, but Zobayda didn't respond. She was staring intently at something on the other side of the fountain.

Droplets of sunlit water tickled Petrello's face as he walked closer to the raised pool surrounding the fountain. A stone mermaid rose from the centre and water splashed from the giant conch shell that she held aloft.

As Petrello walked around the fountain, he felt a hot breeze on his ankles. He looked over his shoulder and saw the dragon, Enid, lolloping towards him. She was overweight and slow on the ground, but she could still fly, and her breath had lost none of its fire.

'Come on then, Enid,' said Petrello. 'I know you want to see Gabar.' He rounded the fountain and gasped.

Olga and Lilith were sitting on a bench in front of the fountain. Lilith wore a grin of delight. Olga was rocking with silent laughter. Before them stood Vyborn. At least it was the top half of Vyborn. From the waist down he was covered in short, greyish bristles. His legs had shrunk, his knees had vanished, his feet were hooves.

Vyborn turned a grimly triumphant face to Petrello. 'I'm not nobody any more,' he snorted.

'N-no,' Petrello stammered.

'He's found his vocation!' Lilith said. 'Don't you agree, brother?'

'V-vocation?' said Petrello.

'His talent,' said Lilith. 'The gift that was due to him, to all the king's children.'

'Perhaps not all.' Olga hid her mouth with her hand, but her words were deliberately clear, and she directed a scornful glance at Petrello.

He hardly noticed. He couldn't tear his gaze away from Vyborn, though he desperately wanted to. His brother's torso was slowly changing; rough bristles covered his chest and arms, his hands turned black and hardened into

82

hooves. When Vyborn's face disappeared behind a mask of coarse hair, Petrello backed away.

A snout grew in the centre of Vyborn's new face, and two tusks appeared on either side of it. Enid grumbled in her throat. Her smoky breath was filled with sparks.

In a trembling voice Petrello asked, 'How did this happen?' He nodded at his brother. 'Did you do it, Lilith?'

Lilith smiled with satisfaction. 'There's a lot that I can do, but not this. Poor little Vyborn, he wanted so much to be special, to have friends . . .'

'So we said, "Then try, Vyborn,"' Olga piped up. '"Maybe you could be different. Think of something."'

'He won't get friends looking like that,' said Petrello.

The new Vyborn could understand him, it seemed, for the wild boar lowered its head and with a ghastly grunt dashed at Petrello.

He leapt back, but not before Enid had aimed long jets of fire at the boar. With a shriek of pain, the boar froze in its tracks and Vyborn's face emerged from the bristles shouting, 'Next time I'll be a serpent, and then you won't get me.'

Petrello turned and, with Enid grunting in his wake, ran out of the courtyard and through the great arch that had once been the main entrance into the castle. Since the spirit ancestors had continued to build, the tall carved doors were now to be found permanently open and in the very centre of the castle.

Beyond the arch, five passages led into the further reaches of the building. Petrello entered the centre passage. It took him to his favourite place, a room identical to the golden chamber in his father's African palace; a room of golden furniture and walls painted with scenes from that hot, faraway kingdom. Camels adorned in gold and silk paced beside small, sunlit houses; monkeys swung from vine-covered trees, exotic birds swooped through a vivid blue sky, and scaly creatures peeped between multi-coloured flowers.

Today Petrello and the dragon didn't linger in the chamber of pictures. They passed the shining tables and the couches covered in cloths of gold. And then Petrello was opening the door into the cameldrome.

Gabar, the camel, was dozing beneath a large fruit tree. The king sat beside him, one hand resting on the camel's neck. All around them, banks of sand rose and fell in smooth golden waves, while high above a slight ripple in the sky was the only hint that an enchanted net covered the cameldrome, keeping its precious inhabitant warm and dry.

'Petrello!' The king leant forward, smiling. 'And Enid.'

Petrello plodded across the man-made desert. Each step he took seemed to sink further into the dense, soft sand. Enid spread her wings and flew to the camel that she adored, settling beneath his long neck with a contented grunt. The camel opened his eyes and burbled fondly at her.

All Petrello had wanted was his father's company, to talk with him about the Seeing Crystal, but he couldn't rid his mind of the scene he had just left; the awful image of his younger brother slowly turning into a wild boar.

The king was pleased to see him. 'Come and sit with us,' he said and, lifting a handful of sand, he let it spill through his fingers. 'You look worried, Petrello. You take our problems too much to heart. There's always a solution, and we'll find it eventually.'

Petrello plunged through the last drift of sand. 'It isn't just the crystal and the bellman. I saw something, Father, and I'm ashamed that I want to wipe it out of my head.'

The king frowned. 'What did you see?'

Petrello hesitated, and then said, in a rush, 'Vyborn.

He turned into a wild boar. It was horrible; the bristles, the snout, the hooves, the tusks.' He covered his face with his hands.

He heard his father sigh. He heard him say, 'That's not so bad. But better if he'd chosen to be a bird or a butterfly. He has obviously become a shape-shifter. Perhaps it had to happen to one of you.'

'But he chose a wild boar!' Petrello's hands dropped to his sides. 'And he attacked me.'

'I see,' said the king gravely. 'Vyborn is very young. It could be that his decision to be a boar was influenced by youthful confusion, or a sense of fun.'

Petrello didn't like to point out that there had never been the slightest sign that Vyborn had a sense of fun. 'Perhaps,' he said. 'But Lilith and Olga never use their talents in a helpful way, and Borlath's fiery fingers always hurt.'

For a moment the king looked sad, and then he said, 'But Amadis . . .?'

Petrello smiled. 'Oh, yes. There's Amadis.' He wished he hadn't mentioned Borlath and his sisters. To lift his father's spirits he would have told him about Guanhamara and the rat, but he couldn't find a way to do that without confessing to their spying. So instead he asked, 'Will it happen to all of us, Father? I mean, having the ability to do what seems impossible?'

The king spread his hands. 'I have no idea.'

'So you don't know if I will be . . . empowered? Or Tolomeo? At the moment neither of us knows if we'll ever be able to do anything special, or useful.'

'I can tell you one thing, Petrello,' said the king, 'If you and Tolomeo eventually develop any unusual talents, you will use them wisely. I know this and it comforts me.'

Chapter Seven

Guanhamara's Demon

Two days passed. One of the Knight Protectors still had not returned: Sir Peredur. Peredur was known for his solitary quests. He often took up the cause of some poor family who were being bullied by their masters. Nevertheless, Sir Edern was anxious.

The king couldn't decide what to do. His chancellor advised letting the matter of the crystal rest. 'The wizards can make a new Seeing Crystal,' said Lord Thorkil.

'Easier said than done,' muttered Eri when the king relayed the chancellor's suggestion. 'Perhaps there is only one Seeing Crystal in the whole world.'

Eri had found the crystal on one of his long walks into the mountains. Llyr had been with him. He was only four years old but he could walk as far as any man. As they picked their way across a shallow stream, Llyr had noticed a patch of quartz sparkling beneath the water. Eri gathered some of the shining stones and brought them back to the castle.

It was only when he was cleaning the quartz in one of his potions that a soft tinkling sound could be heard. Llyr pointed to one of the crystals. As Eri lifted it out of the liquid, light spilled through it, on to the wall, and an image appeared: soldiers, riding through a forest.

'It sees,' Llyr said. 'Soldiers are coming.'

It was true. From that day on, the crystal had been used to warn them of any approaching stranger. It had never failed.

The Knight Protectors were all for riding to Castle Melyntha.

'But what if the crystal isn't there?' said King Timoken. 'We can't attack without a reason. I don't doubt that the eagles saw Rigg and his abductors on the castle road, but we need more proof. The crystal might still be here, hidden by whoever took it.'

John the guard might have told them more, but he had inconveniently escaped. The soldier who had been guarding him was overcome in the middle of the night; knocked senseless by a blow to his head. His keys had been taken and John set free. The stricken soldier wasn't discovered until morning. It was feared that he might never regain his senses.

Never before had the king and his court had so many problems to deal with. In the meantime, with everyone in the castle so distracted, Vyborn discovered how to have fun. Encouraged by Olga and Lilith, he practised his new shape-shifting talent almost the whole day long.

The boys in Vyborn's bedchamber were kept awake all night by boar grunting, owl hooting, bat screeching and donkey braying. Wings scratched their faces, tusks pulled off their covers and the donkey seemed to fill every space in the room with its great head and rough-haired body.

'Perhaps it's not a donkey,' Petrello muttered, burying his head under his pillow.

It was a dark night and Vyborn's shape-shifting couldn't be seen. There were only the familiar animal sounds to suggest what was going on.

'I'll bet you can't become a quiet creature like a cat,' said Tolly, hoping Vyborn would take up the challenge.

'Cats aren't always quiet,' said Gunfrid, who was sharing Tolly's bed.

There followed several moments of grunting and

sniffing. Fingernails scraped the floor, a heavy object rolled and scratched and struggled. Something banged against Petrello's bedpost. What was going on?

All at once, the moon swam out from the grey cloud that had buried it, and Vyborn's human shape could be seen. The light on his face was eerie and cold, and the voice that came from him was an awful yearning, resentful sound.

'I can't,' said Vyborn through gritted teeth. His dark, fathomless eyes glared up at Tolly. 'Why did you say a cat?'

'Just a thought,' said Tolly.

'No,' barked Vyborn. 'You guessed I couldn't. I tried to be a leopard, but I couldn't. Why?' He looked up at Petrello, who had removed the pillow from his head.

'How should I know?' said Petrello.

'Why? Why? Why can't I be a leopard?'

'Leopards are very, very special.' Guanhamara stood in the doorway, a lantern swinging from her hand. 'Leopards are creatures that can never be used by "things" like you, Vyborn, and you'd better get used to the idea.'

'S-s-s-s-k-k-k-gr-gr-gr!' Vyborn's voice went through a series of unidentifiable animal noises. The sounds ranged from a quiet squeak to a deafening roar. And it was while he was roaring that his face and body began to change into a big, featureless lump, a creature that never was, and never could be.

The dark shape lumbered towards Guanhamara, but she stood her ground. 'I'm going to have to teach you a lesson, Vyborn,' she said, her voice very stern.

The lump hesitated. It grunted and sniffed the air. And then it shrieked. Everyone else screamed.

There, standing just inside the door, was a tall, white, writhing monster; a demon with two heads, its eyes red embers, its open mouth awash with fangs, its arms scaly, its fingers bloody.

Petrello knew it had to be one of his sister's illusions, but he couldn't stop himself from screaming.

It was the middle of the night. Blood-curdling screams were bound to cause a stir. But by the time Nurse Ogle appeared on the scene, Guanhamara had tiptoed away, the ghostly demon had dematerialised and Vyborn's head was under the covers.

'What's going on?' Nurse Ogle demanded. 'Are you causing trouble again, foolish Petrello?'

'I am not,' said Petrello indignantly.

'He is not,' said Tolly. 'Nor is he foolish.'

'Who asked you?' snapped the beanpole woman, advancing into the room. She was supposed to care for the children, but in Petrello's opinion she couldn't care less.

'There was a noise coming from this bedchamber, loud enough to wake the dead.'

The nurse lifted her lantern, sending its flickering light across the beds. 'Who's that hiding under the covers?' she demanded.

'Vyborn,' said Petrello. 'He doesn't feel well.'

Nurse Ogle marched over to Vyborn's bed and prodded the body beneath the covers. 'Was it you, boy, making all that noise?'

The others waited to see what would happen. Gunfrid pressed his fist against his mouth to stop himself from screaming again.

Vyborn's small body began to writhe. A head emerged, not Vyborn's head of flat black hair, but a head of bristles, pointed ears and small black eyes.

You had to hand it to Nurse Ogle, thought Petrello. For someone who was looking at a wild boar in a bed, she was remarkably calm. Taking only the slightest step back, she said, 'So we have another off-shoot of King Timoken's enchantments.'

Vyborn grunted. For some reason the awful tusks didn't appear on his cheeks, and his nose still looked rather human. Perhaps he hadn't meant to reveal his newly acquired talent to Nurse Ogle, but was finding it difficult to hold back.

'Maybe he doesn't know he's only half-turned?' Tolly whispered behind his hand.

Petrello suppressed a giggle.

Nurse Ogle sighed. 'Well, boy, just keep the noise down and don't show off. Not in my presence, anyway.'

'It was Guanhamara.' Vyborn's own hair was taking over from the bristles. His pointed ears shrivelled and his eyes looked almost normal.

'What do you mean, it was Guanhamara?' Nurse Ogle peered at Vyborn. 'One girl can't make a noise like that.'

'She made us scream,' Vyborn protested. 'She . . . she brought in a demon. It had two heads that touched the ceiling, and fangs and bloody fingers.'

Nurse Ogle stared at Vyborn. 'Is this true?' She turned to the others.

Petrello shrugged. 'We didn't see.'

'Liar!' cried Vyborn. 'You screamed.'

'There was certainly more than one scream,' said the

nurse. 'So it seems that two more royal children have acquired their endowments, and both on the same day. It must have something to do with that uncomfortable Vanishing.' She made her way back to the door. 'Any more noise and I'll make you all take a potion, one that will give you a horrible stomach-ache for a week.'

They thought she had finished with her dire warnings. No such luck. 'As for you two,' she glared at Petrello and Tolly from the doorway. 'Heaven help us if you acquire talents. They're bound to be nasty. So look out, little waif,' she directed her gaze at Gunfrid, trying to hide behind Tolly. 'You're in for a rough ride, sharing a chamber with these three.'

The nurse walked away. Her rush slippers slapped the floorboards, and her lantern creaked on its rusty handle as she trundled back to her bedchamber at the end of the passage.

Next morning Petrello opened his eyes just as Tolly was leaving the room.

'Are you going to your secret meeting?' Petrello called after his brother.

Tolly didn't answer and then, popping his head round the door, he said, 'Vyborn's taken Gunfrid to the dining hall. He said he was going to show him around.'

'Tolly!' Petrello leapt out of bed and began to throw on his clothes. 'You shouldn't have let them go off together. Vyborn could do anything.'

'He seemed better, if you know what I mean,' said Tolly. 'Perhaps all that shape-shifting last night got it out of his system for a while. I must go. I'm late. Save me some breakfast.'

Pulling on his boots, Petrello left the room. He was just in time to see Tolly turn the corner on to the stairway. By the time Petrello reached the steps, his brother had gone. 'Sometimes I think he can fly,' he said to himself.

In the courtyard, Guanhamara and Elin were tidying Zeba's hair. She was wearing a dress of buttercup yellow, with tight sleeves that were a little too long, and a green velvet hem that she kept tripping over. But she was hardly recognisable as the ragged waif of yesterday.

Petrello noticed his brother, Cafal, watching the girls. He had a strange, gentle smile on his face, as though he were entranced by the scene. Poor Cafal, he had to try so hard to control his unhappy affliction. Petrello had only once seen the were-beast that his brother could sometimes become. But he had heard him, howling in the forest like a creature in great pain.

So much for the gifts that the realm of enchantments had bestowed on the king's third son. It didn't seem fair. But as their father had explained, it was a matter of luck whether his children received a useful talent, or something they'd rather be without.

'How do I look, Prince Petrello?' asked Zeba.

'You look . . . almost beautiful,' Petrello answered lamely.

'Don't say "almost",' Guanhamara complained. 'Zeba is transformed. She looks gorgeous.'

'Yes, of course,' Petrello agreed, wishing he knew how to pay compliments.

'It's just for today.' Zeba ran her fingers over the bright skirt. 'And then I must wear something less splendid.'

'She's to work with the seamstresses,' Elin explained. 'And the others might be jealous.'

Zeba twirled round in her new dress, smiling broadly. 'I'm going to sew,' she sang. 'I always wanted to, but in Castle Melyntha they'd only let me sweep and scrub.'

The breakfast bell rang out. Today it was Selgi's duty. All the children waited impatiently for their turn to ring the bell, but Selgi was the best. He had a way of swinging the bell so that the brass clapper hit the sides in a series of long rhythmical peals.

As children and courtiers hurried to their breakfasts, they didn't look as happy as usual. The bell reminded them of the vanished Rigg, and now there was news that the Seeing Crystal had been stolen. People didn't feel safe any more.

'Have you seen Vyborn?' Petrello asked the girls.

'He was taking my brother to see the helmets,' said Zeba.

'But they're kept in a locked room,' said Petrello, frowning.

Zeba shrugged.

'Save me some breakfast,' Petrello told Guanhamara as he sped towards the armoury. 'And for Tolly as well!'

'Where is Tolly?' she shouted.

'Who knows? But I don't think Gunfrid should be alone with Vyborn.'

Petrello caught a glimpse of Zeba's anxious face, and then he lost sight of the girls as people hurried past them to the dining halls.

'Helmets,' muttered Petrello.

The helmets were kept in a small room just off the

armoury. Petrello found the guard who was supposed to be on duty slumped beside the grilled door. He had a dazed expression on his face, and Petrello noticed that the grille was partly open, with the key still in the lock.

'Have you seen my brother?' asked Petrello, peering closely at the man.

'I saw a goat,' mumbled the guard. 'It had the horns of a devil. When I refused to let it in, it winded me. Butted me right here.' He touched his stomach. 'There was a boy with it, a scrawny lad. He said, "This goat wants you to unlock the door; if you don't he'll butt you again and put his horns right through you."'

'A goat?' said Petrello.

'What could I do?' groaned the guard. 'I mean, what harm can a goat do in an armoury? It can't steal weapons, or put on the armour. And I didn't want to feel those horns in my stomach again, so I unlocked the grille, and the door.'

'And did they go in?'

'Of course they did,' the guard replied sourly.

Before the man could stop him, Petrello slipped through the open grille and took two steps down to a wooden door studded with iron bolts. A great key protruded from the lock, but Petrello had no need to turn it. The door creaked open at a touch.

The room beyond was bathed in brilliant light. Sunbeams glancing through the narrow windows were reflected in the armour placed on stands all about the room. It was as if a headless army stood in shining silence, waiting for their enemy.

As Petrello turned to the arch leading into the Helmet Room, a figure emerged. Lilith. She gave Petrello one of her hollow smiles and asked, 'What are you doing here, brother?'

'I'm looking for Vyborn. The breakfast bell has rung.'

'We heard it. Vyborn is showing your little friend the helmets.' Her jaw still formed a cold smile.

'Why?' asked Petrello.

Lilith lost her false smile. 'And why not?'

'Vyborn came in here as a goat. He injured the guard. Did you know?'

'He is a shape-shifter,' Lilith said, looking pleased. 'It's about time you showed some talent, brother. But then, perhaps it'll never happen for you.'

'Perhaps I'd rather be without.' Petrello made to pass her through the arch, but she stood in his way.

'No need to go in there,' said Lilith. 'The boys are coming now.'

And so they were. Gunfrid came through first, his eyes shining. 'Never thought I'd see so many splendid helmets,' he said. 'All a-twinkling, and with pictures on them, and silver and gold.'

'They're very fine,' Petrello agreed. He waited for a goat to appear, but it seemed that Vyborn was himself again. He came out of the Helmet Room with a look of smug satisfaction. 'Were you worried for your friend? I wouldn't have eaten him, you know.' He gave a snorting giggle.

Petrello didn't bother to reply.

'Hurry up, boys!' Lilith called from the door. 'Or you'll lose your breakfasts.' When Gunfrid and Vyborn followed her outside, Petrello seized his chance and ran into the Helmet Room.

Shelves ran from floor to ceiling on three sides of the small room. Every shelf was filled with helmets. They sat neatly, side by side, on their metal stands. Nothing appeared to be out of place.

Petrello paced beside the shelves, staring at each helmet in turn, until his gaze came to rest on his favourite. It belonged to Amadis. A small golden eagle sat on the crest and strands of gold ran from the base to the crown, forming a net over the silvery steel. Each strand was embossed with silver eagles and swallows with garnet eyes. At the back of the helmet a fringe of bronze petal-like shapes stood out from the base like a shining skirt.

A similar helmet had been made for Borlath, but he had had it melted down and fashioned into armlets. His preferred helmet was plain steel banded with iron.

Cafal never wore armour.

Petrello walked around the room, and then returned to stare at the helmet belonging to Amadis. It looked as it always had. Shining. Beautiful. But something was wrong. Petrello put out his hand. He almost touched a golden strand with the tip of his finger, but his hand dropped to his side. A shiver of apprehension crept down his spine.

He was being foolish again, Petrello told himself.

But later he wondered why the guard had never mentioned Lilith. How did she get into the armoury? And why? Had she seen the open door and slipped through it while Olga had distracted the man?

Petrello didn't discuss his fears with anyone else, even Tolly. They meant nothing, he decided, but in the schoolroom he couldn't concentrate on his lessons, and was told off more than once by Friar Gereint.

It was an uneventful day, and by the time Petrello went to bed he had assured himself that there was really nothing to worry about.

Chapter Eight

A Sword Fight

The night was peaceful. Vyborn's imagination had run dry. He couldn't think of any more shapes to shift into, not satisfactorily anyway.

Petrello was the first to wake. He slipped out of bed, dressed himself as quietly as he could, and then crept back under the covers. Today, he decided, he would discover the reason for Tolomeo's early morning disappearances. But he would have to be very careful not to let his brother know he was being followed. Tolly was obviously determined to keep his morning activities a secret.

Fortunately, Tolly woke up before the other two. Petrello closed his eyes. He heard his brother get dressed; a light creak betrayed Tolly's almost silent footsteps. The door opened and closed. Petrello opened his eyes.

Tolly had gone. Petrello threw back the covers and leapt to the door.

'Where are you going?' Gunfrid asked sleepily.

'Sssh!' Petrello answered. With infinite care he opened the door. He didn't bother to close it. Tolly had reached the corner leading to the stairway. Petrello waited until his brother was descending the steps, then bounded after him. Hardly daring to breathe, he slipped down the narrow spiral. Tolly's head was still in view.

At the bottom of the stairway, Tolly strode into the courtyard. Petrello stayed in the shadowy cloisters. Tolly began to run. Keeping his brother in sight, Petrello put on a spurt and bumped straight into a large basket of washing.

'Watch out!' cried the woman behind the basket. She lifted it in her thick arms and glared at Petrello.

'Sssh!' he hissed. 'I mean, sorry. Sorry, sorry!'

He tore on, not losing sight of his brother for a second. Tolly raced into the next courtyard. Here, smiths and carpenters were already at work. Petrello had no trouble in concealing himself behind benches and worktables as he followed his brother into the third courtyard.

Aunt Zobayda hadn't emerged from her chamber

overlooking the fountain. Her garden was deserted. Water splashing into the pool disguised Petrello's footsteps as he crept round the fountain. Where could Tolly be heading? he wondered. Surely not into the cameldrome? But, yes, that's exactly where Tolly was going. He went through the arch and entered the passage leading to the king's golden room.

Petrello was close on his heels. Once in the king's room he kept close to the wall of pictures while Tolly opened the door to the cameldrome. Tolly slipped through the door and closed it behind him.

Petrello hesitated, but he was in luck! Gabar and Enid were arguing. Only the king and Amadis knew what the camel and the dragon argued about so often, but they always made quite a rumpus. Amadis said it was generally a friendly sort of tiff, and the animals made up afterwards. Today, they drowned out any sound that Petrello might have made when he opened the cameldrome door. He closed it carefully and followed his brother into the sand dunes.

It was easy to hide behind the great banks of sand, but Petrello was now more mystified than ever. Could Tolomeo converse with animals, like the king and

Amadis? If so, why did he want to keep his talent secret?

Tolomeo was now completely hidden in the dunes. Petrello tried to listen for those soft, ploughing footfalls, but Gabar was grumbling so loudly it was impossible to hear anything else.

Petrello cautiously climbed a bank of sand, meaning to peep over the top, but the sand suddenly gave way and he found himself falling into a deep rift. A low growl came from above him and, looking up, he saw three leopards staring down at him. He was not afraid of them; they had never been known to hurt anyone, and yet he felt at a definite disadvantage. He gave them a tentative smile and put a finger to his lips.

A soft rumble came from each spotted throat. Petrello felt foolish. How could they understand his clumsy gesture? And yet they were not like other creatures. They had been wrapped in the king's enchanted cloak when they were tiny cubs. They had followed him from Africa, and spoke with him often. One had a coat as pale as a star, another had an orange patch beneath his chin, and the third was the deep copper of a setting sun. Their names were Star, Flame Chin and Sun Cat.

The big cats bent their heads towards Petrello; they

sniffed the air, and then silently slipped away.

Petrello breathed a sigh of relief. Surprised by the leopards, Gabar and Enid had stopped quarrelling. Now Petrello could hear the soft plush, plush of sand as someone made their way across the cameldrome.

There was only one place Tolomeo could go. He was heading for the fifth courtyard. No one went there. Petrello had only glimpsed it once, after the spirit ancestors had made an overnight visit, and surprised the king with two more towers and three walls that surrounded yet another courtyard.

No one lived in the towers overlooking the mossy flagstones of the fifth courtyard. No one occupied the rooms set into the wide walls that enclosed it. What purpose could Tolly have for going there? Petrello would soon find out.

There was no door into the fifth courtyard. Sand from the cameldrome spilled through a wide arch and drifted across the flagstones beyond.

Petrello hid behind the dividing wall and, very slowly, peeped through the arch. He saw Tolly making for a door in one of the furthest towers. Before he reached it, the door opened and someone stepped out.

Petrello's mouth fell open. It was the queen. Gone were her blue robes, her jewelled belt and her ermine-lined cape. His mother was wearing a coarse brown shirt, green velvet breeches and leather boots. Her hair was piled into a hare-skin cap, with what looked like a squirrel's tail hanging down her back. What was going on?

Tolly's high voice carried across the courtyard. 'Soon I want a real one, Mother.'

'This one will do,' she said. 'Let us hope you will never need to use steel.'

'But if I do, I shall be ready.'

'You will, indeed. And I shall give you the finest ever made in Toledo.'

What were they talking about? Petrello risked a quick peep round the arch. He saw his mother hand Tolomeo a wooden sword. It was finely made but surely not sharp enough to do any damage.

Tolomeo leapt away and began to slice the air with his slim wooden sword. The queen smiled and picked up another makeshift weapon; a sword made of some dull metal with a blunt end. No sooner had Petrello taken in the details of the two swords, than Tolly and his mother were engaged in a spirited fight.

Forgetting to hide himself, Petrello stuck out his head, all the better to see the enthralling combat. He was amazed by his brother's skill, by the accuracy of those deft little lunges and the crafty pricks he landed on his mother's shoulders, on her arms and on her back. The queen, often laughing, parried Tolly's blows, drew back, whirled, lunged and twisted, all the while giving him encouragement and advice: when to strike, how to think, when to leap and how to thrust.

At last the queen cried, 'Enough! You win!' and throwing down her sword, she pulled off her leather gauntlets. When Tolly did the same, his mother said, 'We have an audience, Tolomeo. Let's ask him for his opinion.'

Caught in his mother's eye, Petrello had no option. He stepped through the arch and walked self-consciously towards the combatants.

'You followed me,' Tolly accused his brother.

Petrello shrugged. 'I was curious. Why didn't you tell me?'

Tolly looked at the queen. 'Mother told me to keep it a secret. She didn't want our father to know she was . . . she was . . .'

'Practising,' said the queen. 'But he guessed.' She

smiled. 'How could we keep it from him? He knows everything.'

'So, what do you think, Trello?' Tolly picked up his sword and gave his brother a light poke in the ribs.

'I think . . . well, I'm astonished really.' Petrello swung from foot to foot. 'I mean, you're brilliant, Tolly. But how?' He looked at his mother.

'Instinct,' said the queen. 'I noticed the way that Tolomeo walked. I watched the movements of his eyes, his leaps and runs. I had the carpenters make a dummy sword, small enough for a boy of nine. Our lessons began in secret, and my instincts were proved right.'

'Didn't you think the rest of us were worth a try? Me, for instance?' Petrello kicked the ground with his toe. 'Maybe I could use a sword like Tolly.'

'No, Petrello.' His mother shook her head regretfully. 'None of you showed any of the signs.'

'Is it a gift?' he asked. 'Like Borlath's and Lilith's, like Olga's and Amadis's, and now Vyborn's?'

'No,' she said. 'It is a gift inherited from me, and from my father, the greatest swordsman in all Castile.'

Petrello couldn't be described as jealous, but his mother's words hurt somehow. They gave him a small ache, deep in his chest. 'I see,' he said.

'It doesn't mean that I can't teach you, Petrello,' his mother said quickly. 'If that's what you would like. And I'm sure that, one day, you could be a swordsman.'

'But not like Tolly,' he muttered.

'Perhaps not,' she said, with a gentle smile.

Before he could stop himself, Petrello was telling his mother about Guanhamara and the rat, leaving out the spying, of course. And then Tolly recounted the events of the night, when their sister had stopped Vyborn's shape-shifting with an illusion that sent him running for cover.

'Nurse Ogle came,' said Petrello. 'But I don't think she believed Vyborn's story about Guanhamara's monster.'

There were tears of laughter in the queen's eyes when she said, 'I'm not sure that I would have believed a description like that.' She looked thoughtful for a moment. 'So, your sister is an illusionist. I had been wondering lately if she would show any of the signs that her sisters eventually revealed.'

'Guanhamara's talent isn't cruel like theirs,' Petrello said fiercely.

'No,' said his mother, 'I'm sure Guanhamara will use her gift wisely, though I must admit, she has a great sense of fun. I'm going to get changed now. You two run along or you'll lose your breakfast. Nurse Ogle might not be in the best of moods today.'

The brothers made their way back through the cameldrome. Neither of them spoke. Above them, the gossamer net of blue sky rippled lightly in a breeze from the air outside. They could feel the watching eyes of the great cats upon them, but saw neither tail nor whisker of them. The camel was running, all alone, on a wide stretch of sand. Occasionally he gave a grunt of happiness. The dragon was asleep in a tree, her thick tail hanging from a branch like a net of creepers, the breath from her snout a delicate mist in the warm air.

'I'm sorry I didn't tell you,' Tolly said when they reached the arch into Zobayda's garden. 'About the sword and everything.'

'I understand.' Petrello tried to sound unconcerned. 'Mother told you not to.' He opened the door and walked into the third courtyard.

Aunt Zobayda was sitting on her usual seat near the fountain. She wore a deep purple robe, the hem and cuffs embroidered in gold. An ermine cape covered her shoulders, and her greying hair hung to her waist in a long, thick plait. Her hearing wasn't so good these days, and she wasn't aware that the boys had entered her garden until they greeted her. She looked up from her needlework and gave them one of her warm welcoming glances. 'Have you been visiting the camel?' she asked, with a smile.

They ran and sat either side of her, both talking at once.

'Hush, boys!' Zobayda held up her hands. 'Quiet and slow, if you please. Petrello first.'

Now that the queen knew about Guanhamara's gift, Petrello saw no reason to hide it from his aunt. She didn't laugh as his mother had done, but clearly enjoyed the story of Vyborn and the monster.

'Your father discovered his peculiar powers one by one, and they came out of necessity,' she said. 'But it seems that some of you are using your inherited gifts a little frivolously.'

'Not us,' said Tolly. 'My gift is only for sword-fighting, and it was our mother's idea.'

'I know,' Zobayda chuckled. 'The queen thinks your lessons are a secret, but I have been watching her for many mornings now, slipping out of the royal apartments,' she nodded at a tower across the courtyard, 'and creeping away with her sword and a bundle of male attire. And not long after, you would follow; very stealthily, I must say, Tolomeo.'

Tolly grinned. 'You know everything, Aunt Zobayda.'

'Almost.' She turned to Petrello and asked, 'What of you, Petrello? Have you any secrets to tell?'

'None,' he mumbled. 'Maybe I am the one who will never achieve anything. Nurse Ogle calls me foolish.'

'Give me your hands,' said his aunt.

Knowing that she could sometimes foretell the future, Petrello eagerly placed his hands in hers. She held his fingers tight, and he could feel her ring press into his forefinger. He stared at the ring; it was silver and shaped like a wing. The tiny face of a jinni peeped from the top, and one of its small feet protruded from the bottom. Petrello's fingers began to throb. Tolly was staring at him anxiously, but Zobayda's gaze was grave and intense.

Distant thunder rumbled through Petrello's mind. He tossed his head but the storm would not be dislodged. It rolled closer. It whined in his ears and tugged at his hair. He felt a great wind whirling round his legs and, for a moment, thought that it would knock him off his feet. Hard, frozen rain lashed his face and the pain in his fingers became so cold and sharp he wondered if they might break, like icicles.

'It's hurting,' Petrello breathed.

His aunt loosened her grip a little, but didn't let go of his hands. The look in her eyes seemed to express bewilderment.

The storm in Petrello's head abated, his fingers were still cool, but not frozen.

'What do you see, Aunt Zobayda?' he asked.

'I see an army,' she murmured, and the furrow between her eyebrows grew deeper.

'An army?' He liked the sound of that word. It was exciting.

Aunt Zobayda shook her head, slowly, and added, 'It is in the air, Petrello. The army is in the air.'

'How can that be?' He eased his hands out of her grasp. 'It makes no sense. Why did you see such a strange thing? What can it have to do with me?'

'Petrello, I have no idea,' she said. 'I can only tell you what I saw when I touched your fingers. But what did you see?'

'Nothing. A storm raged in my head. I felt a mighty wind, and thought my fingers were turning to ice.'

116

'Hmm.' Aunt Zobayda spread her own fingers and regarded the silver ring. Again she said, 'Hmm.'

'Your ring has a powerful shine today, Aunt,' said Tolly. 'Is it playing tricks?'

She gave a little grin. 'Who knows?' She turned the ring on her slim brown finger. 'This was given to me by the last forest jinni the world will ever see. It is his image. I sense that he is still watching over us.'

The noises from the next courtyard had, almost without their noticing, become quite a commotion.

'You've missed your breakfasts, no doubt,' said Aunt Zobayda. 'Better run along, boys. It sounds as though something serious is afoot.'

The brothers jumped and ran to the entrance but as they went through the arch, Petrello heard his aunt call, 'Don't fear your gift, Petrello. Don't reject it, for it could save us all.'

What could she mean? Puzzling over his aunt's words, Petrello followed his brother through the maze of carpenters' benches, wagon wheels, barrels and tanners' baths. Flames from the blacksmith's furnace warmed the air and sparks flew in all directions. The noise intensified as they got closer to the first courtyard. Zobayda was right.

The deafening activity could only mean that preparations for an expedition were underway.

There was no doubt about it. The horses were out, stamping on the cobbles, snorting and coughing. Grooms ran around them, carrying armour, harnesses and weapons. The Knight Protectors were all there, arming themselves with their grooms' help, flexing their necks and shoulders, punching the air and steadying their mounts.

Gunfrid squeezed through the crowd and came racing up to Petrello and Tolly, calling their names.

'What's happening?' asked Tolly, although it was plain to see that an expedition was, indeed, about to take place.

'The king was anxious for his knight Peredur,' Gunfrid said breathlessly. 'He hasn't returned. So the king and his knights are riding to Castle Melyntha. Sir Peredur might have been captured, though your brother, Amadis, says the eagles haven't given him news of this, but –'

'Gunfrid!' Petrello spoke so sharply, Gunfrid clamped his mouth shut in astonishment.

Petrello felt unaccountably afraid. Gunfrid was carrying a familiar gold and silver helmet. 'What are you doing with that?' He pointed at the helmet.

'Amadis said I might help the groom, so that one day I could be his –'

'Amadis must not wear it!' The words flew out of Petrello's mouth, almost before he knew they were there.

'Why?' Gunfrid gazed at the helmet, turning it in his hands. 'It's strong and beautiful.'

The same sense of dread that had assailed Petrello before swept over him now as he saw the helmet, shining in Gunfrid's small hands. But before Petrello could utter another word, Gunfrid said, 'Look at me!' and put the helmet on his own head.

For a moment a smile danced on the boy's lips and then, as the helmet slipped further down over his pale face, his mouth turned a ghastly grey; his skin wrinkled and his whole body contorted, as a dreadful trembling spasm took hold of him. With a piercing cry, Gunfrid fell to the ground. He lay on his back, as still as death, all his limbs as stiff as sticks.

Chapter Nine
The Enchanted Helmet

Petrello dropped to his knees beside the motionless boy. He must remove the helmet. He knew it had caused Gunfrid's horrible fit. But the helmet now had a mind of its own. No matter how hard Petrello tugged, it wouldn't come off. In spite of being too big for the boy's small head, the helmet clung like a giant limpet to a tiny rock.

Tolly ran to get help. In a second Amadis was there, tapping Petrello's shoulder, pulling his fingers away from the helmet. 'Let me do it,' Amadis said, expecting his treasured piece of armour to slip into his hands.

'Strange,' he exclaimed. 'It fits the boy.' He looked at Petrello. 'What happened here, brother?'

Petrello told him, in a rush, finishing, 'It's been bewitched, Amadis. I felt it, but couldn't stop Gunfrid.

I knew there was something wrong, but I couldn't say why. Unless . . .'

'What are you trying to say?' Amadis stared intently at Petrello.

'It's nothing. But earlier I saw Lilith in the Helmet Room, and knowing what she can do . . .' Petrello felt almost ashamed. 'It's nonsense. I'm sorry I even thought of it.'

'Of course it's nonsense.' Amadis let go of the helmet and straightened up. 'We need the king's help.'

He had hardly spoken when the king was at his side.

'Who is that hidden in your helmet?' asked the king. 'Is he ill – or –' He looked more closely at the boy on the ground.

'It's the waif from Melyntha, Father,' said Amadis. 'He put on my helmet, and this happened. We can't remove it.'

In one swift movement the king bent and lifted Gunfrid in his arms. The boy's head lolled back, the weight of the helmet dragging it down. His arms and legs were still rigid and it looked as though the king were carrying a boy made of wood.

The three brothers followed their father into the Meeting Hall. Laying Gunfrid on the long table, the king quickly unfastened his cloak and threw it over the stricken boy. Then he placed his hand on Gunfrid's chest, in the place where his heart was struggling to beat.

'He's not dead,' said the king, 'but I have never seen a child afflicted like this. Some wickedness has been used.'

Amadis hesitated before he said, 'Petrello saw something, Father.'

The king turned to Petrello. 'What did you see?'

Petrello reddened. All at once he began to doubt himself. Why had he imagined that Lilith had tampered with the helmet? 'I . . . I'm not sure,' he stammered.

'Come on, Petrello. Have confidence in yourself. Did you see someone else with this helmet?' The king pulled the cloak away from Gunfrid's head and gave the helmet another light tug. It still wouldn't come off the boy's head.

'No,' said Petrello. 'But I saw Lilith in the Helmet Room, that's all.'

The king frowned. 'And what were you doing there?'

Petrello had no choice but to tell his father the truth. How he had followed Vyborn and Gunfrid to the armoury and how Vyborn had turned into a goat and frightened the guard into unlocking the door. 'And

Lilith was there,' he went on, 'and when I saw Amadis's helmet, I felt, I don't know –'

'It was meant for me, Father,' Amadis broke in. 'If it were not for that boy, I would be lying there paralysed, half-dead.'

The king gave a sigh that was more like a groan. 'Why? Who would wish to harm you, Amadis?'

Amadis shrugged, and then, as if struck by a sudden idea, he said, 'The only thing that marks me out from others is my ability to speak with animals.'

'Ah!' The king put a finger to his lips and paced beside the table, glancing occasionally at Gunfrid's motionless body.

The brothers remained silent, reluctant to break into their father's thoughts.

'I begin to see a pattern now,' the king said at last. 'They are trying to remove anything that could warn us of approaching danger. First the crystal and now Amadis and the eagles.'

'They?' Petrello ventured. 'Who are they?'

'Is Lilith part of a conspiracy?' asked Tolly, his eyes round with alarm.

The king spread his hands. 'Another puzzle for

Wyngate.' He lifted one of Gunfrid's rigid hands. 'Fetch Llyr for me. My cloak is not enough for this poor lad.'

'I'll go.' Petrello ran into the courtyard with Tolly close behind.

'What's going on, boys?' called Sir Edern. 'Is the king detained?' The big knight was already mounted and obviously eager to set off. Sir Peredur was a great friend, and both knights would have laid down their lives for each other.

'A plot has been discovered.' Tolly's high voice carried above the crush and clamour of impatient knights.

'A plot?' roared Sir Edern, leaping to the ground.

Hearing Sir Edern's powerful shout, other knights began to dismount.

'You shouldn't have told them,' Petrello said as the boys sped across to the wizards' tower.

'The knights will have to know,' Tolly panted.

They had reached the steps leading to the Eyrie.

'Our father isn't going to accuse Lilith, is he?' Tolly said as they mounted the narrow steps.

'I don't think he can,' Petrello agreed. He had seen the sorrow in his father's eyes before, when one of the others used their talents thoughtlessly, or for some cruel sport. It was as though the king blamed himself for their behaviour. But poisoning? Could Lilith really have intended to do such a thing to her own brother?

'Remember the rash that covered Guan's face?' said Tolly. 'That was Lilith. She admitted it.'

'Yes. Dusted a little something on to that pretty necklace,' said Petrello, remembering. 'Our mother scolded her and she was better for a while. It was lucky that Eri found a herb to cure the rash.' Petrello took the last step up to the wizards' door, and knocked.

'Who is it?' Llyr sounded tired and distracted.

'It's me,' said Petrello. 'And Tolly.'

'Enter, Me and Tolly!' This time there was a hint of a smile in Llyr's voice.

The Eyrie was in even more chaos than before. Petrello had to push the door against a tide of discarded robes and boots. He stepped over the garments only to find himself crunching shells and dried herbs beneath his feet. Eri, bent double over an open chest in the corner, was mumbling oaths in ancient Welsh. The boys recognised some of the words and Petrello couldn't help grinning at his brother.

'So, young princes, have you come to help us tidy our

muddle?' Llyr was placing shells in a row on his table. He liked things to be well ordered. Every crystal, every bone, stone, seed, shell and fungus had its place.

'Are you still searching for the Seeing Crystal?' Tolly asked.

'I am not,' said Llyr, 'but Grandfather won't give up. He thinks a squirrel or a magpie might have moved it.'

'Or one of those black kittens on a rat hunt,' muttered Eri. He stood up, rubbing his back.

'The king needs you,' Petrello said, and he quickly told the wizards what had happened to Gunfrid.

'Shivering stars,' said Eri. 'Take the heather, Llyr. Quick now.'

'I know what to do, Grandfather.' Llyr gathered up several sprigs of heather and thrust them into a bag. Four iron bowls followed the heather. Then Llyr's eyes searched the table, his fingers touching the stones and the shells. Nodding to himself, he picked up several tiny bones and put them in the bag. 'Ready,' he said, striding to the door. But all at once, he turned and hurried back to the table. 'Hoof fungus,' he said, and tossed a handful of curled fungi into the bag.

Petrello and Tolly sped down the stairway with Llyr

almost treading on their flying jackets. They ran across the courtyard, through the crowd of bewildered knights and restless horses and past the grooms and stable boys. The guard outside the Meeting Hall let them in without a murmur.

The king and Amadis were standing either side of the eagle helmet. Gunfrid's pale chin and bloodless lips could be seen poking out beneath the nose piece.

Llyr stared at the small, chalk-white chin. He touched the thin lips with the back of his hand and looked at the king.

'My cloak is not enough.' King Timoken looked distraught.

Llyr merely nodded. He took the four bowls from his bag and handed two each to Petrello and Tolly. 'One on the sill, one by the fireplace, one at the door, one at his feet. So the spell cannot be corrupted from outside.'

Tolly ran to the door and then the window. Petrello took one of his bowls and placed it by the fire. The other he put very carefully on the table a few inches from Gunfrid's small feet. While the boys were busy, Llyr took out the sprigs of heather and laid them on the cloak that covered Gunfrid's body. He broke them up and divided them into four small piles, ordering the boys to place a pile in each bowl. He did the same with the tiny bones, then he went to each bowl and crumbled the hoof fungus on top of the heather and bones. When all this was done Llyr looked at the king and asked, 'Will you light them for us, sire?'

Without a word the king moved to the door. He bent down and with one finger touched the contents of the bowl. The heather took light. It smouldered and glowed. The king went to the other three bowls and repeated the action. Soon the contents of all four bowls were smoking and crackling. A pungent earthy smell began to fill the room.

'Tell the knights to stand down,' the king told Amadis. 'I cannot leave the castle until this poor boy is well again.' He sat in his heavy oak chair, with its ornately carved back, and leant his arms on the table, close to the boy's head.

While Amadis went to speak to the knights, Petrello and Tolly hovered by the table, unsure what to do.

'You had better go to your lessons, boys,' said their father. 'There's nothing to be done here until your friend revives.'

As the boys left the room, their father began to murmur in the language of his African kingdom. And in the background, very low and quiet, came a chant from Llyr, the music in his throat so gentle it could have been drawn from the breath of trees.

'I don't want to go to the schoolroom,' said Tolly as they made their way past the disconsolate knights. They were always in high spirits before an expedition, and the change of plans was disappointing. It took some time to prepare horses and armour, and to be told that all the preparations had been for nothing irked the knights.

'One more day lost for Peredur,' grumbled Sir Edern, patting his stallion's nose.

The horse snorted, aware of his master's irritation.

'The expedition isn't cancelled,' Amadis said. 'It's merely delayed.'

'For how long?' asked Edern.

'Until the boy is cured,' said Mabon the archer. 'It makes sense, Edern. We can't go without Timoken, and he must find out what sort of mischief is afoot. Someone has tampered with that helmet, and until we know who, or why, it is surely safer not to put ourselves at risk.'

'Who knows what sickness that orphan may have

brought us,' Edern grumbled. 'How do we know it was the helmet that laid him out?' He looked at Amadis.

Amadis spread his hands. 'It seems obvious.' He turned and saw his younger brothers. 'Your new friend is in good hands,' he told them. 'Time for lessons now.'

Petrello sighed and Tolly groaned. They headed for the schoolroom. They had to pass the chancellor's office on their way and saw the grey men gathered outside the chancellor's door. They were murmuring to each other, their low voices contrasting oddly with the loud bluster of the Knight Protectors. They stopped speaking when the boys passed. Petrello could feel their eyes on him and he half-expected a scornful remark or even a command from the gloomy Chimery. But the grey men said not a word. They watched the boys until they reached the schoolroom door, and then Chimery was heard to mutter, 'Not long now . . .' The rest of his words were lost in a guffaw from one of the others.

'What did he mean?' asked Tolly as he stepped down to the schoolroom.

'No idea,' said Petrello, opening the schoolroom door.

They entered at the back of the room and quickly slipped on to the bench behind the nearest table. Ahead of them were another three tables, where children aged eight to eleven sat with their hands in their laps, and their eyes fixed on Friar Gereint. The friar sat at a high desk in front of the class. He was very short-sighted and could never make out the children at the back of the class. If he heard the door close, he would call, 'Who's come in? or has someone gone out? Speak!' He did this now.

No one answered.

'Come on. Speak!' Friar Gereint's bad sight made him irritable. He always suspected a trick.

'It's Petrello and Tolomeo,' answered Petrello, not wanting to put any of the other children in the awkward position of having to tell on them.

'Thank you.' The friar relaxed. He was a very short, very stout person, but when the king first met him, he had been a skinny boy with a beautiful voice. Twenty years of good food and little exercise in a monastery had changed him beyond recognition.

'Princes or not, you're late,' said the friar. 'Petrello, please recite the *Ode to Prince Griffith*, composed by Sir Edern's father, the late great poet Elvin.'

Petrello gave an inward sigh. The *Ode to Prince Griffith* was extremely long, and he had never quite mastered it.

Prince Griffith was a Welsh Briton who had once owned Castle Melyntha. When he was killed in a battle, the conquerors took over his castle and most of the Britons had fled or been killed. Petrello's father, being an African king, had even more reason to flee. He had escaped with the wizard, Eri.

Petrello cleared his throat and began. '*Glorious was our prince, our golden-haired warrior. Fearless was he, a prince without equal. Inconsolable are his people . . .*'

Five minutes later, Petrello was still struggling with the third verse. Guanhamara, sitting beside him, knew the ode better than anyone; she kept trying to whisper the right words to her brother, but it was no use. He stuttered, paused, stumbled and squirmed. Friar Gereint's loud sighs didn't help, nor did the giggles from the smallest children at the front. And then, suddenly, Petrello saw Zeba sitting very quiet and still at the end of the table in front of him, and he realised that she didn't know what had happened to her brother.

Petrello closed his troubled mouth and sat down.

'Well done,' said Guanhamara.

'Hardly,' whispered Petrello.

'Given up, have you?' asked the friar. He clicked his

tongue, shook his head and sighed. 'Suppose I gave up trying to teach you?'

Petrello didn't know what to do. He could only think of Zeba. Would it frighten her to know what had happened? She should be told, he decided. She would want to be with Gunfrid.

Petrello stood up. 'There is some grave news that concerns Zeba,' he said.

Zeba leapt up, her face pinched with anxiety. 'Gunfrid?' she cried.

Friar Gereint banged his desk with a mallet. 'Trying to change the subject, are we, Prince Petrello?'

'No, Friar Gereint. It's true. Gunfrid is . . . has been taken ill.'

With a wild scream Zeba bounded to the door; flinging it open, she leapt through and left it banging behind her.

A babble of excitement broke out. Children gasped, murmured and chattered.

'Hush!' commanded the friar. 'Illness is not unknown here. But the king can always cure it.'

'I don't think he can,' Petrello said quietly. 'Not this time.'

Chapter Ten

Breaking the Spell

It seemed to be a very long day. Knights, courtiers, workmen and children were all quieter than usual. Even the dogs were subdued. The king seldom left Gunfrid's side, and when he did he spoke to no one. His sombre mood reached through every room, every tower and every courtyard, and the smell of Llyr's incense hung in corners and seeped into the very stones of the castle.

Lilith was nowhere to be seen. Was she afraid? Petrello wondered. Afraid that she'd gone too far this time. He remembered the seeds she'd put in Elin's shoe. Poor Elin's foot swelled up so much she could hardly walk. She limped for weeks and then there was Selgi's sickness and Cafal's dreadful itching. After the queen's scolding, Lilith hadn't used her cruel power. Perhaps she'd had nothing to do with the helmet after all.

Petrello wished he hadn't seen her in the armoury.

When lessons were over Petrello hurried to Aunt Zobayda's garden. His aunt was wise. She would put his mind at rest, one way or another.

But when he reached the third courtyard, Zobayda was not on her seat, and a shrill voice could be heard coming from the Royal Tower.

Petrello walked closer. There was a guard at the entrance to the tower. 'The queen wants privacy,' he told Petrello.

'I understand.' Petrello moved round the tower until he was out of the guard's sight. As luck would have it, he now stood directly beneath the window of the queen's chamber. He could hear her voice quite clearly.

'I guessed as much,' moaned the queen. 'You poisoned your brother's helmet. But why?'

'I've told you. It was an accident.' Lilith's slightly husky voice rose indignantly.

'How could that be?' the queen demanded.

'I don't know my own strength, do I?'

'Stupid girl. What did you do?'

'I just dropped in a few rose petals,' Lilith said casually. 'Five to be precise; they were dry but still sweet-smelling.'

'Impossible,' said the queen. 'Roses could never be used for such an evil purpose.'

'It's not the petals, Mother,' Lilith said disdainfully. 'It's the words I use with them. A buttercup would have the same effect, if I spoke to it. I admit I was surprised. Those little petals clung to the helmet quite beautifully, though I never asked them to.'

'Ugh!' exclaimed the queen. 'Have you no shame?'

'No harm was done,' Lilith replied. 'That boy is an orphan, a waif from Melyntha. What use is he?'

'Use?' cried her mother. 'He is a human being, in our care.'

There was no reply to this. Petrello stepped closer to the tower, but, all at once, the window above him was opened and he found himself staring up at Lilith.

'Spy!' she hissed. 'Worm! Have you nothing better to do than snoop, foolish Petrello?'

Petrello fled. He wanted to get rid of the ugly words that had come from Lilith's mouth. Forget them. Pour them out. Never hear them again.

'What is it, little brother?' Guanhamara caught his hand as he ran towards the Meeting Hall.

Petrello gasped for breath. 'Guan, is he any better?

Gunfrid? Has he moved? Is the helmet off?'

She shook her head. 'I've taken water to Llyr and our father. I thought I saw the boy's hand move, just a little, but Llyr said it was only my hope, nothing more. Zeba was there. She was sitting very still, staring at the helmet on her brother's head, as if the shock had frozen her.'

'Poor thing.'

'And Gunfrid looked frozen too. His hands were blue, and his mouth and chin grey with cold.'

'A freezing spell,' Petrello muttered.

'Trello, you look frightened. Are there yet more horrors in store for us?'

Words tumbled out of Petrello's mouth. Trying to convey the ugliness of Lilith's tone, he related the conversation he'd overheard in a jumble of breathy sentences. But his sister had no difficulty in understanding him.

'Poor Mother,' said Guanhamara when Petrello had stumbled to the end of his account.

'And poor Father,' said Petrello. 'What will they do, Guan?'

'What can they do?'

The king hardly ever punished his children, and when he did, they knew it was only so that he shouldn't lose face in front of his courtiers. The punishments were always light: mending garments, going without meat, keeping silent until sunset and, very rarely, solitary confinement for a day.

'I've never known our father's cloak to fail,' said Guanhamara. 'Lilith's spell must be mighty powerful.'

Petrello tugged her sleeve as the queen strode past, dragging Lilith with her.

'You'll undo what you have done,' said the queen, tugging Lilith's hand.

'I can't,' said Lilith sulkily. 'I told you.'

'You'll have to.'

The guard outside the Meeting Hall opened the door to let the queen and her daughter through, closing it hastily behind them.

'Can't we . . .?' asked Guanhamara.

The guard shook his head.

'We're Gunfrid's friends,' said Petrello.

'No use, young man.' The guard placed himself squarely in front of the door handle. 'There's magic going on in there; we upset it at our peril.'

No one could prevent Petrello and his sister from listening. They stayed close to the door. They heard a low mutter from the king. They heard the queen, her voice loud enough for them to hear her words. 'It seems obvious to me. Lilith must undo what she has done.'

'I can't.' Lilith's tone was weary and sullen.

'You won't, you mean,' retorted her mother.

'No. I really, really can't,' Lilith insisted. 'Don't you understand? When something's done, it's done. How can I take it back?'

Llyr said, 'Change the flow of words. Speak your cruel instructions backwards. Wizards can unwind a spell.'

'I'm not a wizard, am I?' Lilith said.

Someone tapped Petrello's arm and Tolly appeared beside him.

'Anything happened?' asked Tolly.

'Lilith did it,' Petrello told him. 'She's in there now, trying to undo her spell.'

'She's not,' said Guanhamara. 'She won't, or she doesn't know how.'

'Wow!' Tolly's voice carried across the courtyard, and the guard gave him a warning frown.

'There's serious work going on,' grunted the man. 'Move off, if you're going to make a noise.'

As the three children were dutifully moving away,

the supper bell rang out and they walked together to the dining hall.

Even the youngest children were quiet that evening. By now they all knew about Gunfrid and the helmet. Petrello heard one five-year-old girl whisper, 'What if it never comes off?'

'The smith will cut through the metal,' Guanhamara reassured her. 'It's quite easy.'

'But what will the boy's head be like after that?' asked the girl.

Guanhamara hesitated for only a fraction of a second, but Petrello saw the look of uncertainty in her eyes before she answered, 'Gunfrid's head will be perfectly normal. Just like it was before he put the helmet on.'

Would it? Petrello wondered. Would Gunfrid be as he was before? Lilith must have extraordinary power to create a spell that could resist all Llyr's wizardry and also the magic of the king's cloak.

The children walked into their bedchambers in an anxious silence. Tolly looked at the extra pillow on his bed and said, 'I'll have more room now, but I'd rather have Gunfrid.'

Petrello couldn't sleep. The moon was full and he could see his brothers' heads on their pillows. Vyborn lay perfectly still. Not even a grunt escaped him; either he couldn't decide what shape to take, or he was exhausted by his exertions of the night before. Tolly was restless. He twisted and turned, one hand constantly reaching for his back.

'Tolly, what is it?' Petrello whispered. 'Are you awake?'

'Itching,' Tolly murmured sleepily. 'Something on my back.'

'Tics,' said Petrello. 'D'you want me to pull them off?'

'Mm.' Tolly wriggled upright.

Kneeling on his brother's pillow, Petrello pulled his nightshirt up at the back.

'Near my shoulders,' said Tolly.

Petrello stared at his brother's shoulder-blades. Two bony knobs appeared to be pushing their way through Tolly's skin. A small gasp escaped Petrello before he could stop it.

'What is it?' said Tolly. 'Tell me.'

'I don't know. Just your bones, I think. They're more knobbly than . . . than . . .'

'Knobbly?' cried Tolly.

'Shh!' hissed Petrello. 'You'll wake Vyborn. We don't want another donkey in the room.'

'But what's on my back, Trello?'

'Just bones. Your shoulder-blades. Don't fret, Tolly. I'll look again in the daylight.' Petrello went back to his own bed.

'It's Lilith!' Tolly whispered hoarsely. 'She's done something to me. I know it.'

'No. It's nothing, Tolly. Go to sleep.'

Tolly lay down and pulled the covers over his head. For a long time he rolled around, sighing faintly to himself, and then, at last, he lay still.

Petrello felt more awake than ever. He slipped out of bed and crept to the door; opening it softly, he tiptoed across the passage and peered through the windows that overlooked the courtyard. The door of the Meeting Hall was in deep shadow but candlelight could be seen flickering in the windows. A guard sat by the door, his head on his chest, a pike lying across his knees. All at once, the guard stood and opened the door.

Someone moved through the shadows and walked into the moonlit courtyard. Petrello could see the glint of gold in his father's black hair. The king paced across the cobblestones. He lifted his face to the moon and seemed to speak to it. His skin was shining and, with a shock, Petrello realised that his father's face was bathed in tears. Once or twice he had seen the king's eyes glisten with sorrow, but this was real grief.

Petrello took a step back and clutched his throat. The king barely knew the stricken orphan, and yet he was as distressed as if Gunfrid were his own child. *Everything has failed*, thought Petrello, *and my father blames himself. Gunfrid must be dead.*

A movement in the corner of his eye drew Petrello's attention to the entrance into the second courtyard. A leopard appeared in the archway. It bounded over to the king and rubbed its head against his tunic. It was Star, the leopard with a pale gold coat. A second later his brothers came leaping through the arch.

The three leopards circled the king, and he stroked their heads as they passed. He murmured something to them, and smiled at last. Then he turned and walked towards the hall where Gunfrid's body lay. The leopards followed him in single file: Burning Sun, Flame Chin and Star. They went into the Meeting Hall and the door was closed behind them.

Petrello stared at the windows of the Meeting Hall. He longed to see what was happening in there. Slowly, the candlelight faded. There was not even a glimmer of firelight to lessen the inky darkness beyond the windows. The need to see into those windows became too great for Petrello to resist. He ran down the steps and across the icy, moonlit courtyard.

Choosing the window furthest from the guard, Petrello stood on tiptoe and peered through the glass. He could see nothing, but sensed a darkness as dense and stifling as a blanket. Where the first light appeared he couldn't tell, but gradually he began to make out details in the hall. He could see his father standing by the far wall. Eri and Llyr stood on either side of him. Their eyes glittered and the stars on their blue cloaks gleamed softly.

The king had removed his cloak from Gunfrid's body and thrown it round his own shoulders. Zeba stood in front of him, her head lolled and her eyes were closed. The king's hands rested on her shoulders.

As the light increased, Petrello could see Gunfrid's body on the table. How frail and defenceless he looked. His cold blue arms were as rigid as sticks, his pale chin incongruously tiny beneath the swallow helmet. He was still held fast in Lilith's dreadful spell.

Petrello squinted into the darkness, searching every corner of the hall. There was no sign of Lilith or the queen, but his intense gaze suddenly found the source of light. It was coming from a moving object, just lower than the table top. Two, no three moving objects. Leopards. They were pacing around the table and a strange light came from their bodies; every second it grew brighter. The leopards' steady pace increased, it became a gentle run, and now their coats were glowing. Faster they went, faster and faster. Soon, all Petrello could see was a continuous line of brilliant light. Every detail of the leopards had been swallowed in golden fire.

Faster and faster. Brighter and brighter. The long table was enclosed in a wall of flames. Pressing his head against the windowpane, Petrello could feel the heat. The flames grew, sending dazzling sparks up into the high rafters. And when the sparks floated back to earth, they looked like flakes of golden snow. The tiny pieces of gold dropped gently on to Gunfrid's cold limbs; they floated on to the helmet and dusted his small chin. Slowly, the fingers that had been clenched so tightly began to uncurl. Gunfrid's whole frame was shining like a golden statue.

Zeba's eyes were open now. She stared at the falling gold and then at her brother. She saw his moving fingers and, running through the wall of fire, grabbed his hand.

The golden snow stopped falling and the flames died. The blazing line of light became three leopards slowly pacing. They stopped at last and stood shoulder to shoulder at the foot of the table.

The king stepped forward. He went over to Gunfrid and, placing his hands on either side of the helmet, he smiled at Zeba and, very gently, pulled the helmet off her brother's head.

Chapter Eleven
Lilith's Punishment

In the fading light Petrello saw the king step back, holding the eagle helmet. He turned it over and looked into it, his expression grim. In the next few seconds Gunfrid slowly sat up. He had lost his golden look, and appeared to be the pale, stunned boy he was before. He rubbed his head, shook one hand vigorously, and grinned at his sister.

Petrello sank back on his heels. His toes felt sore and cold, and his eyes were longing to close. Stifling a yawn, he ran back to bed. Tolly was fast asleep, but Petrello had to tell someone the news. He shook his brother's shoulder, whispering, 'Gunfrid's alive. The helmet has come off.'

'What?' Tolly lifted his head.

'Gunfrid's awake,' said Petrello. 'The helmet has come off.'

'Did Lilith break the spell?' Tolly propped his chin on one hand.

'No.' This wasn't going to be easy to explain, Petrello realised. 'It . . . it was something else.'

'What?'

'Well, I think the leopards did it.'

'Ergh?' Tolly sat up. 'Are you joking?'

'We always knew they were different. Remember? They're three hundred years old . . .'

'Like the camel,' said Tolly.

'And our father,' Petrello reminded him.

Tolly was now wide awake. 'But how could leopards break a power like that, when even Llyr and our father couldn't do it?'

'I only know that they did,' said Petrello. He told his brother everything that he'd seen in the Meeting Hall that night.

'Gold?' said Tolly in an awed voice. 'Gunfrid was cured with leopards' gold?'

A muffled voice came from Vyborn's pillow. 'I'm not asleep, you know. I heard every word, and leopards can't make gold.'

'I'm too tired to argue,' Petrello said sleepily.

'And it's too late for you to be a donkey.' Tolly wriggled back under his covers. 'And if your tusks pull my bed about I'll set the leopards on you.'

'Huh!' grunted Vyborn. But he must have taken Tolly's threat to heart, because in another minute all three boys were asleep, and they didn't wake up until well after sunrise.

The castle was full of the news by the time Petrello and Tolly went down to breakfast. The court's mood had lightened. Gunfrid might have been a small orphan of no consequence; it was the strength of the spell that had struck him down that was so alarming. It was naturally believed to have been the wizards and the king who cured the boy. The king thought it best not to tell everyone the truth immediately. Lilith's awful power must not be allowed to spoil the news that had, temporarily, lifted people's spirits.

Petrello and Tolly knew the truth, of course. And so did Vyborn. Petrello decided not to tell anyone what he had seen, and advised Tolly to do the same.

'Why?' asked Tolly.

'If Father wanted people to know about the leopards, he'd have told them. And I don't want him to think that I was spying.'

'Oh, yes,' said Tolly, suddenly understanding. 'But we can tell Guan? She can keep a secret.'

'Yes,' Petrello agreed. 'Guan, and no one else.'

'Vyborn knows,' said Tolly as they reached the dining hall. 'Even if he didn't believe you, he heard, and he might tell.'

'I'll talk to him. Now's as good a time as any.' Petrello deliberately took the empty place beside Vyborn.

Vyborn looked at Petrello suspiciously.

'About last night,' Petrello said casually. 'You didn't believe what I said, did you, about the leopards?'

'No,' said Vyborn. 'It's silly.'

'It was a joke.' Petrello grinned apologetically. 'But now I feel foolish. So don't tell anyone about it, will you?'

Vyborn picked at his bread. 'I like to make people laugh. So I'll tell them a funny story if I want to.'

'Not this one,' Petrello said severely.

'Yes, this one. A funny story about leopards making gold.'

'No!' said Petrello.

Vyborn turned to him. Petrello's heart sank. His brother's face was dotted with sprouting dark hairs. The hairs began to grow at quite a rate, especially under Vyborn's chin.

'Vyborn, no!' warned Petrello.

'Yes,' grunted his brother as two horns thrust their way out of his forehead.

Most of the children had already seen Vyborn's nasty shape-shifting, but not Alcida, Selgi's sister, who was sitting opposite Vyborn. She stared at Vyborn's horns, her eyes so round they almost popped out of her head. Her mouth dropped open and she screamed.

Alcida's scream sent other children toppling off the benches.

'What's going on?' Nurse Ogle demanded from the head of the table.

It was Selgi who pointed at Vyborn, crying, 'He's doing it again.'

With an angry, burbling sort of bellow, the goat jumped on to the table. He stamped on a platter, lowered his head and thrust his horns towards Petrello's chest.

Petrello threw himself backwards and somersaulted on to the floor.

'Did you set him off again, foolish Petrello?' Nurse Ogle shouted, as screaming children ran from their breakfasts and bounded up the steps.

'Didn't mean to.' Petrello stood up, grabbed a hunk of bread and raced after the others.

Tolly, close behind, asked, 'What did you say to him?'

'Hardly anything,' said Petrello, gasping for breath.

Apart from Nurse Ogle and the goat, Guanhamara was the last to leave the hall. 'This is getting boring,' she said. 'Can't he do something a bit more interesting than a goat?'

'Don't,' begged Petrello. 'Imagine a warhorse in your bedchamber.'

'Or a bear,' added Tolly.

Guanhamara laughed. 'Why was he trying to attack you, Trello?'

'It's a long story,' sighed Petrello.

Guanhamara took his arm. 'So tell me.'

Petrello led his brother and sister to a quiet corner of the courtyard, and there he told Guanhamara everything that he'd seen the night before.

'The leopards!' Guanhamara clasped her hands and gave a little jump. 'I knew they would do something one day. They've been so secretive till now. Lilith said the king's stories about them couldn't be true.'

'They made gold,' Petrello stated. 'I saw it. But I don't

think our father wants anyone to know. And I don't want him to think I was spying on him.'

'It'll be our secret. Let's go and see Gunfrid before the school bell goes. He's probably in the sanatorium.' As she spoke, Guanhamara began to hurry across the courtyard.

The boys followed her, but not before Petrello had seen a black goat emerge from the dining hall. The goat stood eyeing the people who were hurrying about their business: knights, scribes, masons, grooms, chancellor's men, cooks, dressmakers, jewellers, cleaners and children playing tag. At last the goat spied Petrello.

'Run!' cried Petrello as the goat galloped towards him. 'Or we'll get a goat's horns up our bottoms.'

Her face brimming with defiance, Guanhamara swung round. In a voice ten times deeper than her normal tone, she uttered three sounds, none of them recognisable. The goat stopped in its tracks, blinked and then, lowering its head, it came on. Guanhamara's words became a rumbling roar as a huge creature materialised before the goat; a giant bull, its horns tipped with shining spikes. The earth trembled as it pawed the cobblestones, and the clouds of steam erupting from its nostrils grew into a tower of sizzling, flashing water.

Peering round the boiling tower, Petrello saw the goat's backside disappearing fast into the second courtyard.

'That should do it,' said Guanhamara, her voice still disconcertingly low.

The bull faded, until all that was left of it was a hovering puff of steam.

'Not real.' Guanhamara grinned as she clutched a handful of empty air.

Unfortunately, Vyborn-the-goat wasn't the only one to be scared out of his wits. People who had been busily hurrying through the courtyard had all stopped to watch the unbelievable appearance of a giant bull in their midst. They were now staring at Guanhamara, frowns of horror on all their faces.

'Sorry,' said Guanhamara, her usual sweet voice sounding a little sheepish.

'Let's go.' Petrello pulled her arm.

'Maybe you shouldn't have done that, Guan,' said Tolly as they made their way to the sanatorium.

'What else was I supposed to do?' said his sister. 'I've discovered my inherited talent. I can only suppose that I'm meant to use it.'

'You could say that the same applies to Vyborn,' murmured Petrello.

Guanhamara laughed.

The sanatorium was situated in a long room at the foot of the wizards' tower. Here, Llyr and Eri could speedily access their pharmacy if a patient needed their urgent attention. Today only one of the ten beds was occupied. Gunfrid sat on the edge of his bed with Zeba beside him, their pale legs dangling over the side of the bed. Gunfrid had lost his awful, greyish pallor. He said it was due to 'something hot and stinky' the wizard Llyr had poured down his throat.

'But he can't walk yet,' said Zeba, casting an anxious eye on her brother's legs.

'They're no use, see.' Gunfrid attempted to raise his leg. His foot straightened a little and his leg moved an inch before dropping back again.

'Your brother, Amadis, has gone to the carpenters,' said Zeba. 'He says they'll make a chair for Gunfrid, with arms an' all.'

'And wheels,' said Gunfrid, 'so Zeba can wheel me around.'

Amadis came in with a smile on his face. But it was a

grim smile. Although Amadis was trying hard not to show his anger, Petrello could see a cold fury in his brother's dark berry eyes.

'Your chair shall have gold on it, Gunfrid,' said Amadis, 'and your name shall be engraved in the wood, and you shall have a red velvet cushion with golden tassels. I've told the seamstresses exactly what to do. You shall be the most comfortable boy in the castle.'

'Thank you,' said Gunfrid, a catch of surprise in his voice.

Zeba gave a small cough. 'They say that Gunfrid's poisoning was meant for you, Amadis.'

'It was my helmet,' he said.

'Lilith did it,' said Tolly. 'She's confessed.'

Amadis didn't reply. He looked into the distance for a moment, rubbed his chin with the back of his thumb, then turned on his heel and left the room.

'He seems mightily troubled,' Zeba remarked.

'Who wouldn't be,' said Guanhamara.

The school bell began to ring and, promising to return later, Guanhamara and her brothers made their way to the schoolroom. They were almost there when a loud commotion from the next courtyard caused them to stop and listen.

Deep voices were raised in anger, and someone was screeching like a demon.

'We have to find out what that is,' said Guanhamara.

Her brothers agreed and all three ran towards the entrance to the second courtyard.

Lilith stood in the very centre, her hands resting on her hips. Olga hovered behind her, an awkward smile on her lips. Lilith began to scream at a blacksmith who was trying to pull his unlit furnace further away from her.

'What's the matter with you?' shrieked Lilith. 'Why are you looking at me as if I've got two heads. Anyone would think I was a monster.' She made a little run at a carpenter who leapt back, sending his workbench flying.

'Funny looks, that's all I get,' cried Lilith. 'Do you think I'm going to stick spells on all your backs? Silly fools.'

Olga giggled nervously.

Lilith suddenly caught sight of her sister and brothers lingering in the archway. 'And what do you want, children? Come to see the fun? You should be at your lessons.'

'We thought you were in trouble, sister,' Guanhamara said innocently.

'Trouble? Don't be stupid.' Lilith swung round and pinched Olga's arm. 'Do something, Olga!'

'Yes, Lilith.' With a nasty grin, Olga stared at a large wagon. One of the smiths was trying to fit a new wheel on to the shaft. All at once, the wheel wrenched itself out of his hands, spun in the air and came flying at Guanhamara.

Guanhamara ducked and the wheel crashed to the ground behind her. Petrello saw Guanhamara's fingers flexing. He could see the anger in her eyes as a series of monstrous images ran through her mind.

'Don't, Guan,' he whispered.

'Why should they get away with it?' she hissed. 'I can do more than them, now.'

'Do it, then,' said Tolly with an encouraging grin.

'It's not worth it.' Petrello tugged his sister's arm.

Reluctantly she allowed herself to be drawn away, and they ran to the schoolroom.

'I could have made them so, so sorry,' Guanhamara grumbled. 'I wish you'd let me do what I wanted.'

'There's been too much trouble today already,' said Petrello. He could hear Lilith and Olga still laughing

158

behind them, and understood how angry Guanhamara felt. But he had a terrible sense of foreboding. The court had suffered so many shocks, all at the hands of the royal children. How could the king bear any more?

Petrello's fears were soon realised. Lessons had hardly begun when Cedric, the king's messenger, came into the schoolroom. Everyone turned to look at him as he walked past the long tables. He wore a crimson tunic embroidered in gold, and an undershirt of gleaming yellow. A line of pearls adorned the band of his black velvet cap and also the cuffs of his buttercup shirt. Cedric was full of his own importance and proud of his appearance. He hadn't set foot in the schoolroom since he was twelve years old. Never mind that there were three princes and a princess present, Cedric's pointed nose was held very pointedly in the air.

There was an expectant hush as Friar Gereint unfolded the paper that Cedric had handed to him.

The friar looked up and said, 'Guanhamara, Petrello, Tolly and Vyborn, you will please attend the king in the Hall of Corrections.'

'Hall of Corrections?' squeaked Tolly.

'Now?' asked Guanhamara.

'Hall of Corrections. Now!' Friar Gereint affirmed.

Cedric marched out and the four children followed him. As soon as they were in the courtyard, Cedric nodded imperiously at the Hall of Corrections and, turning his back on the children, strode away, his nose still in the air.

'Why the Hall of Corrections?' said Tolly. 'Have we done something wrong?'

'You're always doing something wrong,' muttered Vyborn.

Tolly caught Petrello's warning eye and didn't bother to reply.

The guard gave them a suspicious look as they filed into the hall, and Petrello remembered the rat. The king was already there, sitting on one of his high-backed chairs at the far end of the room. The queen was beside him. Petrello had half-expected the chancellor to be in attendance, but their parents were alone.

The king beckoned and the children moved closer to him. All at once there was a shout from outside, followed by a roar of anger. A heated argument began and Cafal came loping into the hall.

'Cafal, what is the altercation?' asked the king.

'It's about the w-wolf, Father,' Cafal stammered.

'Borlath doesn't want it to come in – nor d-did I. But the guard wouldn't pr-prevent it.'

The king couldn't suppress a smile. 'Greyfleet will do no harm, Cafal. You know that.'

'I suppose,' mumbled Cafal.

The next moment Borlath burst into the hall, followed by Amadis and his wolf.

'Greyfleet must remain by the door,' the king commanded.

Amadis murmured softly to the wolf, who dropped to his haunches just inside the door.

Olga shuffled in. Giving the wolf a wide berth and a grimace, she joined her brothers and sisters. They stood in a half-circle. Amadis and Guanhamara in the centre, Cafal and Olga at either end.

'Is Lilith not with you?' the queen asked Olga.

'Indisposed,' mumbled Olga.

The queen clicked her tongue.

For a few moments the king tapped the arms of his chair. His heavy rings on the wood made the sound of a small drum. At last he said, 'You will be wondering why I have chosen the Hall of Corrections to talk to you.'

'Why?' asked Borlath in a surly voice.

'Because you, my children, need correction,' said the king.

'Some of us are men and women, now,' Borlath argued. 'We can live as we wish, without correction.'

The queen's eyes flashed. 'King Timoken is still your father. He is your king.'

Borlath grunted. Cafal sniffed.

The king looked hard at his children, searching each face. 'Some of you have forgotten the advice I gave you when you were younger. Can anyone tell me what it was?'

Why did no one speak? Was it guilt, or obstinacy? Or was each one reluctant to shame the others? Petrello remembered every word the king had said, but he couldn't bring himself to speak.

It was Guanhamara who broke the awful silence. 'You told us that one day we might develop a powerful talent, quite outside the range that other people might expect. And that if we did acquire this talent we must be thankful for it, and never use it to cause grief or pain or worry. And we promised to abide by your rules.'

The king had a special affection for his youngest daughter. He tried not to show it, but anyone could see how his face softened when she spoke. 'Yes, Guanhamara,' he said. 'And I believe that recently your imagination has taken flight?'

'It has, Father.' Guanhamara smiled. 'And I'm sorry if I did something to offend, but I only used my talent in . . . well, mostly, in defence.'

'And perhaps some fun,' said the queen.

'But I didn't break my promise,' said Guanhamara. 'At least I didn't mean to.'

The king turned his attention to Vyborn. 'And you, Vyborn, you have caused great distress.'

The others looked at the king's youngest child. Vyborn screwed up his nose and looked at his feet. Petrello had an awful feeling that Vyborn was going to grow hooves again, but his feet stayed well inside his boots.

'I don't want to punish any of you,' the king went on, 'and so I am commanding you to honour your promises. The people who live in our castle are not to be tormented or harassed or put to any inconvenience. Is that understood? You are no better than them, you just happen to be the children of someone who was favoured by a very special being many, many years ago.'

Silence again as the king's children considered their father's words. Borlath swung from one heavy foot to the other. Cafal tried unsuccessfully to copy him. Greyfleet gave a soft whine and Vyborn sneezed. Tolly scratched his back.

They were about to be dismissed. It only remained for each of them to reaffirm their promises, but all at once Guanhamara said, 'And what about poor Gunfrid? Will Lilith be punished? Because what she did was more than torment, it was attempted murder. And we all know that it was Amadis she meant to harm.'

For a moment the king looked utterly disconcerted. Petrello's heart went out to him. He could see that his father didn't know what to do. If he punished Lilith, whose life would be in danger when she chose to vent her fury?

The queen came to the king's rescue. Looking at her second son, she said, 'Let Amadis decide.'

The king frowned. He was afraid for Amadis. 'What do you say, Amadis?' he asked.

'I accept,' Amadis replied. His face was impassive. Petrello sensed that his brother had been expecting this.

The king gave him a grateful nod. 'You may all go now,' he said.

They filed through the door, Borlath striding out

first, as though a minor irritation had kept him from his duties, whatever they were. He ignored Lilith sitting on a bench beside the arch into the second courtyard. She was swinging her legs as she casually bit into an apple.

The others stopped and stared at her. Petrello heard the sharp intake of breath from Amadis, who stood behind him.

When the king and queen emerged from the Hall of Corrections they immediately saw who the others were looking at.

'Lilith, I thought you were indisposed,' roared the king.

'I was not disposed to attend your meeting,' countered Lilith.

A look of rage passed across the king's face. He clenched his fists and uttered a stifled roar. But it was not as loud as the sound that came from Amadis: a soaring, crying wail.

And instantly Petrello knew what would happen, what his brother had been planning all along. He could feel it in the air, hear the wings slicing through the wind, and when the eagle began to swoop he watched in horrified fascination.

Lilith looked up. She saw the eagle and stood. She

took two quick paces and then it was on her. The eagle sank its talons into the shoulders of her green and gold silk dress, and lifted her. Spreading its wings, it rose into the air, while Lilith screamed and kicked and cursed her brother Amadis. But soon her voice was just a tiny whine, her figure a dot hanging beneath two wide wings, higher than any bird in the bright morning sky.

Chapter Twelve

A Serpent in the Solarium

It was such a shocking thing. Even the king was speechless; and then the wailing began. Olga, her face creased with fury, dashed to the place where her sister had left the ground. Tugging her ragged black hair, jumping up and down in a frenzy, she screamed, 'What have you done? You'll pay for this, Amadis. You're wicked, wicked, wicked!'

'I'm sorry, Father.' Amadis turned his back on his shrieking sister. 'I've broken my promise not to harm.'

'You did what had to be done,' said the queen.

'There seemed to be no other way,' Amadis admitted. 'Yet I know it was wrong. I swear the eagle won't kill Lilith. She'll be removed to a place far from here. It'll give us time to collect our thoughts before she can do harm again.'

'It will.' The king's voice could hardly be heard above Olga's screams. He strode up to her, put a hand on her shoulder and said, 'Olga, calm yourself. You'll see your sister again.'

'Wicked, wicked, wicked!' wailed the girl. 'Punish him! Punish Amadis!'

'Quiet, Olga,' the king commanded.

'No, no, no!' she screamed, tearing herself away from her father's strong hand.

There was no pacifying her. Courtiers hurried away from the dreadful spectacle of a princess gone mad. Soon the courtyard had emptied. Only the king and queen and their eight children remained.

Olga's distress was painful to watch. Lilith was her idol, the centre of her world. How could she exist without her? She had never been pretty, but anguish made her gruesome, her eyelids swollen beneath her heavy brow, her wide mouth a gaping wound. As she dashed away from her family's gaze, the queen guessed what might happen. 'No, Olga!' she cried.

It was too late. By the time her family had caught up with her, Olga was already in the second courtyard, a playground of possibilities for someone like her, and she immediately took advantage of it. Benches and tables went flying across the cobbles, iron wheels, pokers, furnace grates, planks, ladders, everything was moving. There were cries of pain as the smiths and carpenters had their tools wrenched away from them and into the air, and then sent back to strike them. A man lay on the ground moaning, another with a bleeding head took shelter behind an upturned wagon.

The king, grasping his head, shouted until he was hoarse; the queen tried to grab her demented daughter and, for her pains, was tripped by a rolling log. The king ran and, lifting the queen in his arms, carried her to safety.

Amadis bounded over to the man on the ground and helped him into the storeroom behind his forge.

Petrello, Tolly and Guanhamara watched from the archway, not knowing what to do. Behind them, Cafal began to sniffle like an animal. Vyborn jumped up and down, squealing like a pig, delirious with excitement.

Help came at last from an unexpected quarter. Borlath marched up to his sister and, grabbing both her hands, stared into her face, saying, 'Olga, your sister will come back. Remember what I told you. Not long now.'

Petrello remembered that last phrase. There was something sinister about it. But it had the desired effect on Olga. She became very still, closed her mouth and stopped crying.

'Guanhamara,' said Borlath, 'take your sister to her bedchamber.'

Guanhamara swallowed hard. 'Me?' She looked at her mother.

The queen, on her feet again and dusting herself down, said, 'We'll go together.'

'She won't cause any trouble now.' Borlath looked at Olga, his gaze intense, unblinking. 'Will you, Olga?'

'What?' she mumbled.

'You won't cause any trouble now, will you?' Borlath shook her arm, put his face close to hers. 'Will you?'

'No,' said Olga, her voice quiet and flat.

The queen looked at Guanhamara.

'Here goes,' Guanhamara whispered to Petrello. 'Wish me luck.'

But Olga was now quite calm. Her mother and sister took her hands and led her quietly away.

All this time the king had been watching Borlath with undisguised surprise.

'I think Borlath put Olga in a trance,' Petrello said in a low voice.

'Didn't know he could do that,' said Tolly.

'Another string to his bow,' Petrello remarked. 'I hope he doesn't use it too often. And did you hear what he said? He used the same words as the chancellor's man. Chimery. "Not long now."'

'It sounds bad, Trello. But why does it sound bad?'

'Off to your lessons, boys,' the king commanded. 'And let's have no more trouble today.' He frowned at Vyborn as he said this, and Vyborn gave a submissive nod.

But Petrello noticed that his youngest brother glanced at Borlath before leaving the scene, and Borlath returned the look with a secretive sort of smile.

It stayed with Petrello, that smile. It unsettled him. The look that passed between Vyborn and their oldest brother gave Petrello an uncomfortable feeling in his stomach. He couldn't concentrate on his lessons and Friar Gereint called him foolish at least three times. But Petrello found that he didn't care. He was far more concerned with the strife that seemed to be building within his family.

At the end of the day, when Petrello stepped out of

the schoolroom, there was only one person he wanted to see. The king.

Tolly and Selgi were busy playing their game of Blagard. Each had a bag of ten stones. Tolly's were red, Selgi's black. Selgi had invented the game, which became more complicated every time they played. Petrello had given up trying to understand it, but Tolly threw himself into the contest with gusto. The two boys sat cross-legged on the ground, throwing their small stones into the air and watching where they fell. Tolly always shrieked the loudest when his piece landed in the right place.

Guanhamara, arm-in-arm with Elin, asked Petrello if he was coming to visit Gunfrid.

'No,' said Petrello, 'I have to do something.'

Guanhamara put her head on one side, the way she always did when she was trying to fathom her brother's mood. 'Want any help?'

'No.' Petrello smiled at his sister, to soften his reply.

'Don't miss your supper.'

'I won't.' Petrello watched his sister and her friend walk towards the sanatorium, and then he made his way to his aunt's garden.

Zobayda was sitting in her usual place beside the

172

fountain. Her favourite toy, a wooden camel, stood beside her, its head touching the violet silk of her robe, where it covered her knees. Zobayda's husband, Tariq, had made the camel long ago, before he died. Sometimes Petrello wondered if a little of Tariq's spirit remained within the wooden toy.

Zobayda was aware of everything that had occurred in the past two days. Often, it seemed that, even from a distance, she knew what had happened before she was told.

'Troubling times, Petrello.' Today Zobayda's face betrayed her great age. She looked very weary, and the lines on her dark skin appeared to be deeper than before.

'Something is happening to our family,' said Petrello. 'A sort of madness had entered some of us, and I'm frightened, Aunt.'

'Of course you are.' She covered his hand with her long, beautiful fingers and Petrello felt again the strange, warm pressure of the jinni's silver ring.

'It's all his fault, isn't it?' said Petrello, staring at the tiny face peeping above its silver wing.

'Petrello, how can you say that?' Zobayda took her hand away. 'If it were not for the jinni none of us would be here. Your father and I would never have escaped the army that captured our palace and killed our parents.'

Petrello bit his lip. 'I'm sorry. But because our father has one foot in the world of enchantments, it seems that the life that other world has given us has done us harm.'

'We can never be sure how the realm of enchantments will endow us. We must just be thankful that some of it is good.' Zobayda gave him a solemn smile. 'You came here to see the king. I think he might have gone into his Solarium.'

'But we are not allowed –' Petrello began.

'Today . . . today.' His aunt frowned and rubbed her forehead. 'Today I believe you must. The king will understand.'

'You know everything, Aunt.' Petrello already felt better for seeing her, but on his way over to the Royal Tower, he suddenly stopped and, turning to his aunt, said, 'You told me once that I might save you all, but I can't do anything, Aunt Zobayda. Nothing, nothing, nothing. I'm just foolish Petrello.'

'Be patient,' said his aunt. 'You have a gift, Petrello, though as yet, I don't understand it.'

Petrello gave her a small wave and continued on to his parents' apartments. The guard outside was sitting on a stool, chewing sorrel. 'The queen is not in residence,' he told Petrello. 'She is with the Princess Olga.'

'It's the king I wish to see,' said Petrello.

'Not in residence,' said the guard.

'But my aunt . . .' Petrello looked back at his aunt.

'Your auntie's eyesight isn't that good,' said the guard, rather rudely, Petrello thought.

But Zobayda was nodding and smiling at him, and all at once Petrello had an overwhelming feeling that his aunt wanted him to go into the Solarium, whether his father was there or not. So he had to find an excuse very quickly.

'It has nothing to do with Princess Zobayda's eyesight,' Petrello said haughtily. 'She lent my father a precious book, and wants me to fetch it for her.'

The guard looked at Zobayda. She smiled, nodded and made a small pushing motion with her hand. 'Very well,' he said, 'but be quick about it.' And, watching Petrello closely, he opened the door and let him through.

The king's Solarium was on the ground floor. Behind the twisting stairway to the upper floors, there was a small door. Petrello knew it led to the Solarium, but he had never opened the door, never even touched the handle.

No child had. It was an unspoken rule. But his aunt's insistence gave him courage. He put his hand on the brass ring, turned it lightly and the door swung open.

He was met with a darkness so complete he couldn't see one tiny detail of what lay beyond. Perhaps there was nothing but a void waiting to swallow him up. Petrello put one foot over the threshold. He was met by a scent. What was it? *Can you smell the sun?* he wondered. Because that was all he could imagine. It was such a warm, fresh comforting scent.

Before Petrello knew it he was making his way down a long passage. Dull light from the open door behind him showed the faint outlines of a bricked wall; beneath his feet there were more deep red bricks. The passage turned abruptly and deprived of light from the doorway he was once again plunged into the dark. With one hand on the wall, he felt his way onwards. The passage narrowed. He could touch both sides with his elbows.

A pillar blocked his way. He sidled past it and stepped into a bright circular room.

Frescoes of an African kingdom adorned the walls: flat-roofed houses, palm trees, camels, monkeys and exotic birds. Dark men in white robes. Petrello trod carefully across a floor paved in mosaics. Lines of red, orange and yellow radiated from a huge red circle, and the same pattern was repeated in the high, vaulted ceiling, only here the central circle was not made of glass, it was open to the soft, sunset sky.

Four highly polished chests stood against the wall, forming a long, low table. And this was covered with precious objects: coloured jars, painted wooden boxes, golden caskets, and silver trays that held tiny creatures carved from wood and stone. At one end sat a large glass marble, a beautiful object that demanded to be touched. Petrello put out a hand, but, quicker than lightning, the gleaming head of a serpent rose from behind the chest and struck his fingers.

'Ouch!' Petrello put his bruised fingers into his mouth. 'Why did you do that, Solomon?'

Solomon was the king's pet snake and guardian of his treasures. He seldom left the Royal Tower, and when he did he was usually draped about the king's shoulders. He was a big snake, longer than the king when they were lying down together. His skin was silver and black, his eyes like beads of jet. Only the king knew where he came from.

'All right, I won't touch the king's treasures,' Petrello told the snake.

A tiny fragment of Solomon's silver skin had brushed off on Petrello's middle finger. He regarded the small patch of silvery dust, and almost without thinking, went to the wall to wipe it off. There was a painted bird on one of the frescoes and he followed the outline of the bird with his finger. He was delighted to see how the silver dust made the bird sparkle.

And then Petrello found that he wasn't touching the hard plaster beneath the fresco.

He could feel another finger, and it wasn't his.

Chapter Thirteen
Touching the Future

Petrello stepped back. He looked at his hand then at the bird on the wall, with its dusting of silver. He could see no finger poking through the painted plumage, and yet he had felt one. Definitely. Unless he was going mad.

'What's going on, Solomon?' He turned to the snake, now coiled protectively about the king's treasures. 'Did you see . . .?'

Petrello looked back at the fresco. 'Oh!' he gasped.

Before him stood a boy. He was taller than Petrello and had pale skin and large mud-coloured eyes. His hair was dark and stuck out like a brush.

'Where have you come from?' It was Petrello's first thought.

The boy stared at him wordlessly.

Petrello tried again. 'How did you get here?'

This brought a puzzled frown to the boy's face.

So he was a foreigner. He was certainly wearing an unusual outfit. His tight breeches were a faded and rather dirty blue. He wore no tunic and no shirt. Instead, the upper part of his body was clothed in a grass-stained white garment, with short sleeves.

The boy was now staring intently at Petrello, his gaze travelling from Petrello's curly head right down to his leather boots. He smiled and spoke a few words. Petrello thought he recognised one of them, but the boy's language was still foreign to him.

Perhaps signs would work, Petrello thought, but before he could try one, footsteps could be heard approaching the Solarium and both boys turned to the entrance. A moment later the king appeared.

'Father,' began Petrello, 'I can explain. Aunt Zobayda said I should –'

The king raised his hand for silence. He looked astounded. When at last he found his voice, he murmured, 'This has never happened before.'

'I don't know where he came from,' said Petrello, looking at the boy. 'But –'

The king shook his head. 'I don't mean that. I know

180

where Charlie came from, we meet often. But it has only ever been us two.'

'Often?' said Petrello in a small, surprised voice. 'But who is he?'

The boy was looking from the king to Petrello, with a big smile on his face.

'He is my descendant,' the king told Petrello. And then he began to speak in the boy's unknown and mysterious language. The boy nodded and grinned at Petrello, before answering the king in long, excited sentences.

'What is he saying? Why is he here?' Petrello could hardly contain himself.

'It would take a very long time for me to explain it all,' said his father. 'Charlie lives nine hundred years ahead of us, in another era. He speaks our language but it has changed considerably over the centuries. He is of my blood and through all those long years a small part of the world of enchantment has reached some of my descendants. Charlie has been gifted with the ability to travel through images. He can touch one and travel.'

'Is the bird still there, so many centuries ahead? Don't things fade and crumble?'

Petrello glanced at the bird with its dusting of snake silver.

The king smiled. 'Not these frescoes, it seems. Our spirit ancestors have a power beyond our comprehension. They made these,' he nodded at the painted walls, 'so perhaps they will last forever.'

'I touched the bird, and then Charlie's finger,' Petrello said, still bewildered by what had happened.

The boy's expression had changed. He was staring at Petrello with interest and amusement. He spoke again to the king, and the king, looking at Petrello, said, 'Well, well! How extraordinary.'

'What?' asked Petrello.

'Charlie tells me that you remind him of a great friend of his. He can't explain why, for this boy doesn't have your dark skin and black hair. His eyes are wide and blue, and his hair the colour of corn.'

'And his name?' asked Petrello.

Charlie seemed to understand this. 'Tancred,' he said, adding several more incomprehensible words.

'And is he . . .?' Petrello suddenly felt as though he was about to learn something vital, something that would bring him closer to understanding himself.

'Does Tancred have a gift?'

'Yes, he is another of my descendants. He can bring thunderstorms, just as I can.'

'I see.' Petrello regarded his hands, flexed his fingers, hunched his shoulders.

The king looked concerned. 'Petrello, it doesn't mean that you will be able to do this.'

'All the same,' Petrello said cheerfully. 'It's interesting.' He gazed at his hands, as though they might give him another clue. When he looked up, Charlie had gone.

'He often goes like that,' said the king. 'He seldom has time to say goodbye.'

'But why?' Petrello stared at the space their visitor had occupied only a moment before.

'He can be interrupted by a friend, or his parents, and then the link is broken, and he is whisked away.' The king looked up at the red sky as if Charlie had ascended into the air. 'He is a good, honest and cheerful person, and his accounts of life nine hundred years in the future contain much comfort.'

Petrello realised his stomach was growling. 'Thank you for allowing me to meet your descendant,' he said.

'It was your aunt's doing.' The king smiled. 'You should

be at supper, my son. I can hear your hunger. And, Petrello, I would like Charlie to remain our secret, for now.'

'I promise not to speak of him with anyone else, Father.'

When Petrello stepped out of the Royal Tower, the guard gave him an odd look, but said nothing. Zobayda had left her seat and taken the wooden camel into her apartments. Night clouds from the north were beginning to drift into the rosy sky, and a chilly breeze had blown up.

Feeling inexplicably cheerful, Petrello strode into the second courtyard, only to find it deserted. The chaos from Olga's furious assault had been carefully tidied and a subdued mutter came from the workers' dining hall.

Petrello was afraid he had missed his supper. The loud calls from his empty stomach were increasing every second. He ran through the next courtyard and furtively opened the door into the children's hall.

Nurse Ogle was busy wiping the youngest child's face. Petrello hunched down and climbed over the bench into the empty space beside Tolly. A bowl of cold soup was waiting for him.

'Where've you been?' Tolly muttered, as Petrello gulped down the soup.

'Tell you later,' said Petrello, before remembering the promise he'd made to the king. He had experienced something astonishing and unbelievable, and yet he must keep it a secret. It would be hard.

'The bread's all gone, but I saved you some.' Tolly took a soggy roll from his lap and put it beside Petrello's bowl.

'Thanks.' Petrello glanced at his brother. Tolly's eyelids were red and swollen. He'd been crying.

'What's the matter, Tolly? Last time I saw you, you were playing Blagard.'

Tolly dropped his head. He toyed with his spoon for a moment, before whispering, 'My back itched. It got so bad I couldn't play any more.'

'I'm sorry,' said Petrello.

'So I went to find Guan,' Tolly went on. 'And she . . . and she . . .'

'She what?'

'She took me to the wizards for some salve.'

'And is your back better now?' Petrello peered into his brother's unhappy face.

Tolly shook his head and a tear dropped into his bowl.

'It takes a while for Llyr's salves to work. I know because when I bruised my knee –'

'Nothing will work,' Tolly broke in. 'We were on the steps to the Eyrie. The pain was so bad. It was really, really bad, Trello.' Tolly looked across the table at Guanhamara sitting opposite.

Guanhamara smiled encouragingly. She mouthed the words, 'Don't worry. It will be all right.'

'What does she mean?' Petrello asked his brother.

Tolly shook his head. More tears fell. Children were looking at him. Tolly suddenly twisted round, swung his legs over the bench and ran out.

'Tolomeo, you have not had permission,' shouted Nurse Ogle.

'He's not well, Nurse,' said Guanhamara.

'What's it to do with you?' snapped the long-faced woman.

Petrello wanted to race after his brother, but he was afraid he'd make the situation worse.

'No cheese for him tomorrow,' grunted Nurse Ogle. 'Take your bowls to the pump, children. Petrello, take your brother's.'

Petrello quickly gathered the bowls and ran to wash them at the pump. A queue had formed and Guanhamara was on the end of it.

'What's wrong with Tolly?' Petrello asked his sister.

'I can't tell you here,' she said. 'Let him show you.'

'Show me?' Petrello was mystified.

'Poor Tolly.'

Guanhamara looked so solemn, Petrello began to imagine the worst. 'Has the plague come?' he asked. 'Or some other horrible affliction? He had lumps on his back . . .'

'Sssssh!' His sister looked around but no one appeared to have heard them. There was always a lot of howling, squealing and laughter at the pump, as children tried to splash each other.

'He'll be in the bedchamber,' said Guanhamara as they put their clean, wet bowls back on the table. 'I'll come with you.'

They found Tolly lying on his stomach, his face turned to the wall. He'd taken off his jerkin and his loose white shirt was bunched over his shoulder-blades. Petrello sat on the edge of his brother's bed. He looked at Guanhamara, who stood by the door.

'Does it still hurt?' Petrello asked his brother.

'The pain is going,' Tolly mumbled, 'and now I'm a freak.'

'You're not,' Petrello said firmly.

Tolly turned his head and, muffling his voice in the pillow, he said, 'Look!'

Petrello lifted his brother's shirt above his shoulder-blades. In the fading daylight, he saw quite clearly that the small bony lumps he'd glimpsed in the moonlight were now covered in glossy black feathers.

'I'm a freak,' Tolly sobbed. 'Trello, I'm a freak, aren't I?'

'No,' Petrello said fiercely. 'You have wings, Tolly,' and in a tone of wonder, he added, 'They'll grow and you'll be able to fly.'

'I don't want to,' Tolly cried. He sat up and, throwing an arm over his shoulder, tried to reach the offending wings, as though he wanted to tear them out. 'The jinni's tricked me. You've all been gifted in wonderful, secret ways.' He stared at his sister. 'But everyone can see what I am. They'll laugh. Father can fly, but he doesn't have wings. Why has this happened to me?'

'Tolly, I don't have any gift at all,' said Petrello.

'Lucky you,' Tolly muttered.

At that moment Vyborn came in. At least half of Vyborn. He'd managed almost to become a dragon. The scales were there, and the crest on his head, and there was a bit of a tail and one wing. But only one half of his face was a dragon's, and only one arm and one leg, so he was all lopsided. If anyone looked a freak, it was Vyborn.

Guanhamara tried not to giggle but it was impossible. Holding back for a second made it worse. When she finally gave in her high-pitched squeals made Petrello fall to the ground with laughter, and then even Tolly began to giggle.

'Stop it!' screeched Vyborn. 'Stop it! Stop it! Why can't I be a dragon?'

'Because you can't remember what Eri's dragon looks like,' said Guanhamara through her giggles, 'and you've no imagination.' Holding her hand over her mouth, she ran into the passage, trying to stifle the laughter that kept bubbling out.

Vyborn stumped over to his bed and sat on the edge, a dejected, ridiculous half-dragon. Slowly he assumed his whole human form. 'What a day,' he remarked, and flung himself face down on the bed.

Petrello and Tolly grinned at each other, and Petrello said, 'It's going to be all right. Believe me.'

'At least it doesn't hurt any more,' said Tolly.

They glanced at Vyborn, wondering if he'd heard, but

their small brother had already begun to snore. The effort of trying to be a dragon had worn him out.

Later that night Petrello woke up. In spite of the extraordinary events of the day, he hadn't found it difficult to fall asleep. It was the dream that woke him; a dream of feathers. He thought of the cloak that Wyngate always wore; a long cloak of glossy ravens' feathers. If the king could copy it for Tolly, his wings would become part of a long feathered cloak, and no one would guess the truth.

'Yes,' Petrello said drowsily. 'A cloak of feathers.'

While the rest of the castle's occupants were in their beds, the king was getting ready to work. He had many helmets to make, one more precious than the rest. He chose the armoury for his task, and the wizard Llyr to help him.

The king sat behind a square table at the back of the room. On either side of him, candles flickered in tall, three-branched candelabra. Another had been placed on a shelf above. In the centre of the table the eagle helmet gleamed and twinkled, giving no hint of its deadly past.

Llyr had put bowls of smouldering incense before the two doors and on the sill. Pungent smoke drifted around the suits of armour, giving the impression of an army drowning in fog.

'Let us begin,' said the king.

Llyr picked up a large sack and came to stand beside him. The king drew the eagle helmet towards him; he folded his arms about it, closed his eyes and bent his head so that his slim crown touched the golden eagle.

In the language of the secret kingdom, a language that Llyr could barely understand, the king spoke to his spirit ancestors. A moment passed; the king lifted his head and pushed the helmet away from him. And there, before him on the table, sat a second helmet, identical to the first in every detail.

'Tomorrow, early, I want you to take the old one to the smiths.' King Timoken nodded at the object of Lilith's awful spell. 'Tell them to melt it down, burn the poison out of it, and watch them do it, Llyr.'

'I will.' Llyr scooped the helmet into his sack.

'We will do the same with all the others,' said the king. 'We don't know if Lilith has tampered with them. But first, let's take this to Amadis.'

Leaving the sack by the door, Llyr picked up his staff and they stepped out into the courtyard where the black horse Isgofan stood, quiet and patient, with the wolf Greyfleet beside him. Already mounted, Amadis wore his chain mail beneath a padded yellow tunic. It was decorated with a wolf and an eagle, in red and gold thread. The wolf and the eagle appeared again on the shield that hung from his saddle. His head was bare and his thick hair looked white-gold in the moonlight.

'You're still determined to do this tonight, Amadis?' asked the king. 'In another day we could ride out together.'

'I must leave now, Father,' Amadis solemnly replied. 'I have harmed my sister and until I have redeemed myself, I cannot think of returning.'

'Amadis, she would have harmed you,' said Llyr.

'Nevertheless.' Amadis gave the wizard a rueful smile.

'But alone?' said Llyr.

'I shall not be alone.' Amadis glanced down at Greyfleet, and almost as a reminder there came a cry from the eagle circling above him. 'They are my ears and eyes,' he said.

The king handed his son the newly made helmet, saying, 'The only magic in this is for your protection.'

'Thank you, Father.'

When Amadis had put on the helmet, he turned his

horse towards the South Gate. Llyr strode before him and, at a light touch from his staff, the tall doors swung open.

Amadis rode out of the castle with Greyfleet keeping pace beside the horse. As Llyr and the king watched them enter the forest, seven dark forms rose out of the grass at the edge of the trees: Greyfleet's brothers. The wolves followed horse and rider into the shadows, and soon the only creature to be seen was a night owl, perched in a high branch, calling advice to the prince who could understand him.

Chapter Fourteen

A Cloak of Feathers

Friar Gereint's teeth had been giving him trouble for some time. Next morning, when angry roars from the courtyard began to disturb his lesson, the friar's toothache became unbearable. Eventually his head sank on to his chest and, waving his hand at the children, he muttered, 'Class dismissed. Leave! Leave! I must be alone with my teeth!'

'Go and see the wizards, Friar Gereint,' Guanhamara suggested. 'They're good at extractions.'

'Mmmmmmm!' moaned the friar. 'How shall I eat without teeth?'

Guanhamara had no answer for this. She quickly left the classroom and joined her brothers outside. They were rather enjoying the spectacle of Borlath in a rage. Roaring and spitting oaths, he stormed about in angry circles while small tongues of flame flared from his fingertips. Everyone who had to pass him gave a little leap of fright or surprise, especially the ladies who feared for their fine silk dresses.

The king appeared from the sanatorium, where he'd been checking on Gunfrid's progress. Borlath charged towards him.

'Amadis has gone!' roared Borlath. 'Why wasn't I told?'

'Why should you be told?' said the king. 'Your brother made his decision late last night.'

'We were to leave together. All of us. It's not right for Amadis to be alone.'

'He is not alone,' said the king. 'And well you know it.'

'Eagles and wolves,' Borlath muttered as he marched off. 'Otters and hares, ducks and geese, voles and sparrows. I'd rather have an army.'

The children looked at each other. Guanhamara raised her eyebrows and said, 'Amadis gone? I wonder why?'

Petrello shrugged. He felt uneasy. Beside him, Tolly rubbed his shoulder and whispered, 'When shall I ask about the cloak?'

'Now,' said Petrello, when he saw Borlath striding into the second courtyard.

As their father walked towards the kitchens, the children ran to catch up with him.

'Father,' cried Tolly, 'may I speak with you?'

The king turned. 'What's the trouble, Tolomeo?'

Tolly, glancing at the passing courtiers, said in a low voice, 'I have a problem that is secret – and personal.'

The king frowned. 'Come into the cloister.'

They followed their father into the covered walkway that ran beside the wall. The king continued on his way, but slowed his pace as Tolly began to talk. Petrello and his sister, walking behind, could hardly hear Tolly's hushed voice as he described the tiny wings that had sprouted from his shoulder-blades. And then Tolly's voice rose suddenly and a shuddering sigh escaped him. 'I can't bear it that people will see my wings and think I'm different, peculiar, not normal. I'm a freak, Father, aren't I?'

The king stopped. He turned to Tolly and, putting a hand on his shoulder, said, 'You are not a freak, Tolomeo. You have wings, and soon you will be able to fly. We shall fly together, you and I. Imagine how wonderful that will be.'

Tolly stared at his father and a slow smile began to light his face. But the king's words had a different effect on Petrello. They made him feel inexplicably lonely. How amazing it would be to fly with his father.

'Trello said that if I had a cloak made of feathers, like Wyngate's, people wouldn't notice my wings,' Tolly said earnestly. 'Not while they're growing, anyway.'

'I see,' said the king. 'People's stares will make you feel uncomfortable.'

'And they will stare, won't they, Father?' Guanhamara put in.

'For a while, yes,' the king agreed. 'Let us pay a visit to Wyngate; the library is on our way.'

Wyngate was at his usual table, books, maps and pages spread before him. But when the king and his children entered the library, they found the Book Guardian on his hands and knees before the entrance. He immediately became very flustered and got to his feet, holding a large book, some of whose pages lay scattered on the floor.

'Forgive the state we're in, Your Majesty,' whined old Moreau. 'That sudden Vanishing caused such a displacement, many pages have been loosened and I've been at my wits' end . . .'

'Your guardianship is faultless, my dear Moreau,' said the king. 'Please don't let us interrupt you.'

'Thank you! Thank you, Your Majesty.' With a deep bow, Moreau backed away to his desk, where he began to rearrange the loose pages of the large book.

Wyngate was so engrossed in his work, he was totally unaware of all that had been going on behind him. When the king touched his shoulder, he jumped off his stool and his feathered cap went flying. Guanhamara caught it with her thumb.

Before the king could say a word, the investigator exclaimed, 'King Timoken, I might have known it. You have come at exactly the right moment.' Guanhamara handed him his cap and he continued almost without taking a breath. 'Thank you, Princess; as I said the right moment exactly, because only a blink of an eye ago I discovered a place where another crystal might be found. I say "might" because, of course, one can never be sure.'

'That is very good news, Wyngate,' said the king. 'May I borrow your cloak for a moment?'

Wyngate looked puzzled. 'What has my cloak to do with a crystal?'

'Nothing at all,' said the king. 'Nevertheless, may I?' The king held out his hand.

'None of these birds, or should I say feathers, I mean none of the birds whose feathers are here in my cloak . . .' Wyngate often rambled in this way. He was quite relaxed about it. 'Not one met its death at my hands. I want you to know that.'

'I do know it,' said the king. 'But please may I borrow your feathered cloak?'

'Naturally.' Wyngate stood up, carefully removed his cloak, and handed it to the king.

The children stroked the cloak's shining feathers, Tolly with a gleam in his eye.

'It's so beautiful,' sighed Guanhamara.

The king felt he should explain why he wanted Wyngate's cloak. It didn't seem fair to use it without its owner sharing their secret, so the king leant close to the investigator and said in a low voice, 'My son, Tolomeo, is about to fly.'

Wyngate's eyes widened. 'Wings?' he whispered, glancing hastily at the Book Guardian.

'Indeed.' The king's eyes danced. 'But we want to disguise them for a while.'

Wyngate looked at Tolly. 'It will be too long for him.'

'I can correct that,' said the king.

'Of course.' Wyngate smiled at Tolly. 'I shall be pleased to share my feathers with someone so exceptional.'

Again, Petrello felt that surprising twinge of loneliness.

The king was already at work. The children loved to see the way he multiplied. Even though it was a useful, everyday sort of magic, it set their minds alight thinking of possibilities. What fun they could have had, multiplying every object in the castle. The king never used his gift for fun and he told them it was impossible to multiply a living creature.

Turning his head the slightest fraction, the Book Guardian glanced sideways. He could only see the king's back, but he could tell that something rather unusual was going on. Why had Wyngate taken off his cloak? Oh, there he was, putting it on again. Nothing special about that, then. Moreau went back to work. He heard the king thank Wyngate, and then the little group of children were running out of the library.

'Don't run!' The Book Guardian couldn't stop himself from reprimanding the children, even though the king was present.

'Sorry, Moreau!' said the boy in the cloak of feathers.

'Cloak of feathers,' Moreau said to himself. 'Did that child have it on when he came in?' He looked at Wyngate, shook his head and continued to glue loose pages into the precious book.

'Well done, Moreau,' said the king, striding past. 'Your library is excellently arranged.'

'Thank you, Your Majesty.' Moreau almost fell off his stool with pride.

The king had already joined his children in the courtyard when they heard Wyngate's shout. The investigator came bounding down the steps, crying, 'Wait, King Timoken. I forgot to tell you – it may have no bearing on Rigg's disappearance, and yet . . .'

'Tell me,' said the king.

The children moved closer as Wyngate lowered his voice. 'Once or twice, when I visited the wizards, Rigg was there. He liked to look at Eri's books. He could read and write and was interested in wizardry. It occurred to me that Rigg might have seen the list of ingredients for Eri's potion.'

'Which potion, Wyngate?' asked the king. 'There are so many.'

Wyngate pulled his feathered cap down over his ears. 'The mixture that added potency to the Seeing Crystal.'

The king rubbed his forehead. 'I remember. The crystal already made a sound that alerted us, but before it was dipped in Eri's potion, the approaching dangers were never clear.'

Guanhamara couldn't help herself. With a little jump she asked, 'So do you think that Rigg was abducted and maybe tortured until he told – whoever they are – about the secret ingredients of the potion that helps the crystal to see?'

The king and Wyngate looked at her. They had almost forgotten the children were listening. The boys shut their mouths tight, surprised by their sister's boldness. They expected a reprimand, but none came.

'It's possible,' said the investigator. 'But Rigg was loyal through and through. He was as stubborn as a mule. He would never betray the wizards' secret, unless . . .' He frowned suddenly and stared into the distance.

'Children, you should be at your lessons,' said the king.

'Friar Gereint has toothache,' Petrello told him.

'Then go and see Gunfrid. He misses your company. I must have further discussions with our investigator.' The king waved the children away, adding, 'Take care of that cloak, Tolomeo.'

'I will, and thank you, Father.'

The three children ambled towards the sanatorium.

One question was on all their minds. It was Petrello who voiced it. 'Who knew that Rigg knew the recipe for the Seeing Crystal?'

'Only the wizards, surely,' said his sister.

'There must be someone else.' Petrello recalled the investigator's expression. There was something about it that suggested he had an idea who the traitor might be.

In the sanatorium they found Zeba pushing Gunfrid round the beds in his new, wheeled chair. He looked very happy with it, but his legs were still weak.

Gunfrid had two other visitors. Vyborn and Cafal, of all people. They were sitting on one of the beds, watching the strange and rather splendid contraption that Zeba was manoeuvring about the room.

'P-poor boy,' Cafal mumbled. 'I'm going to help. Zeba can't push that chair over the big cobblestones.'

Vyborn had been eyeing Tolly's new cloak. Suddenly he jumped off the bed and snatched at a feather.

'Don't!' cried Tolly, whirling round.

'Where did you get that cloak?' Vyborn demanded. 'I want one. Why can't I have a cloak of feathers?'

'You can,' said Petrello. 'All you have to do is turn into a bird.'

'Ooooh, yes!' A nasty expression crossed Vyborn's face and Petrello wished he hadn't spoken.

Too late. Black feathers began to push through Vyborn's cheeks. His nose vanished and a yellow beak poked out from the centre of his face. Glossy wings lifted from his shoulders. Feathers pushed their way through his shirt and he gave a little jump.

Zeba hastily pulled her brother's chair away from the unfriendly-looking bird. It gave another jump, and then a muffled voice, somewhere behind its beak, said, 'Why can't I fly? I'm a bird. Why can't I fly?'

'Because you can't imagine what it's like,' said Guanhamara.

'I'm tired of hearing that.' The bird lunged at Guanhamara and pecked her arm.

'Ouch!' She leapt back, and then began to giggle.

The bird flapped its wings furiously. It squawked and screamed. Cafal ran from the room. His own beast-like form came to him unbidden, at night, when the last thing he wanted was to be a wild creature. He had never asked for the terrible peculiarity that he'd been given, and he couldn't bear to see his small brother choosing it, and turning into animals that pecked and scratched and gored and bit.

Seeing Cafal run like that, Petrello had a sudden thought. Rigg was a kind man, fierce but protective. He often took younger men under his wing, taught them how to ring the bells, to make their letters and to read names and signs.

Cafal was often seen with Rigg. Had Rigg, thoughtlessly, but out of friendship, told Cafal that he knew the secret of the Seeing Crystal?

Chapter Fifteen
Quelling the Storm

Rain fell in the night; heavy persistent rain. It continued well into the morning. The king could have stopped it, but he had much on his mind. He sat in the Solarium with Solomon on his shoulders, consulting the ancient serpent on a matter that he found too difficult to resolve: the behaviour of his children.

The rain dripped on to the blacksmith's furnaces and the charcoal became too wet to light. At midday the helmets that the king had commanded to be melted were still waiting in their damp sacks. Llyr did his best with gorse and broom and bones, but after a brief flickering the fires died again. The magic in Eri's fingers worked a little better, but eventually the fires fizzled out. He tried with a mixture of hellebore and bloodstone dust, but even this potent mixture couldn't keep the fires alight. It seemed as if the weather had been conjured by some malignant force in the misty, dripping forest.

The damp did nothing to help Friar Gereint's toothache. Too afraid to visit the wizards, the friar took to his bed and classes were cancelled again.

In the sheltered passage behind the furnaces, Petrello watched the wizards' efforts.

Llyr's fair hair, now dark with rain, hung in wet strands on the shoulders of his cloak. In vain he struggled to keep his hood from falling back. Eri had tied a moleskin shawl over his head, and sprinkled his cloak with the scales his dragon shed every summer. He looked an odd sight, but he was doing better than his grandson.

'Shall I tell the king?' Petrello asked tentatively. He didn't want the wizards to think he had no faith in their abilities.

'We've sent messengers twice,' snapped Eri.

'Oh.' Petrello stepped further back into the sheltered passage. The blacksmith's son, Rintail, joined him.

'Why don't they give up until the rain stops?' Petrello asked Rintail.

'King's orders. Got to melt the old helmets as soon as possible,' said Rintail. 'There might be spells in 'em.'

'Spells?' Petrello murmured thoughtfully. Now it all made sense.

'How's your other sister?' asked Rintail. 'Not the poisoner, I mean the one that made everything move. My poor dad's arm was awful bruised.'

'I think she's asleep,' said Petrello. 'The wizards gave her a potion.' He'd seen Llyr take a brown bottle along to Olga's bedchamber, and Guanhamara said she'd peeped in after Llyr had left, and Olga was lying very still.

'Hope the potion keeps her down,' Rintail muttered. 'Couldn't do with all that banging and bruising as well as the wet. I could do with some hot soup. How about you?'

'I don't think we'll get any yet,' said Petrello, stamping his feet. He discovered that he was standing in a puddle. The courtyard was awash with mud. The cooks couldn't cook. No one could work. The sun was shrouded in iron-dark clouds and the candles burned so unsteadily, they melted away almost as soon as they were lit.

Petrello decided to go and see his father. Perhaps he'd have better luck than the messengers. But first he went to his aunt's apartments, and there he found his mother and his aunt cutting and sewing, their heads bent close to their work. Zobayda's usually cheerful room was dismally dark. The toys on their shelves were mere shadows, and of the five candles in the stand behind the queen, only two remained, and they shed a fitful, glimmering light.

'Your brother's shirts,' said the queen as Petrello stepped closer. He could see now that his aunt was cutting narrow slits at the back of Tolly's shirts, while his mother sewed pieces of fabric at the top of each opening. 'To hide his wings,' she told Petrello, 'until they grow too big, of course.'

'But he has the cloak,' Petrello reminded her.

'He can't sleep in it,' said Zobayda. 'And if Vyborn knew about the wings, he would tell the entire court.' She paused in her work and added, 'Your father's in the Solarium.'

'Ask him to stop the rain, Petrello,' said his mother. 'We've had enough.' She put down her needle and rubbed her eyes. 'Tell him to give us some light.'

For the second time in his life Petrello walked down the dark passage and round the pillar into his father's Solarium.

The king was pacing his bright room, murmuring to the snake coiled about his shoulders. While everyone in his castle worked in sunless gloom, here it seemed that sunlight had been captured. The sky, seen through the circle in the roof, was as dark as night, yet here every colour was as bright as ever.

The king didn't smile when Petrello entered. He looked troubled, his thoughts far away.

'Mother sent me,' Petrello explained.

The king didn't answer, he continued to pace, while the snake whispered into his ear.

'It's so dark,' went on Petrello. 'And your sister can't see to do her needlework, and the wizards can't light the furnaces because it's so wet, so the helmets you ordered to be melted are still waiting, and . . . and we can't even have hot soup.'

The king stopped pacing. He lifted his head and suddenly began to laugh. 'Perhaps you should have mentioned the soup first,' he said. 'I'm sure it's more important to you than helmets or needlework.'

Petrello flushed. It was true. He felt cold and damp inside and out.

'It seems that I must go to work,' said his father. 'Come with me, Petrello.'

'Yes, Father.' Petrello had never watched his father work the weather. Not close up. Like everyone else he had seen a distant figure, high on the battlements of the Royal Tower; he'd seen a faraway glint that might have been a swirl of a gold-trimmed cloak, as his father swept it through the air. But he could only imagine what might be happening, up there on the tower, before the weather changed.

The king placed Solomon on his treasure chests. Bending over the snake, he gently stroked its silvery head and whispered something. Solomon closed a jet-black eye and curled himself into a rope-like coil.

'Come, Petrello!' The king led the way down the passage and through the door to the beginning of the long, spiralling stairway.

They were in the half-dark again, but as they climbed the steps, the king's cloak cast a soft glimmering light on the stone walls, and when Petrello looked closer he could make out the faint golden pattern of a spider's web embedded in the deep velvet of the red cloak.

They passed a door into the royal apartments, and then there were no more doors, but only an endless, twisting climb on knee-high steps with nothing to hold but the rough stone walls of the tallest tower in the castle.

The wind roared at the stone, and the rain thundered

and splashed as though it would beat the tower to the ground. Petrello couldn't hear his father's footsteps, or his own. He threw back his head and looked up. They were on the last spiral. The trapdoor at the top was rattling under the pounding of the rain.

The king reached up and flung open the door. As he climbed out on to the battlements, water sluiced down the steps and Petrello almost lost his balance.

'Take my hand, Petrello.' The king grasped his son's hand and pulled him up through the trapdoor. Petrello was met by such savage wind he almost toppled back again. But the king held him steady, while he closed the door with his foot.

Petrello made his way to the protecting wall. If it hadn't been as high as his shoulders, he imagined that he would have been blown away. His father came to stand beside him. Petrello had never seen him look so jubilant; his smile was broad and his teeth gleamed in his dark face; his eyes were wide and eager.

'Now!' The king took off his cloak and, holding it by its golden collar, high over his head, he let the wind billow into it, shaking and tossing the red velvet as though it would tear it from the king's grasp. And then the king began to call. Long, beautiful commanding sounds came from his mouth, like the words of a triumphant song. He began to stride across the roof, with the cloak whirling above him and the words rising through the storm, until all Petrello could hear was the song.

Looking through one of the openings in the wall, Petrello could see the grey land far below. Trees had fallen and the fields were strewn with leaves and branches. The forest stooped and twisted as though its trees were in agony. But as the king's song filled his ears, he saw a stillness creep over the forest. The rain stopped battering his shoulders and, gradually, the darkness rolled away and sunlight brought the land to life. It was green and bright again.

I will never be able to calm a storm like that, Petrello thought. *Why did my father bring me up here?* He looked at his hands and wondered about the boy called Tancred; a boy who was not yet alive.

'Come, Petrello!' The king was putting on his cloak. 'What did you think when you saw the weather change?'

'That it was something I will never be able to do,' said Petrello, flexing his fingers.

'Would you like to?'

'More than anything.'

'Then – maybe . . .' The king opened the trapdoor. 'Let's get to the bottom of this tower. We shall ride out very soon.'

'You and the Knight Protectors?' asked Petrello, as he skimmed down the steps ahead of his father.

'The Knight Protectors, yes. And in five years perhaps you will be one of them.'

Five years sounded a very long time. Petrello wanted to be a knight sooner than that.

Once on the ground, the king went to find his knights. Sunshine filled the courtyards and a castle in gloom came to life again. Fires burned brightly, and one by one the old helmets were melted down. The eagle helmet was the first, and Llyr watched closely as the metals spat and snarled on the blacksmith's furnace. A rivulet of glowing green stuff dripped from the grating to the bucket, and the blacksmith declared that he had never seen the like of it. 'Must be something awful wicked in that helmet,' he muttered gloomily.

The cooks got to work and soon there was hot soup and warm baked bread for everyone. But the knights' platters were filled with venison, and they were told to eat their fill. The king could wait no longer. They must find Rigg and the Seeing Crystal, even if it meant riding all the way to Castle Melyntha.

'And our friend Peredur,' Sir Edern reminded everyone, as he stuffed half a leg into his big mouth. 'He must be found.'

After the midday meal, the horses were brought out, and the children watched the squires help the knights into their chain-mail suits and padded tunics. And then the new helmets were brought from the armoury; each one was different, their gold and silver decorations copied from creatures of the air, the forest and the fields. Mabon the archer wore a helmet engraved with bears; Edern's was crowned with a silver falcon, though his shield was emblazoned with an eagle.

Borlath eyed his plain steel helmet with its band of iron. 'There was no need for a new one,' he grumbled. 'Lilith wouldn't have harmed us.'

'Then why did she try her tricks on Amadis?' asked Mabon.

Borlath turned away.

The twenty-one knights were armed and mounted when the king arrived on his camel. The queen walked at his side. She looked as if she were trying to hide a frown. Gabar's harness glowed with coloured ribbons and silver bells. A red and gold blanket covered his back, and his wooden saddle was hung with golden tassels and decorated with pearls. He looked very pleased and proud.

The king wore no helmet. He trusted in the luck the jinni had invested in his red cloak. The front of his tunic was embroidered with a deep red sun, and his round shield bore the same image. From a plain leather scabbard, his sword hilt could be seen, glinting with jewels.

Cafal had wheeled Gunfrid out to see the king and his knights depart, and the orphan gazed at the troop in astonished awe.

'How fine! How fine!' Gunfrid kept saying. 'I never seen nothing like it, never, never, never. The knights at Melyntha were nothing like this.'

On the other side of the courtyard the chancellor and his men watched the spectacle unsmiling. They would not be accompanying the king into the forest. As the chancellor pointed out, someone would have to defend the castle; a Vanishing would not be enough, if it came too late.

King Timoken gazed down at his queen. She lifted a

hand and clung to his, before he gently drew it away and put on his gauntlet.

'Let us depart!' The king's deep voice carried into the air, cheerful and determined.

A wave of cheering broke out. The great doors of the South Gate were opened and the king led his knights out of the castle.

Good luck, Father! Petrello said silently.

Beside him, Guanhamara eased her hand into his. He could feel her trembling.

'What is it?' he asked his sister.

'Trello,' she whispered. 'I think I have another power, and I don't like it.'

He looked into her anxious face. 'What kind of power?'

'I am seeing into the future, unless it is my imagination that is frightening me.'

'Our father can't be killed, remember,' said Petrello. 'The jinni saw to that. He is immortal.'

'Yes,' said Guanhamara, her voice very small. 'But we are not. And anyway, living forever doesn't mean that you'll have a happy life.'

Chapter Sixteen
Wizards' Smoke

Three days passed. Guanhamara wouldn't tell her brother what her dreams had shown her. She became quiet and pensive, spending most of her time with Elin. No word came from the forest. Perhaps this was a good sign. Two messengers had accompanied the king, and the queen had asked her husband to send news of their progress. She spent most of her days in the castle gardens, snipping at dead flower heads with her pearl-handled scissors, or tugging out the weeds. There were two gardeners to help her but she liked to be involved in the cutting and planting.

On the evening of the third day, Petrello and Tolly slipped out of the East Gate and joined their mother in the garden. She was picking herbs down by the yew trees, every now and then gazing out at the forest. She was pleased to see the boys and held out her arms, then clasped both of them close to her.

'I can feel your wings, Tolomeo,' she said. 'Let me see.'

He turned around and from his back two wings lifted above the glossy feathers of his cloak.

'How they've grown!' exclaimed the queen.

'And I can spread them, Mother. Look!' Tolly's black wings opened like wide feathered fans, the tip of each wing rising above his head.

'My dark angel,' sighed the queen. 'Have you tried to fly?'

Tolly frowned and looked at his feet. 'Not yet.'

Petrello knew that his brother was afraid to try. He thought he might come crashing to earth if he couldn't control his wings. After all, I'm not a bird, he told his brother.

'There's no news from Father, then?' said Petrello.

'No.' The queen stared over the gate at the forest that spread as far as the eye could see, its many shades of green becoming a soft blue in the distance. 'I wish the leopards had gone with him,' she said.

'Why didn't they?' asked Tolly.

'The king wanted them to stay here to protect us.

219

The Vanishing might not be as speedy as it should be, without the crystal's warning.'

They were about to turn away from the gate when a horse walked out of the forest. It began to trot, somewhat wearily, up to the South Gate. The rider was a knight, for they could see his mail suit shining in the evening light. His head was bowed and he slumped in the saddle, as though he barely had strength to hold the reins. Behind him, lying over the horse's back, was a body.

'Mercy!' cried the queen. 'Quickly, boys. We must find out who it is.'

They ran up the path, climbed the stone steps to the East Gate, and hurried into the courtyard. The doors of the South Gate had been opened to let in the knight and his weary horse.

'It's Sir Peredur!' called one of the guards.

'Peredur!' cried the queen, 'But how . . .?'

Hearing her voice, the knight looked up, raised a hand, and then the effort proving too much, fell forward on to his horse's neck, before sliding to the ground.

The queen knelt beside her friend. 'Peredur,' she said, taking his bare hand. 'What has happened to you?'

Peredur's eyelids fluttered and he groaned, 'They're dead.'

'Who?' The queen's fingers dug into Peredur's hand. 'Who is dead?'

Peredur's painful grin revealed his long, wolfish teeth. 'The abductors. But Rigg is still alive. Save him, Berenice.'

'Rigg?' She looked at the body on the horse. Two guards were already lifting it down.

'Careful,' said the queen. 'Take him to the sanatorium. Immediately.'

'Yes, Your Majesty,' replied the guards.

Petrello, standing beside the queen, suddenly became aware of the chancellor's men, pressing close behind him. A groom ran up and led the exhausted horse to the stable. And then the chancellor arrived. He stood opposite the queen, his legs apart, his thumbs in his belt, and his pale blue eyes were hard as stone.

'Stay with Mother,' Petrello whispered to his brother. 'I must fetch the wizards.'

Pushing through the group of grey men, Petrello ran towards the Eyrie. He didn't hear the stealthy run of the man behind him, and was about to leap on to the stairway, when someone stepped in front of him.

'Where are you going, Prince?' asked Chimery.

'To see the wizards,' Petrello replied.

'Why?' The man brought his lined, lean face close to Petrello's. 'Why, I say?'

'You are aware, sir, that two men are badly wounded. They need the wizards' help.'

Chimery's dark eyes narrowed. 'Perhaps . . .'

Petrello's fingers ached. 'Not perhaps. Definitely.' He dodged round Chimery, who, all at once, gave a small stagger.

Petrello leapt up the steps to the Eyrie. He paid no attention to the sudden breeze that appeared to knock Chimery off balance. In fact, he was barely aware of it. He reached the top of the stairway, banged twice on the door and, without waiting for an invitation, burst into the Eyrie.

'Shivering stars, young Petrello,' said Llyr, weighing chalk dust on his copper scales. 'What's the trouble?'

'Sir Peredur has returned,' gasped Petrello, bending to get his breath. 'He's badly wounded, and so is Rigg.'

'Rigg?' Eri got up from his couch so suddenly he trod on Enid's tail. A burst of hot steam issued from her snout, blowing the chalk dust into Llyr's face.

'Stop that!' cried Llyr, rubbing his eyes as he glared at the dragon.

'My fault! My fault!' mumbled Eri. 'Rigg, you say? Rigg has returned?'

'Rigg and Peredur,' said Petrello. 'But Rigg seems close to death. My mother commanded the guards to take him to the sanatorium. We must save him.'

'Of course we must!' Llyr began to pack his medicine box. 'Rigg knows it all: who let the strangers in and who abducted him.'

'He is a good man who deserves to live,' said Eri, slightly reprovingly. He fetched his staff and dusted it with his sleeve.

'Quickly! Quickly!' cried Petrello. 'I think the chancellor isn't happy with Sir Peredur's arrival. He looks as though he wishes him dead.'

'The devil he does.' Llyr pushed a phial of orange liquid into his leather box and hurried after Petrello, who was already leaping down the steps.

It was left to Eri to collect the bowls, the heather, the bones and the fungus. Ready at last, the wizard descended, with Enid lolloping behind him.

While Llyr turned the corner into the sanatorium,

Petrello waited for Eri, afraid that the old man might fall.

'Go on, go on, boy,' Eri ordered as he reached the bottom step. 'Enid and I will get there in due course.'

There was quite a crowd in the sanatorium. Rigg had been laid on the nearest bed inside the door, with Peredur on the bed next to him. On the other side of the doorway the chancellor sat on a low stool, his eyes darting from Rigg to Peredur and then to the queen. A square and sturdy guard paced the aisle between the rows, and Gunfrid and Zeba had retreated to the end of the room, with Cafal still holding the back of the wheeled chair.

The queen stood beside Peredur, occasionally feeling his forehead.

Llyr was already laying out his potions on the small table between the patients. The wizard kept clicking his tongue, feeling Rigg's head, sniffing his skin and lifting the poor man's bruised and broken fingers.

'Even his feet have been crushed,' muttered Llyr, glancing at Rigg's bloodstained bare toes.

When Eri and his dragon arrived, Enid, caught up in the mood of restless excitement, began to snort dangerously long flames.

'Get that creature out of here!' the chancellor demanded.

'Enid's with me,' Eri retorted. He pulled four bowls out of his bag and handed them to Petrello. 'You know what to do,' he said. 'The door, the sill and the beds.'

'Yes, Eri.' Petrello ran to place the bowls where he knew they should go.

'We've had enough of that rubbish,' the chancellor exclaimed. 'Old spells, they do more harm than good.'

'Thorkil!' the queen said sharply. 'Don't speak to the wizards like that.'

Ignoring the chancellor, Eri proceeded to fill the bowls. When all four had their full quota of fungus, bones and heather, he set them alight with a quick touch of his thumb.

The scent of burnt bones, scorched heather and dragon breath drifted round the beds, and the room filled with soft blue smoke.

Petrello's eyes began to water. He looked up at the low rafters. They seemed to sway and dip towards him. He felt so dizzy he had to cling to a bed rail, rocking on his feet. His fingers ached.

'For pity's sake, put out those fires!' the chancellor shouted through a fit of coughing.

'Better leave the room, chancellor,' Eri advised.

But nothing would dislodge the chancellor. He sat there, watching the injured men like a hawk watching his prey.

He needs to know what Rigg will say, thought Petrello, flexing his fingers. *And he's afraid.*

A draught swept across the floor, and one of Llyr's phials rolled off the table. Luckily, it was corked.

'Close that door!' shouted Llyr.

It was already closed. Petrello and the chancellor looked at the closed door, and then each other. Through a cloud of smoke Petrello could see the chancellor's eyes fixed on him. It was a heartless gaze, full of suspicion.

And then the door opened and Tolly came in with the investigator. In their identical cloaks they looked like a bird and its child.

'I thought Wyngate should be here,' Tolly whispered to his brother. 'Because of the investigation.'

'Good thinking,' said Petrello, looking at the chancellor.

Wyngate bent over Rigg, oblivious to the smoke wafting round the bed.

'How is he?' the investigator asked Llyr.

'Unconscious,' said Llyr. 'His heart beats, but very slowly.'

226

'He looks cold,' Wyngate remarked.

'Very cold,' Llyr agreed. He uncorked a phial, handed it to the investigator then, lifting Rigg's head, he gently opened the bellman's mouth. 'Two drops on his tongue,' he told Wyngate. 'No more, no less.'

Wyngate held the phial steady and, with remarkable accuracy, allowed two drops of the orange liquid to fall on to Rigg's tongue. The bellman's eyelids flickered, his mouth remained open, but he gave no sign that he had swallowed the wizard's potion.

Llyr laid the man's head back on the pillow and closed his mouth. 'All we can do now is wait,' said the wizard.

'A pity the king's cloak is not here,' said Eri. He had pulled a strip of silvery grey stuff from his bag and began to apply it to Peredur's forehead. Petrello knew it was a spider's web.

'Mmm,' Peredur murmured. 'That's better. I'll be back on my horse in no time.'

'I doubt that,' said Eri. 'But perhaps you'll be able to talk in a while, and tell us how you came by your wounds.'

'Devils!' muttered Peredur. 'Took me by surprise. I'd been tracking them for miles. We must have been very near the gates of Melyntha. But I got them in the end.

And then I found poor Rigg. They'd tied him to a tree, maybe thought he was dead.'

Peredur fell back on his pillow, breathing heavily.

'No more talk for now.' Eri applied another web to the knight's hand.

The queen looked back at Cafal and the two orphans. 'Children, we must leave the wizards to do their work,' she said. 'Gunfrid can sleep in the boys' chamber tonight.'

'I will c-carry him there,' Cafal mumbled. He began to wheel Gunfrid towards the door. When he passed Rigg's bed, Petrello noticed that Cafal glanced quickly at the bellman and grimaced, as though he were in pain.

'Petrello and Tolomeo, you too,' said the queen.

The sun had gone down and the evening air was chilly. The wheels on Gunfrid's chair bumped and clattered over the cobblestones. Cafal kept hunching his shoulders. He turned his head left, then right, his expression troubled. He had something on his mind and needed to share the burden.

Petrello touched his brother's arm. 'Cafal, did Rigg tell you about the solution? The spell for the Seeing Crystal?'

Cafal nodded dumbly.

'Did you tell anyone that Rigg knew the secret?'

Cafal nodded again. 'Rigg didn't tell me the spell. He saw it written in Eri's book, but he never, never would tell anyone what it was.'

'But someone else knows that Rigg saw the list of ingredients,' said Petrello.

'Ingredients?' said Gunfrid.

'What are those?' asked Zeba.

'Herbs and things that go into a spell,' Tolly told her.

Petrello explained the importance of the Seeing Crystal, and the solution that made it function so effectively.

The orphans listened, their eyes wide, and Zeba emitted a quiet, 'Oooo!'

No one said a word after that. The wheels rattled over the bumpy ground, and then the children reached the steps to the bedchambers.

'I'll carry you now.' Cafal went round to lift Gunfrid out of his chair.

Petrello suddenly said, 'Who did you tell, Cafal? Who did you tell about Rigg and the spell?'

Cafal violently shook his head. 'No one!' He quickly lifted Gunfrid and began to run up the steps.

'You scared him, Petrello,' Zeba said accusingly. 'Why did you do that?'

'Didn't mean to. I just wanted to know.' Petrello followed Zeba, already climbing the steps behind Cafal.

From behind Petrello, Tolly whispered, 'If Rigg wakes up, he'll tell us.'

Cafal laid Gunfrid on Tolly's bed, then fled without another word.

Before going to her bedchamber Zeba bid the boys goodnight, telling them to look after her brother. She gave Petrello a severe look before she went.

Gunfrid asked Tolly if he slept in his cloak. He worried that the feathers might tickle. Tolly grinned and removed his cloak, laying it carefully at the foot of his bed. Vyborn's head appeared above his covers. He looked suspiciously at Tolly's back, and Petrello was glad to see that the queen's clever sewing had made it impossible to make out the shape of folded wings beneath Tolly's shirt.

The howling came later that night. It was not a wolf, not a fox, not any kind of natural creature. Petrello knew the mournful sounds came from his brother, Cafal.

Once, Petrello would have buried his head under his pillow; he hated those howls; he hated knowing that they came from his own brother.

Tonight Petrello was drawn to the window overlooking

the garden. He knew that Cafal liked to wander there, between the flowerbeds. Perhaps the scent of roses helped to calm him.

Petrello looked down into the moonlit garden. A misshapen four-legged creature ran along the path, its large, dog-like head lowered between its bony shoulders. Now and again it would stop and sniff the plants beside it, and then it would raise its head and howl at the stars.

Poor Cafal, thought Petrello.

A distant movement caught his eye. Something appeared at the edge of the forest: a black horse with a white star on its forehead. Petrello would have known that riderless horse anywhere. It belonged to Amadis.

Chapter Seventeen
The Royal Tower

A shout rang out. The Watch had seen the horse.

Petrello turned from the window. He hesitated. Should he go down to the courtyard? Yes, he must. Without waking the other boys, he tiptoed from the room and crept down the steps into the courtyard. The doors of the South Gate had been opened and the sharp cry of a horse in distress could be heard from outside. And then Isgofan galloped into the castle.

A guard ran to catch the horse's bridle. Isgofan's eyes rolled. He reared and snorted. He seemed unhurt, but terrified.

Petrello kept in the shadows, close to the wall. He saw two grey men run from the West Tower, on the other side of the gate. One was Chimery. They spoke to the guard in low voices. The guard handed Isgofan's reins to Chimery, and then went back to the Watch Tower.

A stable boy appeared, rubbing his eyes. The grey men spoke to him, and the boy led Isgofan into the stables.

The chancellor's men remained in the courtyard for a moment, talking together in low voices. All at once Chimery laughed a deep, sneering chuckle. Petrello felt his blood turn cold. How could Chimery laugh while Amadis was either badly hurt or dead? And who would search for him, now that all the knights were with the king?

Mother should know. Petrello ran. Passing the door to the sanatorium, he heard a low growl. He stopped dead in his tracks, his heart thumping. Three pairs of glowing golden eyes approached him. The leopards were on guard. Whoever wished Rigg and Peredur harm would never get past Sun Cat, Flame Chin and Star.

The leopards sniffed Petrello's arms, his hands, his loose shirt. A continuous deep rumble came from their throats and Petrello worried that the grey men would hear and look in his direction. But if they heard the leopards, they chose to ignore them. Perhaps they had already tried to pass them, and given up.

As Petrello stood rigid in the shadows, he began to realise that the leopards' attention was a show of friendship and protection and their low growls were purrs of affection.

'I must go to the queen,' he whispered.

The leopards' gleaming eyes fixed on his face for a moment, and then they let him pass.

He ran on, through the deserted second courtyard and on into Zobayda's garden. A guard sat in the deep recess before the door to the Royal Tower, a lantern flickering beside him. When he saw the boy in his white nightshirt he gave a cry and stood up, his pike at the ready.

'It's me, the king's son,' said Petrello. 'I must see the queen.'

'What's the world coming to?' said the guard. 'It's the middle of the night. Go to the nurse if you're in pain.'

'I'm not,' said Petrello. 'I have grave news for my mother. The horse Isgofan has come back from the forest without his rider, Amadis.'

'Amadis?' exclaimed the guard. 'He has been hurt then, and fallen, or –'

'Someone should go and search,' Petrello said breathlessly. 'There is a moon, and perhaps Amadis isn't far away. The chancellor's men have seen the horse, but they're doing nothing.'

The man looked concerned. All the guards liked Amadis, they admired him for his courage, his honesty and his affinity with animals. 'Better tell the queen, young man.'

The guard opened the heavy door and let Petrello through.

Petrello leapt up the steps, his bare feet making hardly a sound on the cold stone. The loud squeak of the door into the royal apartments made him wince. Once inside, he could hear the queen moving about in her bedchamber. Petrello knocked on her door.

'Who is it?' called the queen.

'Petrello. I must speak with you, Mother. Amadis . . . Amadis . . .'

The door was opened abruptly. 'What has happened to Amadis?' The queen wore a blue cloak over her white gown, and her corn-gold hair hung in a long plait over one shoulder. She drew Petrello into the room. Again she asked, 'What's happened, Trello?'

Petrello was frightened by the look of alarm in his mother's eyes. A single candle burned on a chest by the door, its soft light illuminating the gold on the canopy above the bed, and casting long shadows on the queen's pale face.

'Isgofan has come back.' Petrello was now afraid of worrying his mother even further, but he had to tell her the truth. 'Amadis is not with him. The chancellor's men know, but they are doing nothing.'

The queen gave a sharp intake of breath. For a moment her hand covered her mouth, and then she said, 'Someone must go and search for him.'

'But it will have to be a knight, a swordsman, and if the chancellor's men won't go, there is only Peredur, and he is too ill.'

'There is Running Hare,' said the queen. 'Petrello, wait outside.'

Mystified, Petrello stepped out of the room. He didn't close the door, however, and could hear the lid of a chest being opened, and then a rustling and a swishing. Another chest was opened with a bang, and then it was quiet in the room, except for a light metallic jangle, like the sound of a buckle on a belt.

'How do I look?'

Petrello gasped. A figure had appeared at the door of the bedchamber, not the queen; this was a young man in a fur cap, his rough shirt pushed into brown breeches. He wore the queen's blue cloak, and a sword in a jewelled scabbard hung from his bronze-studded belt.

'Mother?' Petrello gulped.

The queen smiled. 'I can still use a sword, as you have seen, Petrello. When I have gone I want you to bring your brothers and sisters to this tower. You should all be together. The guard, Egbert, is loyal. He will protect you.'

'Protect us?' Petrello's head was whirling. 'Why? Who from?'

'Events have moved faster than I expected,' said the queen. 'I was afraid this would happen. The chancellor's men are no longer our friends.'

'I guessed,' said Petrello. 'But I didn't think they would harm us.' He found that he was shivering.

'Come with me. Egbert will accompany us.' The queen propelled her son to the stairway. She ran down while he followed, still shivering; shocked by the sudden turn of events.

The guard, taken aback by the queen's unusual appearance, opened his mouth like a fish, and let it hang there. But he seemed to know who she was.

'Egbert, I'm going to the stables,' said the queen. 'Come with me, and then return here and guard my children.'

'Your Majesty.' The guard bowed his head and picked up the lantern.

They walked through the empty courtyards to the stables, and while Egbert led the queen inside, Petrello waited at the entrance. The queen eventually emerged on her favourite horse, a white mare called Elizen.

'Remember your brothers and sisters,' said the queen.

'Even Olga?' asked Petrello.

His mother frowned. 'Perhaps not Olga,' she said. 'She can look after herself.'

Egbert put down his lantern, ran ahead of the horse and drew back the heavy bolts of the great doors. It often took two men to do this, but Egbert was a strong man.

Petrello watched his mother ride up to the gate, and then, all at once, a man leapt out of the shadows and grabbed Elizen's bridle.

'Thorkil, let me pass!' shouted the queen.

'I will not,' said Thorkil, his voice cold and hard.

There was a sudden moonlit flash. Petrello could hardly believe what he was seeing. His mother drew her sword so fast Thorkil had no time to reach his own. There was a roar of pain as the chancellor let go of the bridle, and the queen galloped out into the night.

It was a moment so brief it was almost as if it hadn't happened. But it had. Something broke when the queen used her sword: a link between Thorkil and the king that had become as fragile as an eggshell. And for the king's children, the castle was now a dangerous place.

Petrello didn't wait to see what happened to Egbert. He ran. First to the girls' bedchamber.

A candle burned low in a lantern hanging by the door. On Guanhamara's pillow he could see Zeba's wild hair beside his sister's sleek brown head.

'Guan, wake up!' He shook his sister's shoulder.

Guanhamara raised her head and yawned. She looked up at her brother and passed a hand over her face. 'What is it?'

'We must go to the Royal Tower.' He quickly told her everything that had happened, while she slowly sat up, swung her legs over the side of the bed and stared, unbelieving, at her brother's face.

By now, Elin and Zeba were awake. Alarmed by the desperate urgency in Petrello's voice, they too were yawning and climbing out of bed.

'You should have seen our mother, Guan,' said Petrello. 'Her sword-hand moved so fast I couldn't see it, and Lord

Thorkil was so unprepared, I think she might have sliced his finger off.'

'Good,' Guanhamara said sleepily. 'If we're going to the Royal Tower, then Elin and Zeba must come too.'

'Take the clothes you need,' Petrello advised as he left the room, 'and go quickly.'

He hurried on to his own bedchamber, and there he found the boys already awake.

'Trello, what's happened?' Tolly rolled off his bed and landed on his bottom.

'We have to go to the Royal Tower,' Petrello told him. 'The queen has commanded us.'

Gunfrid, unable to move his legs, looked at Petrello in alarm. 'Must I stay here, alone?'

'No, no, Gunfrid. I'll carry you!' Petrello pulled on his breeches, his boots and his jerkin.

'Are you strong enough?' Tolly eased himself into his feathered cloak.

'Of course,' Petrello replied, uncertain now, whether he could carry Gunfrid all the way to the Royal Tower. And then he remembered Cafal. He would carry Gunfrid.

Vyborn hadn't moved. He sat glaring at his brothers, his cheek propped on his hand.

'Hurry, Vyborn!' Petrello raised his voice. 'Don't just sit there.' Seeing his words had no effect, he strode over to his brother's bed and pulled off the covers.

'Why must we go to the Royal Tower?' asked Vyborn. 'I'm too tired.'

'Because our mother said so, because Amadis has fallen off his horse and is maybe dead or wounded, and our mother has gone to find him, and she has no faith in the chancellor's men.'

'Why?' asked Vyborn sulkily.

'I can't explain,' said Petrello, exasperated by his pig-headed brother. 'Move, Vyborn. For your own sake.'

'No!'

Petrello guessed what would happen, even as he began to pull Vyborn's legs off the bed. He wasn't surprised when the soft feet turned hard, and coarse black hair began to dapple Vyborn's olive skin, but he'd forgotten the other boarish features, and gave a yell of pain when Vyborn dug a fast-forming tusk into his shoulder.

The boar sprang off the bed, knocking Petrello

sideways. It charged past Tolly and went squealing out of the door, along the passage and down the stairway.

'Why is he always a boar?' said Petrello, clutching his shoulder.

'No imagination,' said Tolly.

They grinned at each other, but couldn't quite laugh.

Petrello ran to the bedchamber Cafal shared with his older brothers. Cafal was already dressed. He looked warily at Petrello and muttered, 'What's going on?'

'Mother wants us to go to the Royal Tower,' said Petrello. He tried to sound calm, for he could see that Cafal was in quite a state. He had only just returned from howling at the stars.

'Go away,' said Cafal.

'It'd be better if the family were together, all in one place. Safer.'

'Safe from what?'

'From the chancellor's men.' Petrello knew this wasn't enough to get his brother moving. He had no option but to tell him everything.

Cafal watched his brother's mouth. His frown grew deeper and his long face took on a beast-like aspect. Petrello felt uncomfortable in his presence. The thing that Cafal could become was much more of a threat than the boars and goats that Vyborn opted for.

'Mother gone?' Cafal screwed up his broad nose and began to breathe heavily.

Petrello took a step back. 'She wants us to stay together.'

'No.' Cafal shook his head. 'I'll wait for Borlath.'

Petrello had noticed how his brother liked to look after the orphans. He decided to appeal to his better nature. 'I can't carry Gunfrid all that way. No one else can. And his chair will make too much noise.'

Cafal scratched his head. 'I'll do that. I'll carry the orphan, but I'm not going to stay with you.' He darted Petrello a meaningful look, from under his heavy brows. 'Something might happen to me.'

Petrello suddenly understood. His brother couldn't bear the thought of being seen in his beast-like form. 'If you could just carry him then, Cafal?'

Cafal nodded.

The girls and Tolly had already gone when Cafal carried Gunfrid down the echoing steps. Petrello led the way to the second courtyard, but before they reached the arch, Zeba peered round the wall and whispered, 'I wanted to be sure Gunfrid was safe.'

243

'I'm safe,' said Gunfrid in a hushed voice. He patted Cafal's head and Cafal gave an amiable grunt.

The castle was eerily quiet. Petrello sensed that they were being watched, and yet no one came to stop them. Looking over his shoulder, he saw why.

Two glowing forms were following them. Sun Cat and Star had left Flame Chin to guard the sanatorium while they protected the king's children.

The leopards increased their pace. Now they walked either side of the small group. When the Royal Tower was reached they stayed at the door, while Cafal carried Gunfrid up to the royal apartments. Petrello followed them. Walking into the queen's bedchamber, he found Elin and his sister sitting on the wide bed. Elin looked as if she had been crying.

Cafal laid Gunfrid beside the girls and strode back to the door.

'Stay with us, Cafal,' said Zeba. 'We'll feel safer with you.'

'You must. Our mother said so,' Guanhamara insisted.

'Let him go, Guan,' Petrello said quietly.

Cafal turned his head and gave Petrello a grateful smile. And then he was gone. Petrello ran down the steps after him. Before bolting the heavy door, he looked outside. Zobayda's garden was bathed in a soft golden light, its source the pale-haired leopard that moved silently about the flower-filled courtyard.

High in Zobayda's tower a candle still burned. Looking up, Petrello saw his aunt framed in the window. She raised a hand to him, and he waved back.

We're safe tonight, Petrello thought as he hurried up to the royal apartments. *And maybe tomorrow. But what will happen after that?* At the back of his mind lay a question he could hardly bear to consider. *Will Mother and Father ever return?*

Chapter Eighteen
Zobayda's Ring

The six children slept together on the wide royal bed, limbs tangled, toes touching chins. A mattress of soft foamy feathers cradled their bodies, and a thick woollen quilt kept them cosy.

This must be how a bird feels, when it is newly hatched, thought Petrello. He didn't want to wake up, he was so warm, so very comfortable. He felt he could have stayed buried in those soft embracing feathers forever.

Outside a bird began to sing. A soft grey light crept across the painted walls, but it was hardly dawn. Why had he woken up? Ah, there it was. One of the girls was crying. It was only a small mouse-like sniffle, but Petrello couldn't get back to sleep.

He pulled himself out of his downy cocoon and sat up. The three girls lay at the other end of the bed. Zeba and

246

his sister still had their eyes closed. They appeared to be fast asleep. But Elin had a hand over her eyes, and her shoulders were shaking.

'Elin!' Petrello whispered. 'Elin, what's wrong?'

He realised what a foolish thing it was to say, because so many things were wrong.

Without replying to Petrello, Elin rolled out of bed and ran to the window. She stood there, staring out at the forest, her tears falling freely, her clasped hands twisting and turning.

Petrello reluctantly left the bed and went to Elin's side. 'I know they say your father is always eager for a fight,' he said, putting a tentative arm around the girl's shoulder, 'but I'm sure he's safe with the king. He'll come back.'

Elin nodded. But she still wept.

'Our brave Knight Protectors will return and give the chancellor's men such a beating, they'll leave the castle and we'll all be safe again.' Petrello even managed to convince himself. He felt so much better now.

But Elin wasn't comforted. Her tears fell faster, and she took loud gasping gulps of air, her shoulders rising and falling with each gasp. She suddenly turned her tear-stained face to him and sobbed, 'But what about Amadis?

He went alone, and Isgofan came back without him. Where were the wolves when he fell, Petrello? Where were the eagles and owls, the deer, the wildcats and the serpents that live in the trees? Where were they all? They should have been protecting him.'

Elin's sudden confession came as such a surprise, for a moment Petrello couldn't reply. He should have guessed that she loved Amadis. He just hadn't noticed. And then the answer came to him, and as he spoke he knew it must be true. 'They were there, Elin; all the creatures of the air and the forest. And they're taking care of Amadis right now.'

'Do you really think so?' Elin squeezed out one more tear and smiled.

'I'm sure of it.'

They were about to creep back and get some more sleep when the door opened and a head of tousled brown hair appeared. It screamed.

All the children woke up. Yawning, groaning, grumbling and mumbling, they lifted their heads and stared at the stranger standing in the doorway. And then they realised that she wasn't a stranger at all.

They had just forgotten that Mair, their mother's attendant, slept in the royal apartments.

'Heaven preserve us!' Mair walked into the room, shaking her head at the children peeping out from the royal quilt. 'Where's the queen?'

Petrello hastily explained that Amadis was missing and the queen had gone to find him.

'She's a bold one, your mother,' said Mair. 'What possessed her?'

'The chancellor's men wouldn't go,' said Guanhamara. 'And Mother said we were to stay here together, because . . .' She looked at Petrello.

'She doesn't think we are safe,' finished Petrello.

'Mercy!' Mair sank on to a padded stool. 'It's like Melyntha all over again.'

Petrello knew that Mair had run away from Castle Melyntha, after the queen escaped. She had followed his mother through the forest for many days before she eventually found her, and vowed never to leave her side again. He pointed out that they didn't have to escape from their own castle.

Mair looked at him and rolled her eyes. 'We'll see.'

Her lips formed a tight little line. 'If the chancellor takes over, he won't want a batch of royal children hanging about, will he?'

Guanhamara, wide awake now, leapt off the bed. 'Don't be silly,' she cried. 'You're such a pessimist, Mair. The king will return very soon with the crystal, and everything will be all right again.'

The desperation in his sister's voice made Petrello think she didn't believe her own words. What had her dream shown her?

'The king might be too late,' Mair said darkly. And she left a room of silent, anxious children.

'That woman finds optimism impossible,' Guanhamara said at last. 'We are safe here.' She smiled round at everyone. 'Don't forget the leopards.'

After another bleak silence, Gunfrid said hopefully, 'We are not royal children.'

'They are our friends,' said Zeba, giving her brother a severe look. 'Where would we be without them? You can't even walk.'

Gunfrid pouted and rubbed his legs.

A few moments later Mair returned with a jug of water, one cup and a plate of small honey cakes. She seemed a little more cheerful. 'Share nicely,' she said. 'Later I'll go to the kitchens and see what I can get for you.'

They thanked her and Guanhamara shared out the honey cakes, taking a handful to Gunfrid.

If only someone could tell them what was going on. Petrello went to the window. He could see Zobayda in the tower opposite, and decided to go and see her. Guanhamara joined him at the window and waved at her aunt.

'I'll go and see her,' said Petrello.

Guanhamara clutched his arm. 'Suppose they catch you?'

'They won't. Star will protect me.'

'No,' said his sister. 'Look!'

Petrello looked down into Zobayda's garden. He was just in time to see Star leaving through the arch. His brothers must have called him, or he would never have left his post.

'I'm going anyway,' said Petrello. 'I want to see our aunt.'

Guanhamara shook her head. 'Trello, no, no, no!'

'Is it because of what you saw – in your dreams?' Petrello searched his sister's face.

'I can't make sense of it, but I think our father's

trapped somewhere.' She frowned and, looking over her shoulder, whispered, 'And so are the knights.'

The other children were busy with the honey cakes, breaking the last ones into two and three. Petrello leaned close to his sister and asked softly, 'What did you see?'

'I saw a lake as smooth as glass, and in the centre a white cloud hanging there, hiding everything beneath it and . . . and . . .' she continued in a whisper, 'I think our father was beneath it, no, not think, I'm sure. In fact, I know that the king and his knights are trapped under that cloud. Don't ask me how I know. It was more than a dream, Trello. It was knowledge – given to me.'

'I see.' Petrello paused, uncertain whether to ask his next question. 'And did you know that your best friend loves Amadis?'

Guanhamara grinned and gave him a funny sideways look. 'Of course I know, and so does he.'

'Oh.' Foolish *Petrello, you know so little*, he told himself.

The other children had noticed the two whispering by the window. Elin and Tolly came over to them.

'Why are you whispering?' said Tolly.

'We're wondering what to do next,' said Guanhamara.

'Look!' cried Tolly. 'Our aunt has visitors.'

Looking down Petrello saw two grey men at Aunt Zobayda's door. Where were the guards? he wondered. There was a brass knocker on the door, in the shape of a camel. One of the men lifted the camel and rapped loudly.

Don't open the door! Petrello silently warned his aunt.

Tolly banged on the window. 'Aunt, don't open the door!' he shouted.

But Zobayda couldn't hear. Perhaps she thought her nephews wanted her. A moment later she had pulled back the bolts and opened the door. The children watched in horror as one of the men grabbed Zobayda's right hand and dragged her out.

'What can we do? What can we do?' wailed Tolly.

Petrello was about to run and help his aunt, when his sister gripped his arm and said, 'No, Trello. They'll catch you too. Something's happening.'

Before the second man could catch Zobayda's left hand, she had lifted it up and brought it down on the first man's fingers. There was a bright flash, a scream of pain and the man fell to the ground.

'The ring,' breathed Petrello.

The man still standing was too shocked to move, but then he seemed to recover and tried to snatch Zobayda's arm. She whirled in a circle, too fast for him to catch her, and before he could step back she had touched him with her ring. He yelled in agony and staggered out of the garden, clutching his chest.

Zobayda looked up at the watching children and smiled.

The children cheered wildly. Petrello unlatched the window and flung it open, calling, 'Brave Aunt Zobayda, come and see us!'

'I was just about to,' Zobayda called back, 'when I was so rudely interrupted.'

Petrello ran down to draw back the bolts. When he opened the door his aunt walked in looking as cheerful and unruffled as if nothing in the least unusual had happened.

'It was the jinni's ring, wasn't it?' said Petrello, peering round her at the man on the ground.

'Of course.' His aunt lifted her left hand and turned it this way and that. 'Look at him sparkling. He's always like that when he's had a fight.' She looked over her shoulder. 'Don't worry about the Grey Man. He's not dead. But he'll be harmless for a while.'

Petrello peered at the jinni's tiny face. 'I'm glad you

had him with you, Aunt. The leopard has gone. I don't know why.'

'He must have had a very good reason.' Aunt Zobayda began to climb the steps. 'And your guard is missing. I fear for him.'

'Me too.' Petrello bolted the door and followed his aunt. 'Our mother has gone to look for Amadis. His horse came back alone, and the chancellor's men won't go and find him. Mother said we must all stay together, for the chancellor isn't our friend.'

'I know. I know.'

'How do you know, Aunt?'

'I have windows, I have eyes and ears, and I have a jinni's intuition.'

'Oh.' Petrello was a little mystified, but much impressed.

When Zobayda entered the royal bedchamber she was immediately surrounded by chattering children, all asking questions at once.

'Yes, yes. It was my ring,' she answered, sinking on to the bed. 'When the king and I were young, it saved us many a time.'

They settled beside her on the big bed, and Guanhamara flung her arms around her aunt, begging her to stay with them.

'Of course I'll stay, but not in this room,' said Zobayda. 'It seems you have all made yourselves very much at home here. I'll go and find Mair.'

They followed the king's sister out of the bedchamber and down a passage with several doors opening off it. First Zobayda looked into Mair's tiny room. The queen's attendant had fallen asleep again on her narrow wooden bed.

'We won't wake her,' Zobayda whispered.

There were three more rooms. One for the queen's clothes, her shoes and her jewels, another for the king's robes and a third with long windows on both sides. Here the king liked to read at night. There were shelves of precious books, chests and boxes, a table covered in maps and papers, several tall candelabra, two high stools and a long velvet-covered couch.

'This is where I shall sleep,' Zobayda declared, settling herself among the cushions on the couch.

'Are we prisoners?' Tolly asked.

'You could say that,' his aunt replied. 'But not for long, I'm sure.'

A sudden loud banging on the door sent Petrello

leaping down the steps again. 'Who is it?' he called.

'Don't keep me waiting, boy. Open up.'

It was Llyr's voice, Petrello was sure of it, and yet he hesitated.

Behind him, Tolly said, 'I'm here, Trello! And I have my sword.'

Petrello turned to see his brother descending the stairway, his sword at the ready.

'I remembered that Mother had left it here,' said Tolly, running down to stand beside his brother.

There was another loud bang, and the same voice asked, 'Do I have to use a spell to break down this door?'

Petrello drew back the bolts, but before he could open the door a man burst through it.

'Merciful moons, Tolomeo!' gasped Llyr. 'Sheath your sword before you do some mischief. I'm your friend.'

A friend he might have been, but he didn't look like the wizard they knew. A steel helmet covered his fine fair hair, and at least twenty sharp knives hung from his belt. He was carrying two large leather bags.

'Venison pies!' Llyr announced, waving one of the bags. 'Are you all here?'

'Vyborn wouldn't come, nor would Cafal,' said Petrello.

Llyr nodded. 'And Olga is in my care. What about your aunt?'

'She's here,' said Petrello.

'Take me to her.'

They led Llyr up to the king's reading room. When he appeared at the door, the other children backed to the window, their eyes on the gleaming knives at his waist. But Zobayda greeted the wizard with a wide smile and a cry of welcome.

'Provisions,' said Llyr, putting the bags on the floor.

'What news do you have?' Zobayda begged. 'We have learned not to trust the chancellor's men,' she glanced at her ring, 'but how can we continue like this; virtual prisoners in our own home?'

Llyr sat beside her and removed his helmet. He noticed the children staring at his knives and grinned. 'Yes, I can turn bones into steel,' he said. 'As for news . . .' His cheerful expression fell away, as though it had been a mask. 'It is grave, the news, and I wish I didn't have to give it to you.'

'What? What?' Guanhamara came closer to the wizard. 'Tell us!'

Llyr looked at Zobayda and then at the king's children,

his eyes resting on each face for several moments.

'To begin . . .' He ran a hand through his damp yellow hair. 'Last night Wyngate lay beside Rigg. He lay on the cold stone floor and would not move all night, for he said the bellman might dream, and he might talk in his sleep. He might murmur a word or two that could tell us who opened that window and let two strangers in.'

'And did he?' asked Guanhamara. 'Did Rigg talk?'

'Not in his sleep,' said Llyr. 'He recovered a little, woke up and cried for water. And Wyngate was there with the water almost at once. Poor Rigg was so pleased to see a friendly face he broke down in tears, and that's when Wyngate asked him, "Who let this happen to you, Rigg? Who do we have to fear?"'

There was a tense silence in the room. They waited, almost afraid to know Rigg's answer. Elin and Zeba crept closer, their bare feet making no sound at all on the king's thick carpet.

At last Zobayda asked, 'And did Rigg answer? Did he see the man who let two strangers into our castle?'

'He did.' Llyr buried his face in his hands, shook his head and stared at the sky turning bright in the window.

In a hushed voice, Guanhamara asked, 'Who?'

Llyr took a deep breath and said, 'It was your brother, Borlath.'

Zeba gasped, but no one else said a word. Had they guessed? Had they known all along?

Zobayda said, 'But why? What reason could he have for throwing away our chances; of weakening the strength of our marvellous spell-wall?'

'He told me once,' said Llyr, 'that he had no time for spells and wizards. "We should be able to defend ourselves," he said, "without resorting to magic. Where's the pride in that?" And then he put his face very close to mine and almost whispered, "Imagine what it's like, wizard, to know that you will die before your father? That you will never inherit his castle, his treasures, all this?" And he waved a hand at the courtiers in their bright clothes, the horses, the guards, the dogs and geese and children.'

Zobayda sighed. 'I think I knew but couldn't bear to accept it. Envy is a dreadful thing. Resentment even worse. They warp you. And now he's in the forest with the king.'

Llyr lifted his head and stared at the painted ceiling. 'He's here.'

'What?' Zobayda exclaimed. 'Borlath, here?'

'He rode in a short time ago, alone. The leopards behaved very strangely. They prowled about him, growling. He kept an eye on them and wouldn't dismount until two of the chancellor's men came to help him. And then he told us that all the knights were dead.' There was a cry from Elin, but Llyr pressed on, 'They were set upon by bandits in the middle of the night. The king was captured and badly wounded. Borlath was the only man to escape.'

'Lies! All lies!' cried Guanhamara.

'The king can't die,' Zobayda said quietly.

'It's not that,' said her niece. 'I know the knights aren't dead, and I know the king can be rescued.'

'How do you know all this?' asked Llyr.

Guanhamara twisted her hands together. 'I saw it. I dreamt it. I saw a cloud hanging on a lake as smooth as glass, and I know my father and his knights were there. I know it.' Her eyes filled with tears and she stamped her foot.

'Calm yourself.' Zobayda got up and put her arm around Guanhamara. 'I have dreams and often they come true.'

'But what do you do about them, Aunt? What use are

dreams if we can't . . . If we can't do anything about them?'

Zobayda looked thoughtful. 'We'll just have to think how we can find this cloud that sits upon a lake, and rescue your father and his knights.'

'The eagles could tell us,' said Petrello. 'They can see everything from up there.'

He nodded at the sky through the window.

'I wish I could fly,' said Guanhamara, and slowly, very slowly, she turned her head and looked at Tolly.

Petrello found himself doing the same, and in a moment everyone but Zeba and Elin was looking at Tolly. Poor Tolly's face turned crimson. He stared at the floor and shuffled from one foot to another.

'I'll go,' said Tolly in the quietest voice imaginable. 'But not alone.' And he looked at Petrello.

Petrello felt slightly dizzy. How could he and Tolly fly above the forest? The air wouldn't hold them up so high. Tolly might have wings, but he didn't. And yet he couldn't let his brother go alone. He grinned at Tolly and said, 'Then I'll come with you.'

Chapter Nineteen

The House on Stilts

Petrello and Tolly were alone on the battlements. Llyr had offered to come with them but Petrello said no, they must be on their own. If they failed there was nothing anyone could do.

The sky was a clear blue, the wind so gentle it hardly ruffled their hair.

'D'you think I'm a coward?' asked Tolly, frowning.

'I wouldn't like to go out there all by myself.' Petrello stood by an opening in the wall. The forest was still emerging from the dawn mist, the birdsong lifting out of it soft and muffled. He had suggested they leave from the battlements because he remembered how the wind had pulled the king's cloak into the sky, how it had held it up so powerfully. His hand reached for the sword his mother had left for him. Zobayda had found it in the queen's dressing-room. His name was on a label tied to the hilt. So she had believed in him, after all. He wouldn't let her down.

'D'you think I can lift you?' Tolly sounded doubtful.

'The air will carry us.' Petrello believed this.

Tolly's dark wings were spread behind him. In the airy light the colours in the black shone like jewels. He flapped them slowly, once, twice, and then, suddenly, he was in the air.

'You're going without me?' cried Petrello.

'No, no. I was just trying them out.' There was pride and panic in Tolly's voice. He kicked the air, and rose even higher. 'How do I get down?'

'Wish it!' called Petrello. He had no other suggestions.

Tolly closed his eyes, stopped flapping and landed, rather heavily, on the battlements. 'Ho!' He coughed. 'I'm all shaken up.'

They laughed together nervously.

'Climb on my back,' said Petrello. 'You know, like you do when we're playing horse. I'll hold your legs very tightly; then, when you rise into the air again, I'll come with you.'

'D'you think so?'

'I know so.' If not certain, Petrello was at least hopeful.

Tolly gave a short run; he jumped. Now he was on his brother's back, his arms round Petrello's neck. His wings came down, the tips brushing Petrello's arms. And then they were in the air.

They sailed over the wall and the air held them. Petrello told himself he wouldn't look down, but he did. He could hardly believe what he was seeing: his own feet with nothing solid beneath them, and far below the castle gardens, fast disappearing now. The wind grabbed his legs and they flew out behind him. Now they were over the forest, and he could see deer in a glade, staring up at them.

Something hot touched his foot. He gasped. Were Tolly's wings on fire? Before he could shout at his brother a great whoosh of air knocked them sideways. Tolly shouted, but the wind filled Petrello's ears and he couldn't hear the words.

A huge shape swept through the air above them, flames shooting from its snout. It was Enid, her great wings and tail creating a wild gusty draught.

Once the dragon was ahead of them, she stopped cavorting in the air and began to glide. Petrello was immensely glad to see her. With a dragon on their side, nothing seemed impossible.

They watched the trees pass beneath them, for mile after mile. They saw glades and rivers, rocky hills, banks of flowers; they saw hares running, birds' nests and heronries, but never a lake as smooth as glass. Tolly's wings became as much a part of him as his legs or arms. He began to control them with ease. But although Petrello believed in those great black wings, he never lost the feeling that the strong current of air beneath them was somehow connected to him.

'Let's make some circles,' Petrello shouted to Tolly. 'We've been flying south for a long time, but the lake could be in the east or the west.'

'Agreed!' Tolly took off at a frightening speed. He circled above the trees, he zigzagged, bobbed and tilted. And Enid never left their side. She seemed to be enjoying the exercise; her flames began to shoot alarmingly close and Petrello had to shout, 'No, no, no, Enid!' She seemed to understand and moved off a little.

At least she's keeping us warm, thought Petrello. *Otherwise we'd be freezing cold up here.*

Ravens, hawks, larks and swallows swung away from

the unlikely creatures that frolicked in the air. Even the eagles kept their distance.

Gradually Enid's warmth stopped reaching them. She was still close by, twirling and whirling along, but Petrello's feet were getting colder and colder. The forest below had lost some of its greenness. In fact, the more he stared at it, the less like a forest it looked. Was that snow lying on the topmost branches? It couldn't be. It hadn't snowed for weeks.

Enid's flames began to flicker, like candles in a breeze, and then they died altogether. The dragon made a choking sound. She blinked, coughed twice and then, all at once, she began to drop towards the forest. She flapped her wings, but it seemed to be an effort. The dragon turned her head and looked up at the boys, her expression anxious and questioning.

'Trello, I can't feel my wings,' called Tolly. 'We're going down.'

Petrello sensed something dragging his legs. He kicked out at empty air. And then, below them, he saw a pale cloud, lying in the centre of a lake as smooth as polished glass.

There was nothing they could do to stop their rapid

tumble through the sky. Petrello watched the lake come closer and closer; they were about to fall into the icy-looking water when, with one last desperate beat of his wings, Tolly veered to one side. They landed heavily on a stony beach. Petrello let go of his brother's legs and they rolled apart.

For a moment they were both too stunned to speak. Petrello could see Enid crouching on the stones a short distance away. Her crested head drooped and a low gloomy grumble came from her throat.

'Enid, what happened?' Petrello asked, not really expecting her to hear.

But she lifted her head and ambled over to him.

'It was like a cold power dragging us down,' said Tolly, pulling himself upright.

Petrello sat up and patted the rough scales on the dragon's neck. She grunted with pleasure and a tiny flame appeared at the end of her snout. Petrello was glad to see it. 'I thought you'd lost your fire,' he told her.

Tolly was staring hard at the cloud. Following his gaze, Petrello saw that it wasn't an ordinary sort of cloud. It was more like a giant white nest. Thin, worm-like strands snaked into the air above it, and long feathery stuff extended from all sides. Petrello recognised the poisonous fungus that Llyr kept for rare and powerful spells.

'Can anyone be alive in there?' Tolly murmured.

'Yes,' Petrello said fervently. 'The king. He has his cloak.'

'How do we reach him?'

'We must fly above the cloud . . .'

'And drop into it?' asked Tolly. 'We'd be choked to death.'

'Let's think.'

They turned and walked towards a copse of birch trees growing beside the lake. Enid followed, thumping over the shingle like a heavy bag. They had almost reached the bank when they noticed a man, standing very still, beside a silvery birch.

Even as they looked, more figures appeared. They were much smaller than the first. They massed behind the man as though they were afraid.

Tolly and Petrello stopped. 'Shall we fly?' Tolly whispered.

'I'm not sure,' said Petrello.

And then the man called, 'Enid, welcome! Welcome, princes!'

Tolly and Petrello exchanged glances. It seemed

that the strange man was a friend. They followed Enid's example and continued towards the bank. As they drew closer they could see that the man's dark hair clung to his scalp like a cap of silk. He wore a rough hempen shirt and breeches made of some shiny animal hair. His feet were bare and the skin of his handsome face was pale and sleek. The crowd of children were dressed like the man; some of them looked related to him.

When they reached the stranger, he said, 'You don't know me, of course. I left the Red Castle ten years ago, when you were but a few weeks old; I think you must be Petrello.'

'I am. And this is Tolomeo.'

The man took first Petrello's hand, and then Tolly's. 'I'm Tumi,' he said, 'and some of these rascals are my children.'

All the children grinned at the princes and dipped their heads, as they called out their names. They spoke so fast Tolly and Petrello remembered none of them.

Tumi studied the boys' faces for a moment. 'I saw your wings,' he said to Tolly, 'and knew that you must be Timoken's sons. You are both like him, if a little paler. But then your mother is very pale-skinned. I trust she's well.'

Petrello hesitated, and Tolly said, 'We don't know.'

Petrello added, 'We've come to find our father. We believe he is in that smothering cloud. Our mother and our brother, Amadis, are also somewhere in the forest.'

'But we don't know where,' Tolly burst out. 'And we don't know how to rescue our father.'

'We're in a bit of a fix,' said Petrello.

Tumi's face became very grave. He looked at the cloud and said, 'Yes, certainly a fix. You'd better come home with me, and we'll try and sort this problem out together.' He turned to the children. 'Get your baskets and bring them along, as fast as you can. Don't linger by the water. Ketil, you're in charge.'

The tallest boy in the group said, 'Yes, Father,' and the children all ran down to the water's edge. Here they proceeded to haul in the dome-shaped fish baskets, tied with twine to large pebbles on the beach.

Tumi led Tolly and Petrello round the edge of the lake. Enid came lolloping behind. She never took her eyes off the cloud until they came within sight of a very strange house. It sat above the water on tall wooden stilts, and a plume of grey smoke curled from its round clay chimney. Petrello wondered how they could possibly reach it without getting very wet. But as soon as they were opposite the house, Tumi called, 'Sila, Timoken's sons are here.'

A door opened and a long ladder was thrust out. The end splashed into the water a short distance from the bank.

'Take off those fine boots, young men,' said Tumi. 'We have to paddle now.'

The boys sat down and pulled off their boots, while Enid watched, a slight suspicion creeping into her yellow eyes.

'Can Enid come in with us?' Tolly asked.

Tumi glanced at the trees leaning close to the beach. Petrello could see now that the topmost branches were hung with the deadly fungus that filled the cloud. 'The dragon shouldn't stay out here,' Tumi said. 'Go and meet my wife. I'll deal with Enid.'

Petrello climbed the ladder first. He didn't know what to expect when he reached the top, and was astonished to see such a beautiful room inside the odd-looking house. Coloured carpets covered the floor and the walls were hung with polished shells, beads, crystals and shining stones. In one corner a log burned in a small iron grate, and around the walls there were mounds of bright blankets and cushions.

Tolly stepped into the room. He stood gazing at the walls while a woman, standing by the door, clasped both the boys' hands. 'Welcome,' she said warmly. Her round and gentle face was framed by hazel-coloured curls and soft lines ringed her large brown eyes. 'I'm Sila,' she said, and then, turning to Petrello, 'and you are Petrello.'

'How did you know that?' he asked.

'I knew by the little breeze you brought in with you,' she said. 'We left the Red Castle just after you were born, and I remember your mother saying that you brought a little storm into the world with you. All the pretty covers, the cloths and shawls and baby blankets went flying about the room.'

'Really?' Petrello hadn't known this.

'There, you've done it again,' she said, and Petrello noticed that the crystals, the beads and shells and stones were all jingling in a tiny breeze.

Sila laughed. 'They named you Petrello after the bird that thrives on stormy seas.'

'I didn't know that,' said Petrello. 'I think I must have lost my storminess for a while.'

'They named me Tolomeo,' said Tolly, 'because my

mother came from a place called Toledo.'

Enid's snout appeared in the doorway. She seemed to be smiling, though it was hard to tell. It might have been a grimace for, behind her, Tumi's groans were getting louder and louder. Suddenly, Enid's whole body burst through the door, with Tumi tumbling after her, his hands still on her thick tail. 'Dragons aren't meant for ladders,' he puffed.

Enid shuffled into a corner, looking a little bemused.

A moment later the children appeared with their baskets of fish. As soon as they saw Enid they dropped their baskets by the door and ran to make a fuss of her. They knew she was a dragon because of the many stories their father had told them.

Tumi sat in the open doorway and gutted the fish, while Sila hung a cauldron of water above the fire. And as Tumi worked he told the boys how he and Sila had left the Red Castle to live on the lake, because Tumi missed being near water. Their friends Karli and Esga had come with them, and Timoken himself had helped to build their house, 'With that wonderful way he has of multiplying a plank,' Sila put in.

'All our children can swim like fish,' said Tumi. 'And

I mean fish, for they can stay under water for a long, long time.' He put down his knife. 'And that is how we plan to rescue your father.'

'How?' asked Petrello. 'Why is he there? And what is that cloud? Who made it?'

'Why did they make it?' begged Tolly. 'Our father has a cloak that has protected him all his life, so why not this time?'

'So many questions,' sighed Tumi, and he told them about the Damzel of Decay, the dark spirit of the forest who had for so long hungered for Timoken's marvellous cloak of healing and protection.

'She is sometimes beautiful,' said Sila, 'but her beauty is a mask. It hides a hideous nature. She is very strong and she has demon servants to help her in her dreadful sorcery.'

'We believe she struck a bargain with Sir Osbern D'Ark of Melyntha Castle,' went on Tumi. 'He would get someone in the Red Castle to steal the Seeing Crystal, knowing the king would come looking for it. And the Damzel would seize the cloak before the king had time to act.'

'Without his cloak he is much weakened,' said Sila.

Petrello thought of Borlath. He was ashamed to mention his brother's part in the terrible events.

'How did they get our father and his knights on to the island beneath the cloud?' asked Tolly, looking through a small window between the strands of twinkling crystals.

'The Damzel's demons carried them over in nets of stinking weeds,' said Tumi. 'They are afraid of water.' He walked over to the cauldron and dropped several fish into the bubbling water. 'We saw from our little window and shuddered, not knowing what to do.'

'So they can fly?' said Petrello.

'Servants like that can do anything.' Sila stirred her cauldron fiercely. 'Sir Osbern hopes they will remain there, prisoners of the cloud forever, while he keeps the Seeing Crystal and takes over the Red Castle, a place he has always pined for.'

'A magic castle,' said one of the girls, her eyes shining.

'A castle he would share with Chancellor Thorkil,' Tumi said darkly. 'We heard all this from one of Sir Osbern's grooms. The boy still lives in the forest with his mother, and sometimes she comes to us, for our fish. We always suspected that one day Thorkil would move against the king.'

Petrello and Tolly brought their cushions closer to the fire. Their thoughts had made them cold. They stared at the flames beneath the cauldron, wondering what to do next.

'So the Damzel has the cloak,' Petrello said unhappily.

'No,' said Tumi. 'It wouldn't stay with her. It tore itself out of her grasp. We saw her on the beach, snatching and tearing at it, until it fell apart and floated away.'

'We found it.' Ketil went to a chest and lifted out some thin pieces of fabric. They were torn and ragged, and yet they had a faint golden sparkle.

Petrello leapt over to Ketil and took the flimsy bits of stuff out of his hands. As he held a piece up to the light he could follow the thin gold lines that ran across it. It was part of a spider's web. A ripple of anger ran through him, and all the shells and crystals, all the polished stones and coloured beads jangled and clinked and sang; even the cauldron of fish went swinging.

'My father's cloak!' cried Petrello. 'But how are we to mend it?'

Firelight, shining through the web, made a golden pattern on Tolly's grave face. 'Leopards' gold,' he said. 'The leopards will mend it.'

Chapter Twenty
Leopards' Gold

Not long after the brothers had arrived at the house on stilts, a small slight man with gentle eyes appeared at the top of the ladder. He was followed by a woman with a merry face and thick, dark hair. They had left the castle with Tumi and Sila, and were parents to half the children in the small fishing group.

Karli and Esga were overjoyed to meet two of Timoken's sons, but when Karli heard about the chancellor's treachery he shuddered. Esga looked at him and gripped his hand. She explained to the brothers that even as a boy Thorkil had been a bully. He had made Karli's life a misery, until Timoken came into their lives.

'For a while Thorkil became easier to live with,' said Karli. 'It seemed as though he had cast off his arrogant ways. And then his sister, Elfrieda, married a man called

Chimery, a stranger with a secret past.'

Tumi slowly shook his head. 'Once Thorkil and Chimery got together, we could see that the friendships your father was so eager to foster would one day fracture, and the good and special life we loved would fall apart.'

'Timoken couldn't see it,' said Sila. 'I don't like to say this, but sometimes your father expects too much of people. A goodness they can't live up to.' She smiled at the king's sons. 'But then, why shouldn't he?'

There was a moment's silence, and then Esga, glancing hastily through the small window, announced, 'My brother, Ilgar, is in that cloud.'

'He is a Knight Protector?' asked Petrello.

Esga nodded. 'One of the bravest and the best.'

It was Tumi's suggestion that Tolly should wait until nightfall before he flew back to the Red Castle. Darkness would hide him from anyone on watch.

Tolly was determined to go alone this time. His wings were part of him now, he said. They did whatever he wanted. And it would be easier to carry the web if he didn't have to cling to Petrello.

Petrello suspected this wasn't the only reason. The light in Tolly's eyes told him that his brother relished the thought of an adventure on his own.

There was something else Petrello had to ask about. A part of the king's capture that wasn't clear. 'The horses,' he said, 'and the camel. What became of them?'

'Ah,' said Tumi. 'They behaved rather unnaturally. When the king and his knights were set upon, the horses were screaming. But as the demons carried those poor weed-wrapped men across the water, the animals fell silent. And then, without a sound, they turned, all at once, and went – every one in the same direction.'

Petrello and Tolly looked at each other and Tolly said, 'Amadis called them.'

'Amadis, of course,' said Tumi. 'The boy with white-gold hair, who was often seen with wolves.'

'Who conversed with dogs and cats and horses,' said Karli.

'And eagles and even rats,' added his wife.

'He's alive then!' Petrello jumped up, ready to search for his brother at once. But looking round the sea of anxious faces, he realised that it would not be easy to find Amadis in a forest that stretched further than he could imagine. He would need help, and the light was fading fast.

'Tomorrow,' said Tumi. 'After the king has been released.' He didn't mention how this would happen, and Petrello thought it better not to ask, in case Tumi wasn't really sure of his plan.

Sila began to ladle her fish dish into bowls, and the two smallest children handed them out. Petrello judged them to be about five and six years old, and he thought of Vyborn, who might not have carried a full bowl so carefully.

'This isn't just soup,' Tolly declared, lapping it up. 'It's the most delicious food I have ever tasted.'

'Even compared with those special Red Castle dishes?' asked Sila.

'Definitely,' Tolly insisted.

Petrello agreed. For the fish dish was thickened with the most delicious beans, and flavoured with the sweetest herbs he had ever tasted.

'Herbs from the forest,' said Tumi, 'and beans from the market, where we sell our fish, just as my parents used to do.'

'Before the conquerors came,' Karli murmured.

'We go by boat,' said Sila, noticing Petrello's puzzled frown. 'A river runs all the way from the lake to the town.'

'Isn't it dangerous?' asked Tolly. 'Do the demons and their Damzel ever try to stop you?'

'We are not worth bothering about,' said Tumi. 'We have nothing they need.'

'Until now,' Ketil said quietly.

Everyone turned to look at Tumi's oldest son. He was a lean boy with a thin, serious face, and his voice was already deep. 'If we help the king, the Damzel won't forgive us,' he said. 'We won't be able to live here any more.'

There was a brief hush. The other children stared at Ketil with scared and troubled faces, while the adults scraped their bowls with hunks of bread and wondered what to say.

All at once, the smallest girl cried, 'Unless we kill her.'

Tumi looked up and smiled at his youngest child. 'Then that's what we'll have to do, Adela.'

No one suggested how this could be done. Rescuing the king was uppermost in all their minds.

As night clouds brought a dark shroud across the sky, Sila began to light the rushes. They were held in iron brackets fixed to the walls, and when they flickered into life, their light was reflected in the polished crystals and silvery shells, so that the whole place seemed to sparkle.

Petrello thought it one of the most beautiful rooms he had ever seen, and he couldn't bear to imagine Tumi and his friends and family having to leave it forever.

It was almost time for Tolly's departure. Petrello could sense his brother's nervousness. He kept looking through the window with a half-smile on his face, and his dark eyes were unnaturally bright.

'Are you sure you want to go alone?' Petrello asked. 'I'll come with you, happily.'

'No.' Tolly shook his head. 'I must do this alone, Trello. I have to carry the cloak.'

The other children were aware that their new friend must soon fly out into the night. They crept closer to Tolly and some of them stroked the glossy wings that lay above his feathered cloak.

Tumi crossed the room and opened the door. Framed in the doorway was a brilliant full moon, but below it, the pale fungus that covered the treetops seemed to swallow the light, rather than reflect it.

'Are you ready, Tolomeo?' asked Tumi.

Tolly stood up. 'I am.'

Petrello had been holding the frail strips of his father's cloak. He got up and put them carefully into

Tolly's hands. There were five pieces in all.

'You have great faith in those leopards,' Karli remarked. 'Can they really do what you say?'

'We believe they can,' said Petrello.

'They have to,' said Tolly.

Tumi led the way down the ladder. Petrello and Tolly followed, Petrello carrying both pairs of their boots. The lake was icy cold and held an eerie green light.

'We're coming too,' said Ketil, who was already climbing down the ladder.

He was quickly followed by the rest of the children, and then Karli and the two women came splashing on to the beach. They spoke in whispers now; the presence of the great cloud lying heavy on their spirits.

Petrello helped Tolly into his boots. Then he clasped his brother's hands and felt the life in the king's cloak warm under his fingers. 'Are you sure you can find the castle without me?' he asked, still anxious for his brother.

Tolly nodded vigorously.

'Good luck, then.' Petrello hugged his smaller brother as though it might be for the last time.

'Where's Enid?' Tolly asked.

Petrello looked back at the house on stilts. Enid

hadn't even come to the door. 'She's asleep,' he said, trying to hide his concern. 'I think she needs to get her strength back.'

'Oh.' Tolly grinned. 'Here goes, then.'

Petrello stepped back as Tolly's great wings lifted, and there was a gasp of wonder from the children.

'Good luck! Good luck!' came the hushed calls.

The black wings dipped then lifted, and Tolly rose into the air.

They watched him fly higher and higher, his wings sweeping the cool night air and sending a soft breeze across their faces, and then he swung away and darkness swallowed him.

Petrello walked back towards the ladder. He didn't want to spend another moment in a place where he could see the cloud.

'Now we wait,' said Tumi, putting an arm round Petrello's shoulders. 'Your brother is a brave boy.'

'His father's son,' said Karli, who was following them.

'Yes, Petrello agreed, and this time the little twinge of loneliness seemed to matter less.

Once inside the house on stilts, the children began to fall asleep on their beds of straw-filled cushions. Tumi put a log on to the stove and sat beside it, while Karli and the women rested against the walls.

'Sleep, Petrello,' said Sila. 'We'll wait for Tolomeo. Tomorrow you must be strong.'

'Strong, yes,' said Petrello. His eyes were already closing. He crawled over and lay his head on a cushion beside Ketil. He thought of the cloud, and the king and his knights within it. Were they asleep or were they, even now, struggling against their choking, toxic bonds?

High above the forest, Tolly spread his wings and allowed himself to be carried on the damp south wind. His mind raced. Where should he land? On the battlements? In the first courtyard where the leopards were last seen? He held the pieces of his father's cloak tight against his chest. They gave him courage.

Tolly thought himself quite safe, so high in the dark sky. He had forgotten that someone wanted the bundle of magic that he carried; someone who had seen a winged boy fly into the air with the thing she most wanted in the whole world. The Damzel of Decay would have given her crooked toes, her curling green fingers, perhaps even her cold colourless eyes for the web of the last moon spider, woven into a king's cloak.

A freezing current of air suddenly bit into Tolly's arms. The shock almost made him drop his precious bundle. He flapped his wings and tried to rise higher, but something caught his foot. Looking down, he saw a hideous green creature clinging to his boot. It was a hairless, bloated thing, with long pointed ears and a thin whisker of a tail. Its eyes bulged, its hooked nose drooped and its warty hands were bigger than its long domed head. Tolly kicked out, but it clung tighter and pulled his foot into its cavernous mouth.

Tolly felt himself sinking. Helplessly, he beat his wings; then, turning in the air, he saw behind him an army of the grisly green demons. Two carried between them a blanket of fungus that floated in the air like a great misty net.

For me, thought Tolly, and his terrible fear turned to anger. *They mean to wrap me in their poisonous net and steal the cloak again. Well, they won't because it's ours.*

Belief in himself, and in the magic of the cloak he carried, gave him the strength to climb again into the air, and as he climbed he saw a dark mass of wings moving across the moon.

'Eagles!' cried Tolly, loud enough for the demons to hear.

The great birds swept over him and into the crowd of demons behind. He had never heard such screams, as beaks and talons tore into green warty flesh. The sky was full of beating wings, of thrashing tails, twisting crooked feet and fingers and drifting shreds of fungus. And then the owls came, and crows and hawks and ravens, and the angry screams ringing into the night became howls of anguish and terror.

A white screech owl tore the demon off Tolly's foot and he was free.

Fly on, the birds seemed to call. *Fly on and let us sweep this menace from the sky.*

So Tolly flew on, with a smile on his face. For he knew that Amadis was there, below him in the trees. Who else would have called the birds? And if Amadis was there, perhaps the queen was with him. And Tolly's smile grew wider, until at last he saw the sixteen towers of the Red Castle rising above the trees.

As soon as he saw his home, Tolly knew where to land: in Zobayda's garden where he might see his aunt and sister, safe in the Royal Tower.

He reached the high red walls, flew over them and dropped down beside Zobayda's fountain. A light burned in the high window of the Royal bedchamber, and Tolly wondered if his sister might come and look out. He ran towards the door of the Royal Tower, but something rushed at him from behind a tub of roses. It stood in front of Tolly grunting, lowering its head with its vicious tusks, ready to charge.

'Vyborn?' Tolly whispered. 'Vyborn, is that you?'

The boar moved closer. It lifted its head and glared at him with tiny, spiteful eyes. Tolly could see nothing but hatred in that angry gaze.

'Why are you doing this?' Tolly asked in a reasonable tone. 'I'm your brother.'

'Is that what you are?' A man stepped out of the shadows behind the boar. 'So you have wings, do you, boy? And what's that stuff you're carrying?'

Tolly hugged the cloak tighter. He recognised Chimery, the chancellor's man.

'Give it to me!' Chimery demanded, drawing his sword.

'No,' said Tolly. 'I won't.'

'Oh, I think you will!' Chimery raised his sword. 'Or you'll lose your head.'

Better to lose my feet than my head, Tolly thought as he spread his wings. But before he could lift into the sky, something bright sliced through the air. Chimery clutched his shoulder. Blood seeped through his fingers, as he pulled out a knife.

Seizing his chance, Tolly drew his sword and lunged at Chimery. The man gave a roar of fury and swung his sword at the boy's head. But Tolly was too quick for him. Ducking down, he thrust the tip of his sword deep into the man's stomach. Chimery gave a choking groan and dropped to the ground.

The wild boar rushed away, squealing.

'Well, young Tolomeo, I'm very glad to see you,' said Llyr, emerging from Zobayda's doorway.

'Llyr!' breathed Tolly. 'Your knife . . .' He peered down at Chimery. 'Is he dead?'

'Without doubt,' said Llyr. 'You had no choice. Your mother taught you well.' He picked up the knife, wiped it on his tunic and slipped it into his belt beside the others. 'Now, tell me, what do you have there, clutched so tightly?'

'My father's cloak,' said Tolly.

Llyr touched a thin piece trailing over Tolly's arm. 'This is not the king's cloak. What's happened, Tolomeo?'

'The Damzel took it. The Damzel of Decay, they called her.'

'Ah, Timoken's old enemy.' Llyr gave a grim smile. 'My grandfather has met her.'

'I thought the leopards could make this whole again.' Tolly held up the scraps of cloak. 'You know, the way their gold helped Gunfrid to live.'

Llyr nodded. 'We'll go and find them, but tell me, where's the king? If this is his cloak, what's happened to him?'

'I'll tell you, but first,' he looked up at the candlelit window in the Royal Tower, 'how're my sister and my aunt?'

'Fast asleep, I should think. They're well. My knives and the leopards keep them safe. Now, we must be quick about this leopard spell, Tolomeo. I don't want to use too many knives just yet.'

As they slipped quietly through the second courtyard, Tolly gave the wizard every detail of every scrap of news that he could remember. And while he talked and whispered, he was aware that Eri had joined them. The old man grunted and grumbled as he listened to Tolly's story. He shook his head and clicked his tongue, and when Tolly reached the part where the birds came to save him, in a deep soft voice the wizard exclaimed, 'So Amadis is alive. I knew the wolves wouldn't let him down.'

Then, from Eri, Tolly learned about the monsters his sister had conjured from her high window, and the shapes that Vyborn had assumed to attack her phantom creatures. The way that Borlath strutted and demanded, while Cafal ran in his shadow, doing everything he asked. And then Tolly and the wizards were in the first courtyard, where the leopards kept watch.

As soon as they saw Tolly, the leopards rushed at him. Flame Chin stood and, putting his paws on Tolly's shoulders, sniffed the flimsy pieces of the cloak. He pulled the bundle out of Tolly's arms and dropped it on the ground. Star and Sun Cat pushed their noses into it. Grumbling and growling, they gathered the pieces in their mouths, raised their heads and roared into the night. It was no use trying to hush them. The chancellor's men were already awake.

Tolly could only watch and hope. The leopards moved the precious bits together. They dragged and pushed and stretched them. The shape of a cloak emerged, and the pattern of the web within it became so bright, Tolly could barely look at it. The leopards began to circle it. Around and around, faster; they lost their leopard forms and became a single whirling flame. Tolly could feel the heat on his face.

Shouting could be heard. The chancellor's men had emerged from their tower. Tolly felt the breeze of a knife pass over his head. He heard a distant groan of pain, and then another. He saw Eri's staff twist into a gleaming serpent and strike a sword-hand. He thought he saw Friar Gereint wielding a sword, and through the flames he glimpsed the chancellor's cold grey eyes.

The wall of flames leapt higher. Now there was gold in the air, falling like snow and covering the king's torn cloak.

Tolly's head began to spin. He closed his eyes against the blinding glare of fire and gold. How long he stood there, hardly conscious, he never knew. But gradually he became aware of a hand on his shoulder.

'It is ready,' said Llyr.

Tolly opened his eyes. The cloak lay before him, covered in gold. Behind it the leopards sat in a row, licking their paws.

There was no sign of the chancellor's men.

Llyr lifted the cloak. Gold-dust fell from it and floated out into the dark. The red cloak was whole again.

Llyr folded it tight and put it into Tolly's arms.

'Go quickly!' said Eri. 'And bring the king back with you.'

'I will!' Tolly spread his wings and they lifted him away.

Chapter Twenty-One

Dragonfire

Petrello was asleep when his brother returned. He was unaware of Tolly's head sinking on to the cushion beside him. And yet he did feel something when Tolly pulled the cloak over them both. It was a comforting warmth that seeped into all his bones.

In the early morning, when he was only just awake, Petrello thought another Vanishing had begun. And then he realised that the house on stilts was rocking like a boat.

A low murmur of voices came from beyond a thick rush door at the end of the room. Tumi's voice suddenly became loud and impatient. 'I must. We're doomed already. Only the king can save us now.'

For a moment Petrello lay still, his hand clasping the soft edge of the cloak. Yawning, he let go of it and stood up. The other children had gathered round the window and he tried to peer over their heads.

'The water's rising.' Ketil stood aside to give Petrello a better view.

Petrello couldn't believe his eyes. The lake now covered the beach; it had even seeped into the forest. Some of the smaller trees were already half-submerged. The water had a poisonous green glimmer.

'The house!' said Petrello. 'Is the water –?'

'Almost at our door,' Ketil said grimly.

'I didn't hear rain,' said Petrello.

'The Damzel doesn't need rain,' muttered Ketil.

Tumi came through the rush door. Sila, behind him, looked as white as the moon.

'I'm sorry this trouble has come to you,' Petrello said desperately.

'It's not your fault.' Tumi was staring at Tolly, still fast asleep beneath the red cloak. 'I don't like to wake your brother, but I must take the cloak now, before our house is swept away.'

Karli and Esga emerged from another door. Karli's whole body was covered in the same shiny animal skin that Tumi's breeches were made of. He grinned at Petrello, saying, 'Your father made this from a sealskin.' He stroked the fur of his sleeve. 'So it holds a certain magic.'

Tumi disappeared into his room and Sila said, 'Tumi found a dead seal when he was just a boy, and skinned it.'

'And from that single skin your father made many,' added Esga. Even in this grave situation she still had a merry face, and Petrello noticed that she was looking at the children. She didn't want them to be afraid.

Tumi reappeared, wearing his sealskin bodysuit. It had a hood that he pulled tight over his head. Karli did the same.

Petrello knelt beside Tolly and shook his shoulder. 'Tolly, wake up,' he said gently.

Tolly opened his eyes.

'Well done, brother.' Petrello grasped an edge of the cloak. 'I don't know how you did it, but they need this now.'

'No! No!' Tolly clutched the top of the cloak and wouldn't let go.

'He's hardly awake,' said Sila. 'And we don't know what happened to him last night. He appeared at the door half-asleep and crawled across the floor, your father's cloak held tight.'

'Tolly, let go!' begged Petrello. 'They're going to take it to the king.' He gave the cloak another tug.

Tolly sat up, his eyes wild, breaking out of sleep. 'They did it, Trello. The leopards with their gold.'

Esga bent over him. 'Can we take it, Tolly? Your father needs it.'

Tolly slowly released his grip. Esga lifted the cloak away and handed it to Tumi. 'You'll have to stay underwater all the way,' she said. 'If the Damzel sees you . . .'

'It's what we planned to do,' Tumi replied, looking at Karli.

They walked to the door, and when Tumi opened it, Petrello could see the luminous green water rising and falling only inches below. He could hear it sucking round the wooden stilts and burbling under the floorboards. Soon it would be in the house.

'Ready?' Tumi passed a corner of the cloak to Karli and suddenly they were gone, sliding into the lake like two slippery eels.

'They've gone! They've gone!' cried Adela. 'Will the water kill them, Mama?'

'No.' Sila lifted Adela into her arms. 'They will swim under the water, like you do sometimes. Papa and Karli will swim all the way to the island where the cloud sits, and once Timoken has his cloak . . .' She couldn't finish, for she didn't know how it would all end.

There was no sign of anyone beneath the slow swell of the eerie green water. The watchers couldn't tell where Tumi and Karli might be. From the doorway they could only see the forest; they had to move to the window for a view of the cloud.

The great, white sphere seemed to have expanded. The strands of fungus that snaked out of it had grown. Now they reached into the damp air like long, giant fingers.

There was a sudden bang on the roof, and then another and another.

'Rain?' Esga looked at the rush ceiling.

'Not rain,' said Ketil. 'Demons!'

Three wicked-looking upside-down faces glared in through the window. The children's screams had no effect on the hideous creatures, who began to tap at the pane with their curling claws. Esga rushed at the window, but Sila caught her hand crying, 'Don't let them in!'

They had thought that Enid was asleep, but now she uncoiled herself and lifted her head. She stared at the upside-down faces and suddenly ran to the open door.

Petrello was never sure how it happened, he hardly thought what he was doing, but he knew he had to act.

As the dragon sailed through the doorway, he jumped. Clinging to her scaly neck, he felt the rush of air as her great wings spread either side of him. His left hand holding tightly to one of her spines, with his right he drew his sword.

Enid swerved in the air and swept towards the demons on the roof. Two streams of fire shot from her snout and Petrello saw the hanging demons leap to their feet. They shook their fists and screeched at the dragon, as though their tongues were tearing from their jaws. But when Enid came at them, low and fast, they crouched, and then one jumped. It gripped the dragon's wing and sank black fangs deep into it. Enid screamed and shot into the air, her snout pointing at the sky, her tail hanging.

Leaning from the dragon's neck, Petrello lifted his sword, but he couldn't reach the demons. He leant into the air, further and further, his fingers aching as they clung to Enid's spine. *One more swipe and I'll do it*, he thought. But as he lifted the sword again he began to slide off Enid's back. With one last desperate effort he struck at the demon's head. Its eyes bulged and with a deep gurgle it fell away and dropped into the lake.

Demons can't swim! Petrello thought with grim satisfaction, and against the surge of air from Enid's sweeping wing, he managed to pull himself to safety. The dragon rumbled a sort of thanks and tilted down to make Petrello's grip easier.

He knew the battle wasn't over and, though his heart sank, he wasn't surprised to see another crowd of the Damzel's servants coming at him from the cloud. They didn't fly for they had no wings; they hovered and darted, dropped and spun. Petrello waited, his sword at the ready, and it entered his mind that he might die if the approaching creatures pulled him off the dragon's back.

As the mass of demons came closer, a huge bird appeared in the sky, its wings as black and shiny as a raven's.

'Tolly!' cried Petrello.

'I'm coming, Trello!' called Tolly, and he swept into the mass of demons, his sword striking them so fast they couldn't avoid it. They jumped on to his wings but he beat them off. They grabbed his head, but he still reached them.

Given new heart by Tolly's bravery, Enid's fire returned

and she snorted flames into the crowd, while Petrello struck at warty hands and crooked legs and leering faces. So many demons fell into the lake, their numbers should have diminished and yet the sky was dark with them. Petrello's sword-arm ached so fiercely he could hardly lift it any more.

'Don't give up!' cried Tolly, but Petrello could see that he, too, was growing weary. Soon one of the demons would pull him down by his wings; even now they were tearing at his feathers.

The sky had turned darker than the forest shadows. Far below, only the roof of the house on stilts was visible. The rest of the building had been submerged.

Where were the children? Where were their mothers? Drowned, or swimming for their lives beneath the cruel green surface of the lake?

'Petrello!' Tolly's shout came almost too late.

A fat demon landed on Enid's crest. More hideous than the rest, his blood-red fangs spread his mouth in a fixed and ghastly grin. A long green arm shot towards Petrello, the fingers of the crooked hand curled into a hook. Petrello threw back his head and lashed out with his sword, but still the hand came, grabbing the air in its empty hook, one clawed finger reaching for Petrello's eye.

Petrello slashed again. Quick as lightning the hand withdrew. Petrello leaned back as far as he could, any more and he would lose his grip on Enid's spine. He felt himself slipping and still the clawed finger reached. As he lifted his sword again, his brother's voice carried through the air, 'Lower, Trello! Slice him!'

In his mind's eye, Petrello saw the castle cook slicing ham. Lowering his sword, he sliced.

There was a blood-curdling screech as the crooked hand flew away, and the wounded demon dropped from the dragon's crest.

Petrello lay his head on Enid's scaly neck. Never in his life had he felt so weary. He doubted that he could lift his sword again. Where were the birds? The words came to him from afar. They were Tolly's words. 'Where are the birds? Where are the eagles?'

Amadis can't know, Petrello thought sleepily. *He can't see us. They will only come if Amadis sends them.*

But Amadis had problems of his own. The men from Melyntha had found him.

Sir Osbern D'Ark of Melyntha had made a bargain

with the Damzel. With his help she would capture the African king who owned an enchanted red castle, and had married the girl Sir Osbern had chosen for a wife. All the Damzel wanted in return was the king's cloak, and maybe a young prince or two, with those special gifts that forest-dwellers often spoke about.

Sir Osbern knew that a certain Chancellor Thorkil was ready to betray his king. And he was delighted to hear that the king's oldest son would help the chancellor.

Sir Osbern's part of the bargain had gone reasonably well. His men had stolen a particular crystal, and had abducted the bellman who knew its secret. As predicted, the king and his knights had entered the forest to find the bellman and retrieve the crystal. Unfortunately, a solitary knight had rescued the bellman and killed one of Sir Osbern's men, but the other, though badly wounded, had returned with the crystal.

Sir Osbern waited impatiently for news. At last it came, delivered by a demon.

I HAVE HIM. FOLLOW MY SERVANT.

Sir Osbern's muscles had run to fat, his hair was thin and white, but his greed and his cruelty had only increased. When he and his men followed the hideous hovering thing into the forest, they came across a young knight. His eagle-crested helmet was so bright, his armour so splendid and his ebony horse so fine, he was surely a prince. A prince worth capturing.

As Osbern's soldiers began to surround the young knight, he leapt off his horse, making unnatural animal sounds.

Go, Isgofan, go! cried Amadis. *Go home so they will know.*

Like a bolt of lightning the black horse vaulted over the heads of the soldiers and vanished into the trees.

At an order from Osbern five of the soldiers dismounted and began to advance on Amadis. He reached for his sword but one of the men leapt forward and slashed his wrist. His gauntlet fell, and the man slashed again at the prince's hand. And all the while Amadis continued to call, this time to the wolves.

Out of their hidden places the wolves ran to him. Greyfleet leapt, his jaws closing round the first soldier's sword-arm, and before he could strike again, the other wolves surrounded Amadis in a moving tide of grey and black and brindle.

'Kill them!' roared Sir Osbern.

But as his soldiers reached for their swords, the wolves jumped and tore into their arms.

Run, wolf-friend, Greyfleet grunted to Amadis. *We will follow.*

Amadis wouldn't leave the wolves. He retreated a little way into the trees, ready to do battle with Sir Osbern himself if his friends were harmed. But having delivered their fatal bites, the wolves turned swiftly and ran to Amadis. They took him to a cave they knew, and there he stayed for three nights while his right hand healed. Without a horse it would take him several days to reach the Red Castle, and he dared not risk another encounter with Sir Osbern's men.

On the third night Amadis wandered down to a stream where he bathed his injured hand. The moon was full and bright, and when he looked up into the sky, he saw a winged boy, followed by a crowd of hovering, flitting demons.

It must be Tolomeo, thought Amadis, and he called to the eagles, begging them to rescue his brother.

As the eagles went on their way, Amadis felt an unhealthy draught brush his face. There was a damp, foul-smelling force lurking in the trees. He shivered and ran back to his warm wolf cave.

The following morning there was a great commotion in the forest. Amadis heard a voice he knew and he ran towards it. With the wolves at his heels he bounded over rocks and briars, he leapt over streams and tumbled down banks of wild flowers. *It's Elizen*, he told the wolves, *my mother's horse. They've caught the queen. Help me to save her.*

His call went to all the strongest and wildest creatures in the forest: the stags and the boars, the hawks and the eagles, the wildcats and the foxes.

They found the queen in a narrow glade, surrounded by soldiers. One of them had grabbed Elizen's bridle, and the mare was screaming in distress.

'Mother!' cried Amadis. 'I'm here!'

A deep roar of laughter erupted from Sir Osbern. 'So I have you both,' he boomed. 'Mother and son. I know you now, Berenice, with your fine hair tucked beneath a cap of hare-skin. For this is surely King Timoken's son, with his gift for conversing with animals.'

'Just so,' said Amadis, and he called out in every wild language that he knew. And all the creatures that had followed him advanced on Osbern and his men.

A savage battle began. Creatures were wounded.

Soldiers died. Queen Berenice wielded her sword so fast and so nimbly, Osbern couldn't get near her. Protected by his wolves, Amadis sliced and slashed, working his way closer and closer to the owner of Melyntha. It had become so dark Sir Osbern could only be recognised by his huge bulk.

Why has day become night, wondered Amadis. *Have we been fighting so long?*

How could he know that, high above the forest, his brothers needed his help?

The demons crowding about the winged boy and the dragon all at once began to leave the sky. Where they went, the boys couldn't tell. The hovering creatures seemed to vanish into passing clouds of vapour.

Tolly flew to Enid's side. 'Have we won a battle?' he asked his brother.

'Has Tumi reached the king?' was Petrello's answer.

Their only thought now was to land somewhere safe, but all they could see beneath the clouded sky was a vast expanse of grey-green water.

In the distance, Petrello saw a darkness, greater than the clouds, gather itself into a dense black shape. It was as if the forest canopy had lifted and become a whirling mass of leaves.

And then it came at them, its black sleeves flapping, its face more terrible than their darkest nightmares.

Chapter Twenty-Two
The Damzel's Last Fight

Karli and Tumi had reached the island in the centre of the lake. As they stepped out of the water, they pulled back their sealskin hoods and took great gulps of air; it was foul to taste, but it was air and their lungs were greedy for it.

They climbed a shallow bank, carrying the wet cloak between them, and then they shook out the drops of greenish water and the patches of slimy black weed, until the thick velvet was red again, and the thin gold lines shone out, even in the bleak grey light.

They folded the cloak and Tumi held it under his arm as they stepped further on to the island. Before them sat the great cloud, its curling tentacles brushing the reeds around it. Usually the island rose high above the lake, now it was all but submerged. The wet earth squelched under the men's feet as they made their way towards the cloud.

'Have you a plan?' asked Karli.

Tumi gave him a grim smile. 'My plan was to find the king and clothe him in this magic garment.'

'So we must enter the cloud,' said Karli.

'Indeed,' his friend agreed.

They were now within inches of the curling tentacles. Together they stepped close and immediately, thin, slimy arms wrapped themselves around both men. With their knives under their sealskin suits, they could only use their hands to tear and pull the sticky strands away. When Karli bit into one, a thick white paste oozed out, the taste of it making him retch.

'Foul, foul, foul!' Karli spat out the dreadful soupy stuff. 'But I'm still alive,' he joked, and bit again.

Tumi did the same. The taste was sickening, but it was the only way to rid themselves of their living bonds.

Once they were past the tentacles they found themselves inside the cloud. A dense fog confused their vision, but they plodded on. Afraid of losing each other, they kept close, touching hands every now and then, and whispering encouragement to one another.

'Not much different from being underwater,' Karli said through his half-closed mouth.

'Water smells better,' said Tumi, coughing.

'Where are they? Where's the king?'

'Perhaps the Damzel's tricked us.'

'And caught us like fish in a net.'

'There!' said Karli.

Just ahead of them a dark shape floated: a man suspended in the vapour, his body wrapped in a net of weeds.

Karli and Tumi stood, their eyes half-closed against the mist. What had they expected? Not this: a man bound and floating. Was it the king?

'It's Sir Edern,' whispered Karli. 'See, the red hair.' His toe touched something hard and sharp. Without taking his eyes off the hanging knight, he reached down and lifted up a round metal object.

'His helmet,' said Tumi. He stepped closer to the bound man. It was shocking to see the great knight floating so helplessly. But when Tumi looked into Edern's face, the lids beneath the thick eyebrows flickered and the mouth twitched in a painful grin. He was alive, but only just.

'We must find Timoken.' Karli tugged his friend's arm. 'We can't do anything for Edern until the cloak has done its work.'

Moving on, they passed Mabon the archer, and Esga's brother, Ilgar, both hanging in the choking air like Edern. Stumbling over fallen swords and helmets, they passed little Sir Urien, trussed like a fowl, but still breathing. In the distance they could see other knights, all bound and hanging, trapped in a paralysing spell.

At last they saw the king. Taller than the others, he seemed to stand in the air, his head erect, his expression shocked and furious.

Tumi let the cloak unfold and Karli took one side of it. 'How can we reach his shoulders?' he whispered.

'We leap together,' said Tumi.

They looked at each other, nervous and hopeful.

'Now!' said Tumi.

They leapt, carrying the cloak high; Tumi one side, Karli the other. They hung the red cloak on the king's broad shoulders, and when they landed on the ground they drew the gold embroidered edges together, and wrapped them round the king as tightly as they could, so that only Timoken's head could be seen above the bundle of rich red and glittering gold.

They waited.

And they waited.

High over the cloud, Tolly, Petrello and the dragon, petrified and motionless, drifted on a current of air, while the flapping thing came closer. Strands of white hair floated about its awful face. Its eyes were blank, its lips bloodless.

But its voice was unexpectedly soft. 'Don't be afraid, little princes. The Damzel won't hurt you.'

They stared at her, their eyes wide with terror.

'Clever boys,' went on the silky voice. She floated closer, stretching a pale hand towards them. Her nails were black, and curved like claws.

Enid snorted and sped into the sky, while Petrello clung to her, all the breath knocked out of him.

'Silly dragon! Your time has come. You're growing old and your flames are weakening.' A coldness had edged into the Damzel's voice.

Tolly soared up and flew beside his brother.

'Silly, silly!' croaked the Damzel, all the sweetness in

her voice forgotten. 'Your castle's doomed, your father is my prisoner now. Come and live with the Damzel, she'll treat you well.'

'NO!' cried the boys. And for good measure, Petrello added, 'You must be mad!'

The Damzel screeched. She flew in a circle just beneath them, grumbling and moaning, grinding her black teeth and scratching her long white hair. Looking up at them, she screamed, 'The Damzel will have to come and get you then!'

Beneath the dark shroud they could see her bony shoulders flexing. She gave a hideous grin and, lifting both hands, she flew at them.

With a shriek of panic Enid soared higher. Tolly tried to follow, but the Damzel snatched at one of his wings. He cried out, helplessly, as the black claws pulled him closer.

'Fire, Enid!' Petrello shouted. 'Burn her, scorch her! Save Tolly, Enid!'

The dragon breathed a tiny spark, but she seemed too exhausted and too frightened to do any more. Petrello could only watch in horror as Tolly struggled, his torn feathers drifting away on the wind.

'Tolly! Oh, Tolly, I don't know what to do!' Petrello cried.

A desperate sob tore out of Tolly as the Damzel reeled him in, her fingers tugging him closer and closer.

There was a sudden rumble of thunder from below. The Damzel turned her head. As she peered down at the cloud a bolt of lightning shot out of it, scorching the Damzel's sleeve. With a screech of astonishment she let go of Tolly's wing. Seizing his chance, Tolly flew to the dragon's side.

'No, you don't!' shrieked the Damzel.

But before she could pursue him a figure burst out of the cloud and came flying up at her.

'Timoken!' she screamed.

When the king reached her she locked her long white fingers around his neck. The king twisted his head, but the black-tipped fingers closed tighter and tighter. The king clasped the Damzel's hands, he pulled and tore at them. Gradually, he forced her hands away until he was free. But only for a second, for now slithering behind the king, the Damzel coiled one arm about his head, and with the other she began to tug at the neck of his cloak.

'Father!' cried Petrello. He tried to urge the dragon closer to the fight. 'Enid, save the king!' he shouted into her ear.

The dragon gave a start of surprise and a shower of sparks flew out of her snout. A breeze that came from nowhere blew the sparks towards the Damzel, settling on her head, her shoulders and her back. Fire took hold of her black robes, and she began to scream.

Flames leapt along the Damzel's sleeves and finally she lifted a hand to beat them away.

The king broke free at last and flew a little distance from the burning Damzel. When she came at him again, with a chilling cry, he drew his sword and struck.

The sight of the ghastly head, swathed in its long white hair, would invade Petrello's sleep forever. When it dropped into the lake below, spray hissed and steamed in ever widening circles all around it, like a boiling pot.

The black bundle of the Damzel's body was carried on the wind for a moment before it fell, with a distant splash, into the churning water. The Damzel was gone, and yet Petrello could only think how close he had come to a life more terrible than he could imagine, and he began to shake.

'To earth!' King Timoken called to his sons.

His father's voice cut through Petrello's terror and he found that he could smile.

The king took off his cloak and swung it through the air, calling out in the language of his secret kingdom, and when the boys looked down they saw that the lake water was receding, the cloud was a mere ribbon of mist, and on the island lay twenty mail-clad knights. Their bonds had withered and fallen away, and some of them were beginning to sit up, shaking the last of the Damzel's spell out of their heads. Two figures in shiny sealskin could be seen bending over the dazed knights, clasping their shoulders and patting their hands.

The king, his sons and the dragon landed on the bank beside the house on stilts. As soon as they touched the ground, two women and a crowd of children ran out of the trees to greet them.

After much excited hugging and chattering, Sila called, 'The boats, children! We have the knights to rescue, and I'm sure your fathers could do with some help, after their long swim.'

Five brightly painted boats were carried out from a cave hidden in the undergrowth, and five of the older children each took a boat and began to row out to the island.

'You're always welcome in our home, Timoken,' said Sila. 'Though I can't promise it will be very pleasant after all that lake water has passed through it.'

'You might be surprised,' said the king. 'The Damzel is dead, her power broken. All things should be as they were.'

'You are a very great magician,' Adela said shyly.

The king laughed and put his arms around his sons. 'But what would I be without loyal friends and brave sons?'

'Still a king,' Adela said firmly.

The two women and five remaining children climbed back into the house on stilts, and almost immediately Sila called out that, indeed, the house was just as it had been before the lake rose, apart from a few damp cushions. She invited the king and his sons inside. She had plenty of dried fish, she said, and knew what the king could do with just one apple. But he told her, politely, that he would wait until all his knights were safely ashore.

'And we'll wait with you,' said Petrello.

The sky was now a cloudless blue; the sun was so fierce they had to retreat into the shade beneath the trees. Enid was already there, fast asleep.

Behind the king's broad back, Tolly whispered, 'We have to tell him.'

Petrello nodded. He didn't know how he was going to tell his father about the queen. He couldn't bear to shatter the happiness the three of them had shared since the king's release. But Petrello knew that he couldn't keep the truth from his father any longer.

They had made themselves comfortable on the broad roots of an oak when Petrello said, 'Father, I have something to tell you.'

The king was watching the boats bringing his knights across the water, and Petrello wasn't sure that he had heard. He raised his voice a little. 'It's about Mother.'

'Don't worry,' said the king. 'The leopards will protect her, and the wizards have plenty of unused magic. Eri may be old, but –'

'She's not there!' Tolly broke in, unable to stop himself.

The king frowned at him. 'Not there? Not in the castle?'

'I'm sorry, Father,' Petrello said awkwardly. 'I couldn't tell you sooner, because –'

'Tell me now!' the king demanded.

Hesitantly, Petrello began his account with the arrival of Rigg and Peredur, and then the riderless Isgofan.

'When Mother heard that the chancellor's men wouldn't search for Amadis, she went herself,' Petrello said unhappily. 'They even tried to stop her, but she fought her way past them.'

'She would,' said the king. He got up and began to pace to and fro before them. 'And did Rigg recover? Did he say who took the crystal and let those ruffians into the castle?'

This was the worst part of all for Petrello. He found he couldn't reply.

'Answer me, Petrello. If you know you must tell me.'

Reluctantly Petrello mumbled, 'Borlath. He was in league with Osbern D'Ark.'

The king stopped pacing. He raised his hands to his head and gave a dreadful howl. 'I wondered where Borlath had gone. I was afraid he was lost in the forest, but all the time he knew the Damzel lay in wait for us, and saved his own skin.'

'I'm sorry,' Petrello murmured. He would have done anything to wipe away his father's desolate expression.

'Tell me everything,' the king said bitterly.

And so Petrello haltingly delivered his account of treachery and corruption in the Red Castle. He finished with his journey through the air with Tolly, and their discovery of the house on stilts. And then it was Tolly's turn to speak of his flight to the castle with the ruined cloak, and how the leopards had made it whole again with their spell-binding gold.

'All was well there, Father,' said Tolly. 'Aunt Zobayda and our sister were safe, Llyr has knives . . .'

'Knives from bones,' the king said, smiling at last. 'Llyr has a way with bones. You are a brave boy, Tolomeo. I'm proud of you.'

I wish I had done more, thought Petrello.

The boats were beginning to arrive, and by now, some of the knights had recovered enough to leap into the water. They helped Tumi and Karli draw the boats up on to the shore, and then came bounding towards the king. Edern was the first. He rushed up to his old friend with a joyful roar, hugging him so fiercely the king had to laugh as he struggled for breath.

Petrello and Tolly stepped back into the trees as the other knights came splashing through the water. The king embraced every one of them, and for a while the air rang with their cheerful shouts and raucous laughter. They were together again and the evil in the forest had been destroyed. Many of them hadn't seen their old friends Karli and Tumi for many years, and were overjoyed to be reunited with them.

The jovial mood couldn't last. As soon as the king began to tell the knights what his sons had described to him, their faces fell. Some muttered oaths and shook their fists, others fingered their sword-hilts and their bags of arrows. In a few moments the crowd of happy men had become a troupe of angry soldiers, swearing vengeance.

The king's voice rose above the clamour of his knights. 'We will reclaim our castle. Thorkil has shown his hand and will be removed. But without horses and my camel, we are many days from home. So tonight I shall fly to Melyntha. I'm sure Osbern's stables are well-stocked. As for Gabar, he has a charmed life and will return.'

Tolly whispered, 'Can he really persuade twenty horses to leave their stables?'

'Believe it!' said Petrello.

Mabon the archer suddenly spoke up. 'What about the queen?'

'I'll find the queen,' the king said gravely. 'If Osbern has taken her, he won't survive our next meeting.' He noticed the boys were watching him from the trees. 'Petrello,

Tolomeo, bring us some food. That little house won't hold twenty knights, some of them as heavy as horses.'

The brothers followed Karli and Tumi into the house on stilts, where Sila handed them a basket of dried fish. She only had one apple but, handing it to Petrello, she said, 'Your father will know what to do with this.'

When the food had been delivered the king sent the boys back to the house. He had much to discuss with his knights, and his sons needed rest after their long battle with the Damzel and her demons.

'When will you go to Melyntha, Father?' asked Petrello.

'Nightfall,' he replied.

'Will you bring our mother back?' asked Tolly.

The king looked away from them. He took a breath and said, 'I can't lie to you, my sons. You might not see your mother just yet.'

If they had other questions they couldn't ask them. They returned to the house on stilts and when they had eaten they laid their heads on the slightly damp cushions and fell asleep, oblivious to the chatter of women and the noisy chorus of other children.

It was dusk when Ketil woke them. 'A creature has arrived,' he said excitedly. 'Our mother says it's a camel.'

Chapter Twenty-Three

Petrello's Storm

Half-awake, Petrello murmured, 'A camel?'

'A CAMEL?' cried Tolly, leaping up, and now Petrello was wide awake.

'Mother saw it first,' said Ketil. 'She opened the door to call to our father, who is out there with the king, and she saw this creature.'

'Where? Where?' Petrello ran to the open door where Tolly was standing.

The moon had all but disappeared and the sky was beginning to lose its night-time colour. The lake water glittered with reflected light from small fires dotted round the shore. The knights had left them for a moment while they gathered about the king and his precious camel. The boys' spirits lifted. If Gabar was safe, then so, perhaps, were others.

Petrello was about to climb down the ladder when Sila put an arm across his chest.

'No, Petrello. Listen!'

There was a great commotion in the trees: a thunder of hooves, the whinnying and snorting of many horses and then, suddenly, a white mare galloped into view; her rider was smaller than a knight and wore a brown fur cap.

'Mother!' cried Petrello.

The mare was followed by Amadis, riding Sir Edern's brown stallion. A crowd of horses came jostling and nudging their way behind him. When they saw the lake they trotted to the water and began to drink.

The king ran to his wife and lifted her down.

'We must go to them,' Petrello pleaded, pushing Sila's arm away.

'I can't stop you now,' she said with a smile.

The boys clambered down the ladder and ran through the water without bothering to remove their boots. There was such a crush around their mother, they had to punch their way through the knights.

'Not so rough, young man!' Mabon exclaimed, lifting both boys into the air.

The queen laughed and held out her arms to them.

They ran to her and when she had hugged them they saw that her hands were scratched and her tunic smelt of leather and wolf and horse.

'Mother, where have you been?' asked Tolly.

She drew them to the warmth of the fire and they sat one each side of her, while she told them about her fight with Osbern D'Ark, and how Amadis and his wolves had rescued her.

The king and his knights stood about the fire and listened, interrupting the story with grunts of approval and alarm. Petrello noticed that Enid had woken up and, seeing her friend Gabar, was affectionately nudging his long legs with her snout, while he bent his head and nuzzled her.

'You should have seen our mother,' said Amadis. 'She could overcome us all in a sword fight.'

'I'm aware of that,' the king said, smiling at his wife. 'Is Osbern dead, then?'

The queen shook her head. 'I had to make a bargain.' She put her hand in a leather pouch hanging from her belt, and drew out something flat and glistening. 'The Seeing Crystal!' she said, holding it up. 'Osbern gave it to me in exchange for his life.'

Sighs of wonder and relief came from the group of knights, but Sir Edern muttered, 'He deserved to die.'

'I had to honour my word,' the queen said solemnly.

Amadis stepped closer to the fire and said, 'As the villain rode away, he gave us a parting gift; a warning that he knew would be too late to save us.'

'Save us?' said the king.

'Oh, Timoken,' sighed the queen. 'That wretch sent a message to the king of England, telling him where he could find an enchanted castle, a splendid castle, better by far than any of his own. A thousand soldiers are coming to take our precious home. Without the crystal the wizards will be unprepared; they will know nothing until the army is at our gate, and then it will be too late for Llyr and Eri to reach the spell-wall and bring about a Vanishing.'

Everyone could hear the low growl that rumbled in the king's throat. He paced about while his knights, his wife and his sons watched him, waiting for a sign, for advice, a plan; anything to give them hope.

At last, without a word, he went to Gabar and, speaking very softly, stroked his woolly neck. The camel rumbled back at him and slowly began to crouch.

For a moment they thought that the king had given up, that the task ahead was too hopeless to attempt. They even began to wonder where their next home would be. Petrello thought of Guanhamara and his aunt. What would happen to them?

All at once the king turned from his camel and said, 'Even on horseback we will be too late.'

Did he mean to fly, they wondered? And what then? Could he conquer an entire army on his own?

'Petrello, come here,' said the king.

'Me, Father?' Petrello felt foolish. All eyes had turned to him.

'We're going to fly home,' his father told him. 'I need you to come with me.'

Petrello laid his hand on his chest. He meant to ask if what he heard could be true. But he found it impossible to speak.

'Quickly, my son,' the king commanded. 'Climb on to the camel's back.'

In a fog of bewilderment Petrello walked up to Gabar. 'But what can I do?' he whispered.

'We'll find out,' the king quietly replied. 'Now, on to the saddle.'

Petrello climbed on to Gabar's wooden saddle, and the king sat in front of him. Petrello clasped his father round the waist, the red cloak warm and comforting under his hands.

The group of knights were staring at Petrello, some incredulous, others merely puzzled. And yet the queen was smiling, as if she had guessed what the king intended and knew that it was right. She stood with her hands on Tolly's shoulders, and when Petrello caught his brother's eye, Tolly grinned and nodded, as if to say, 'I believe in you.'

The king made a soft animal sound, and Gabar lifted into the sky. The forest canopy receded and the dawn wind brushed Petrello's cheeks as they raced through the air. He buried his head in his father's cloak and closed his eyes, his mind in a turmoil. What could he do? His trust in the king was absolute, and yet he was afraid that he could never do what his father hoped.

The light was increasing every minute; soon the sun began to show above the distant trees. Beneath them the vast forest rippled like an emerald sea. And then the sixteen towers of the Red Castle came into view.

They were flying directly towards the South Gate, and as they drew nearer Petrello looked east, to where the town of Rossmellon sat in its small valley. The trees between the castle and the town were not so dense and now he could see the movement of mounted soldiers on the wide track, their helmets a dull grey in the early light. The foot soldiers had left the track, however, and were beginning to fan out into the trees.

'Do you see them, Petrello?' asked the king.

'There are so many,' he breathed.

'Too many,' said his father.

As they approached the castle they saw the door into the garden move very slightly. Through its narrow opening a figure cautiously emerged. It was Eri in his blue cloak, his white hair uncovered, his long staff glimmering with magic.

'He'll never cover the whole distance of the spell-wall,' muttered the king.

They were above the garden when Eri saw them. He lifted his staff in greeting, and the king called, 'Go back, Eri. Go back!'

Eri stood motionless, his hand shading his eyes. Gabar flew right above him and then over the castle wall. He landed in the second courtyard, where a sinister silence greeted them. Llyr stood inside the door, a knife ready in his hand. He ran to the camel as they landed.

Before Llyr could speak the king lifted his hand and said, 'Get your grandfather inside. An army is almost at our gate.' He slipped from the camel and lifted Petrello down.

Llyr was on his way back to the door when Eri came in, grunting, 'Whatever next? I must . . .'

'Too late, Grandfather.' Llyr closed the great door behind the old man and quickly drew the iron bar across it.

'What's happened?' asked the old man, glancing at Petrello. 'Where are the others?'

'All safe,' replied the king. 'They're on their way, but we came on ahead. My sons have told me everything.' He touched Petrello's head. 'Is Zobayda safe? And the children?'

The wizards exchanged glances, and Eri said, 'Safe, Timoken, though Borlath is confined in the Hall of Corrections. The guards are all loyal, but some have been killed. Chimery is dead and Thorkil is for the moment locked in his office with most of his men. Friar Gereint has found his sword and stands guard outside the door. A few of the chancellor's men are,' he gave a nervous shrug, 'somewhere about. But the leopards keep watch, and no one can get past Llyr and his knives.'

'Your daughter, Guanhamara, likes to spend time on the battlements,' said Llyr. 'She's up there before dawn most days. It was she who told us an army was approaching, or we would never have known.'

'I made Llyr wait to guard the entrance,' said Eri, 'while I went alone to walk the spell-wall and begin the Vanishing.'

'Dear friend, you would never have completed it.' The king laid his hand on Eri's shoulder. 'We have learned that the king of England has sent his army to take our castle,' he looked at Petrello, 'so my son and I have come to stop them.'

The wizards looked at Petrello and nodded gravely. They didn't seem surprised to hear that he would be helping to defeat an army of a thousand men.

'A few knives would be welcome, Llyr,' said the king, 'to bring the soldiers out of the trees. Do you have enough?'

'A sackful,' said Llyr, his eyes gleaming. 'I'll use Princess Zobayda's tower.'

'No time to lose,' the king told him.

Before Petrello had time to grasp what was happening his father had seized him round the waist and they were flying up to the top of the Royal Tower. When the king set him down, he was so breathless he could hardly stand.

'Look, Petrello! See what we're up against!' The king pointed to the east.

Petrello staggered to his father's side and peered through an opening in the wall. His vision was blurred, his head foggy with shock and the long journey through the air. He rubbed his eyes and stared at the trees below. He knew the soldiers were there, but the army appeared to have doubled in size. The glint of armour spread almost to the town, north and south it bobbed and quivered in the early sun. Soon it would burst out of the trees and cover the meadow and the garden.

The king removed his cloak and swung it through the air, his familiar chant filling Petrello's ears. Black clouds darkened the sky; rain, heavy as iron, thudded on to the trees. A thunderbolt tore into the approaching soldiers, and Petrello could hear their screams. For a moment the army halted, and then they marched again, their shields above their heads, the rain denting the metal but not harming them. The king began to roar, and the rain stopped. A bolt of lightning struck the treetops. Fire spread through the branches and they fell, blazing, on to the army below. Some of the men dropped to the ground, others came on.

There were wagons on the track, carrying machinery that Petrello had heard of but never seen: battering rams, giant catapults, ladders and siege towers.

A knife whistled through the air and, turning his head, Petrello saw Llyr on Zobayda's tower, hurling his magic at the army. The knives struck home, piercing breastplates, helmets, gauntlets, but the soldiers still came on. There were archers among them and a sudden shower of arrows swept towards Zobayda's tower. Most fell short, but Llyr disappeared; whether he had been hit or was hiding, they couldn't tell. Another arrow landed behind the king; a burning rag was tied to it and nearly scorched his cloak. He stamped the flames out, but now the sky was full of burning arrows and the army was in the meadow.

'It's time, Petrello!'

He heard his father's voice and wanted to shrink until he was no bigger than a beetle. What could he do?

'What am I to do, Father?' he asked. 'I have no talent, there's nothing –'

'You can move the air, my son. You have always had the gift, but you have never had to use it – until now.'

'Move the air?' Petrello murmured.

'You've heard of hurricanes, typhoons, cyclones. They're made of moving air; great winds that can sweep men into the sky, winds that can uproot trees and carry houses. You can bring a wind like that, Petrello.'

'Can I?' he whispered.

'Wish for it!'

Petrello felt a hand on his shoulder. He sensed his father's strength warm on his back, racing through his arms and into his hands. He moved his fingers, opened and closed them, and a breeze came out of them. He heard a moan, and then a roar as a wind tore over him, slamming him against the wall. Clouds of dust flew into his eyes, and he closed them and sank to his knees. 'Hurricane!' he croaked.

With his eyes closed he imagined he was quite alone with a wind that was all his, a wild creature that he loved. And while it raged about him, a small being came into his mind's eye; a hairless creature with moth-like wings and huge saffron-coloured eyes. It darted through the trees, holding a giant spider's web that floated behind it, glittering with droplets of water. The image was gone in a second, and he heard the king saying, 'Look, Petrello! Look what you have done!'

'The wind,' he groaned.

'The wind has left us, it's with the army now. Look!' The king put his hands under Petrello's shoulders and lifted him to his feet.

Petrello stared at the sky. A cloud of objects whirled and twisted above the trees, above the meadow. Higher and higher they rose; now they were level with his gaze, now ever higher; soldiers, wagons, helmets, swords, all drifting, turning, floating. The wind carried them back and forth and then they were above the castle, and Petrello turned around to see them blowing over the river, over the forest towards the great grey ocean. Screams like the buzz of tiny insects could be heard for a moment, before they were drowned in the hurricane's roar.

Another sound slipped into Petrello's ear. The king's voice. 'Let them down gently, my son. Scatter them, blow them far from here, but let them live to tell their king.'

'I understand.' Petrello was shaking with exhaustion, but he thought of the soldiers twisting and turning in the air, with nothing beneath them but the sky. They would need a strong and careful breeze to carry them to earth. He had brought the hurricane, now he must control it. He closed his eyes and saw the soldiers floating far, far away, and then they were falling, slowly, gently until they landed, on distant pathways, on mountain passes, hills and fields, in forests, hamlets and castle courtyards. They were crouching in terror, dumb with fright, but safe.

Petrello opened his eyes. The king was looking at him, his head on one side.

'Remarkable,' he said. 'Somehow you managed to leave the horses on the ground.'

'They meant no harm. And the soldiers are safe now. But, Father, do you think the king of England will send another army?'

'He won't risk it. News of an army in the air will be too fantastic to be believed. Those in power will try and forget it. A thousand men were sent to capture a castle and all of them disappeared.' The king smiled and shook his head. 'Let's go down and celebrate.'

This time the king didn't fly. He descended the spiralling steps with Petrello following, still a little dizzy with shock and success. When they reached the royal apartments, Zobayda and Guanhamara were there to greet them, Gunfrid, Zeba and Elin shyly looking over their shoulders.

'We saw it from the window,' cried Guanhamara. 'Men in the sky, wagons, swords, helmets, everything an army carries. Did you put them up there, Father?'

'No,' said the king. 'It was Petrello.'

They all stared at him in astonishment, but Zobayda was smiling. Her arms were folded and Petrello could see the silver jinni on her finger. It looked especially bright.

Chapter Twenty-Four
A Celebration

Before any celebrations could take place, the king had to be sure that his wife and sons and all his knights were safe. It took them two days and two nights to travel through the forest, and in that time the king had much to put right in his castle.

Thorkil and ten of his men were still locked in the chancellor's office, but no one felt safe while four grey men were still at large. The courtiers kept to their chambers; the workmen, the cooks, the musicians, the stable boys and messengers stayed close to each other in their own quarters. Very few risked appearing in the courtyards.

It was Wyngate with his sharp eyes and investigative mind who eventually tracked down the grey men. Two were in the armoury, hidden in spare suits of armour, one was in the blacksmith's forge, disguised as a log, and the last was cowering in a barrel of apples in the stockroom. Terrified by the sight of the angry king and his wizards, they quickly gave themselves up. The chancellor might sneer at ancient spells, but his men knew all too well what they could do.

Released from the locked room, Thorkil emerged looking sullen and defiant. He made no apology and no excuses for his treachery. When he and his men had been relieved of their weapons they were taken to the South Gate and told to make their way, on foot, to Castle Melyntha. 'Life with Osbern will suit you better,' the king told Thorkil. 'But I suggest that you don't travel on the usual route, or you will meet my Knight Protectors, and they're likely to draw their swords at the very sight of you.'

'There will be wolves,' muttered one of the men.

'And wild boar and snakes,' mumbled another.

'And other things,' grunted a third.

'You may take a weapon,' said the king, handing the third man a small knife.

'What about our families?' asked the man, feeling bolder.

'They will come later, in the safety of a wagon.' The king gave the man a hard but reassuring look.

Thorkil said not a word. He marched out, followed by his men, some of whom were shuffling rather pathetically. The great doors closed behind them and the king gave a huge sigh of relief.

'That was well done, Timoken,' said Eri.

'Now for my son,' said the king.

'A far harder task,' Llyr quietly remarked.

Borlath had managed to injure several of the guards before he was finally overcome. Now, confined in the Hall of Corrections, he stormed up and down, scorching and singeing whatever he touched, though he was careful to avoid a full-blown fire, knowing that he would be the first to burn.

The wizards wouldn't allow the king to speak to Borlath alone. They knew their friend might weaken. Timoken still believed he was partially responsible for his son's betrayal. It was the jinni's fateful gift to him, always to have one foot in the realm of enchantments, a place where darkness lurked beside the light.

Guanhamara and her brothers were there, of course; lying flat on the floor above the hall, their eyes pressed to the gaps in the boards.

The king sat at the far end of the hall, with Llyr and

Eri on either side of him. A dozen knives still hung from Llyr's belt, and Borlath glanced at these occasionally as he paced before the five men guarding him, their pikes all at the ready.

The king's voice boomed across the hall. 'Borlath, explain why you conspired with others to take over this castle, to abduct the bellman and murder my knights!'

Borlath stopped pacing. 'Why not mention my other crimes?'

The king was silent. The wizards' chairs creaked. Eri's staff tapped the floor.

'Surely you have guessed,' said Borlath in a sneering tone. 'Why did Lilith put her enchanting petals into a certain helmet? Because I told her to. Oh, she has a wicked nature, I grant you, but it was my idea.'

Unable to keep the confusion out of his voice, the king asked, 'Why?'

'Why? Because I can. Because I will never be king. Because I have to watch wizards defending our castle with ancient magic, because my brother's power comes from wolves and eagles, and I wanted to silence him forever.'

'You wanted Amadis to die?' roared the king.

'Lilith's gift is stronger than she thought,' muttered Borlath.

'I wonder,' said Eri quietly.

'It seems that you no longer wish to live here,' said the king.

'Huh!' Borlath uttered a hollow sort of laugh. 'Not now that my little brothers are flying, and throwing soldiers in the air.'

'You have so much,' the king said sadly. 'You have youth and strength, you inspire loyalty in Cafal, and you have a certain command over others. You could be a great Knight Protector, Borlath.'

There was no reply to this. Guanhamara looked up at the same time as her brothers. She rolled her eyes at them and Petrello shrugged. And then, suddenly, someone below started to speak, and they quickly lowered their heads. Tolly was so fast he banged his forehead on the floorboard.

'We know you are there!' said Eri, from beneath. 'So behave yourselves and take note of what you hear.'

Tolly reddened. He rubbed his forehead while his brother and sister shook with silent giggles.

The king seemed unconcerned about the spies above

him. In a weary, bitter voice he told Borlath to gather the possessions he needed, to fetch his horse from the stables and to leave the castle before dusk.

'I am banished, then,' said Borlath.

'Banished,' said the king. 'You can go to Sir Osbern, if you wish, or try to make your fortune elsewhere. But never return to this castle, or you will spend the rest of your days in a pit so deep and dark you will wish you were dead.'

The three children lying above the Hall of Corrections quietly got to their feet and tiptoed out of the building. They had heard enough. Later that day they watched from the shadows as Borlath rode out of the South Gate. He looked broken and desolate. He could have been a great knight and, although they were glad to see him go, they felt sad that he had chosen to be so alone.

Cafal had crept up behind them, and when Borlath had gone, Petrello asked, 'Are you sad, Cafal, to see our brother go?'

'I am sad that he did what he did,' said Cafal, 'and I am sad that I told him about Rigg.'

There were two more children to reprimand, but the king had lost the will to punish. It was quite obvious that

Vyborn's natural talent couldn't be suppressed, but he promised not to change into anything fierce. He would stick to cats and dogs, he said, and an occasional rat. How long this would last, even Zobayda couldn't predict.

Olga had lost the will to move anything, even herself. She lay on her bed moaning about how much she missed Lilith, and how Amadis had murdered her. And then her younger sister had a vision. Ever since Guanhamara had 'seen' her father and his knights held in a cloud, everyone believed in her visions, though Petrello wasn't sure about his sister's picture of Lilith.

'I see her on a beach,' said Guanhamara, perching on the edge of Olga's bed. 'She's collecting shellfish. She looks a bit cross, but she's well and . . . and, I think, yes, I think she's planning to come home.'

'How?' asked Olga.

'Oh, she'll find a way,' said Guanhamara cheerfully. 'She's very clever, isn't she?'

'Yes,' Olga agreed, almost with a smile.

'But our father says that you won't be allowed to see her, unless you stop moving things about.' Guanhamara had made this up, but she decided it was what the king would have wanted. It certainly did the trick.

For quite some time Olga would only move the smallest objects. She never doubted Guanhamara's vision, because Amadis confirmed it. The eagle had taken Lilith to a seashore, where there was plenty to eat, and a small house nearby. Amadis didn't lie, and an eagle wouldn't know how to.

The celebrations were held three days after the queen, Tolly and Amadis had returned, though the twenty knights accompanying them began their merry-making the very night they arrived. A great deal of wine and mead were consumed, and the bawdy singing lasted until daybreak, but no one in the castle would have dared to complain.

Spring had become summer when the great day arrived. Long tables were carried into the courtyard and covered with cloths of red and gold. Cooks and musicians were up at dawn. The smells of baking and roasting wafted through the courtyards, and the sounds of musicians practising new tunes made it impossible not to hum or sing.

The royal family sat on one table, together with twenty knights, two wizards, the investigator and Friar Gereint. A new chancellor had yet to be appointed.

Gunfrid and Zeba sat between Cafal and Petrello. Gunfrid's legs were improving rapidly with a daily dose of the wizards' new potion. He could even stand on his own; soon, it was predicted, he would be able to walk again.

Guanhamara made sure that her friend Elin had a place beside Amadis, and the girl watched entranced as birds and mice and even a lizard settled themselves on his head and shoulders. A tiny wren perched on his finger, and when he gently held it out to Elin, she blushed with pleasure and asked, 'For me?'

'To make you smile,' said Amadis. Behind him Greyfleet gave an approving grunt.

Gabar paced between the tables, his proud head bending now and then to accept a favourite titbit. Enid followed close behind him, the end of her thick tail giving any disrespectful dog a sharp tap on the nose.

Before the giant puddings were brought out, the king made a speech. At a gesture from Llyr, one of the musicians blew two blasts on his trumpet and chattering courtiers, workmen, children and barking dogs gradually fell silent.

The king began with a promise. Looking at Gunfrid and Zeba, he said that very soon he would rescue their friends, still held as slaves by Sir Osbern D'Ark. There were murmurs of agreement from the knights and the pink-faced orphans smiled their gratitude.

The leopard, Star, sitting beside the king, gave his hand a nudge and he turned to stroke its head. The other two leopards came running up and the king laughed as he bent to hug each one. 'I haven't forgotten you, my friends,' he said. 'You and your rare gold.'

And then the king went on to thank his family for putting themselves in such grave danger. 'Without each other we would have perished,' he said. Looking down the table until he found Petrello, he added, 'We would certainly have lost our home.'

Petrello felt himself held in the king's deep gaze. In his father's eyes he read love and pride, but also a warning. *I will never misuse the gift that you passed to me*, Petrello silently promised.

The king's warm smile grew into a broad and joyful grin, and Petrello realised that everyone was staring at the sky where, only a few days ago, a thousand soldiers had floated and tumbled and spun. And now all eyes were turned to him, and he felt very hot and tearful all at the same time.

Beside him Guanhamara whispered, 'No one will ever dare to call you foolish again. Nurse Ogle will have to bite her tongue so many times, she'll wear a hole in it.'

Petrello laughed until he could hardly breathe, and Vyborn chose that moment to turn into a large ginger cat. It ran the length of the table, overturning several jugs of water, but no one paid any attention to it, and they didn't bat an eyelid when Olga sent a platter full of fruit spinning into Tolly's lap.

'Thanks for that,' said Tolly. He raised his wings and sighs of wonder and admiration filled the courtyard as sunlight coloured every single gleaming feather.